Nora's Ribbon of Memories
D0400267

OTHER BOOKS BY
STEPHANIE GRACE WHITSON:

The Prairie Winds Series

Walks the Fire

Soaring Eagle

Red Bird

The Keepsake Legacies Series

Sarah's Patchwork

Karyn's Memory Box

Stephanie Grace Whitson

THOMAS NELSON PUBLISHERS®
Nashville

Published in Nashville, Tennessee, by Thomas Nelson, Inc.

Scripture quotations are from the KING JAMES VERSION of the Bible.

Library of Congress Cataloging-in-Publication Data

Whitson, Stephanie Grace.

Nora's ribbon of memories:a novel/Stephanie Grace Whitson.

p. cm. — (Keepsake Legacies)

ISBN 0-7852-7187-2 (pbk.)

I. Title. II. Series: Whitson, Stephanie Grace. Keepsake legacies.

PS3573.H555N67 1999

813'.54—dc21 99-36159

CIP

Printed in the United States of America

1 2 3 4 5 6 7 QPV 04 03 02 01 00 99

In loving memory of
Mother
1913–1996

In about 1929, a motherless teenaged girl was dropped off on a street corner, suitcase in hand, and wished a good life by her father, who then drove away, leaving her to make her own way in life. The girl went door-to-door, asking if anyone needed a housekeeper. One woman gave the girl a chance, ordering her to clean a room. When the girl had finished, the woman inspected her work. There were a few pennies lying on the bed. The girl had found them under the bed. The woman scooped the pennies up, congratulated the girl on her honesty, and gave her a job and a home.

The girl eventually married a truck driver with little education and not much to offer other than a strong work ethic and an incredible capacity for commitment that was to last through nearly fifty-five years of marriage. Together, the couple built a life. It wasn't a fairy tale, and they did not always live happily-ever-after. But they raised four children and endured and now they are enjoying an eternity where there is no abandonment, no unhappiness, and no fear.

One of the couple's four children was me.

This book is my way of celebrating my Mother's tenacity. I once read an epitaph that said, "She done what she could." That was my mother. She done what she could. For me, it was enough.

Prologue

1998

"It's a stroke."

Reagan's stomach tightened with dread. Memories assaulted her: a hallway lined with wheelchairs; aged hands reaching for her; meaningless babble escaping from toothless mouths. She had always tried to touch each one encountered on her way to her own parents' room, even if it was only a hand on a slumped shoulder or a gentle squeeze of a wrinkled hand. Always, the thought that her touch might be the only personal kindness they might know for that day brought her near tears.

Reagan forced herself out of the past and back into the moment. Cupping her half-empty coffee cup in her hands, she bowed her head and murmured, "I was afraid of that."

Mason Ritter slumped down into the chair opposite hers. The waiting room was empty except for the two of them. Reagan looked up at the clock. She had been there only about two hours before Irene's brother arrived, rushing through the doors to the intensive care unit to check on his sister before conferencing with various doctors.

"What's the prognosis?" Reagan asked.

"They don't know. Thank God you were there when it happened. They gave her that new wonder drug—what do they call it?"

"t-PA," Reagan offered.

"Yes, that's it. She might not be severely impaired. That's all they can say." The elderly gentleman's hands shook as he raised them to smooth his rumpled white hair.

Reagan tried to remember what Irene had said about her brother. Was he older or younger than Irene? Younger, Reagan thought. In his late sixties, if she remembered correctly.

"Who can I call for you? What can I do?" Reagan offered.

Mason shook his head. "I don't know. Lila called everyone as soon as we heard." Lila was Mason's second wife. Irene hadn't said much about her, only that Mason had remarried not long after the death of his wife of forty years. Reagan remembered a faint tone of dislike in her friend's voice every time she mentioned Lila's name.

Reagan gathered that Lila had been the one who instigated the previous year's auction on the Ritter homestead northwest of Lincoln. Mason had sold the farmland nearly ten years earlier than that. Except for his grandfather's forty acres of virgin prairie and an additional ten acres around the nearly-empty house, there wasn't much left to remind the Ritter family how closely they had once been tied to Nebraska soil.

Irene had been adamantly opposed to the auction. She begged her brother to delay it, insisting she could find room for things in her own mansion in Lincoln. But then the farmhouse was broken into and Lila finally had the upper hand in family discussions. No one wanted to see the place go to ruin, Lila argued. It was poor stewardship to leave the house filled with family treasures with no one there to check on things. Lila made room for a few of the family treasures in her own home. Irene rescued a few things, but not much.

As a sometimes-antique-dealer, Reagan had attended the Ritter auction and purchased a cracked water cooler full of dusty grain bags. Weeks later, intending to plant geraniums in the cooler, she had pulled the bags out and discovered a memory box and a diary. When Irene Peale was notified of the find through the auctioneer and came to reclaim her family treasures, she and Reagan had immediately connected on a level that transcended the generations between them.

Reagan willed herself to listen more carefully to what Mason was saying. "Of course you know that Irene and Henry didn't have children. So there are only a few distant relatives. We've managed to reach everyone who would want to know. Everyone, that is, but Noah. We'll keep trying. Lila has said," Mason said, then hastened to add, "and I agree—that there's no reason for everyone to flock in here. It would make Irene mad, having everyone flutter around. And heaven forbid that she misunderstand and think we were keeping some sort of deathwatch."

In the past months, Reagan had become familiar with Irene's fierce battle for independence. The "seventy-something" widow still lived alone in a historic Lincoln mansion filled with several generations of her husband's family memories. She swam nearly a mile three times a week. On the days she didn't swim, she walked, her brisk gait belying her age. *Mason is right,* Reagan thought. *Irene would despise having anyone fluttering about. Except Noah.* Reagan said aloud, "She won't feel that way about Noah, though."

Mason nodded. "I agree. Noah always spent his summers with Irene and Henry. They have been close since he was eight years old. I hope we can find him soon." He shook his head. "I thought he was staying in Nebraska for a while. But I'm only the boy's father. I never know what he's going to do next." Mason pressed his lips together as if he had just revealed a family secret and regretted it. He continued in a more even tone. "He doesn't have service installed at the farm yet. I've left a dozen messages on his voice mail, at both his condo in Tiburon and the office in Sausalito. It doesn't make sense that he would just turn off his cell phone. Even if he did, he always checks in with his office at least twice a day." Mason shrugged his shoulders. "Maybe all his high-tech machines just aren't working right. Or maybe he's off on a fishing trip. As I said, I never know what Noah is going to do next."

Reagan stood up, talking as she pulled on her denim jacket. "I'll drive up to the farm and see if he's there. If I leave right now, I can be there early in the morning."

"You don't have to do that."

"I know." Reagan reached behind her to lift her long dark hair outside her jacket collar. "I want to. Irene would want Noah here."

Mason nodded and stood up. "Thank you." He patted her arm.

Reagan stopped at the ATM in the hospital lobby and withdrew cash for gas and meals for the next two days. It would be a long drive to the Ritter homestead in Custer County, and she hadn't had much sleep. Once she had found Noah and headed him toward Lincoln and his aunt's bedside, she might need to check into a motel and get some sleep before driving back.

As she drove by the university football stadium and headed north for the interstate, Reagan clicked on a CD. The soothing first notes of John Tesh at the piano helped her settle back and relax.

She reached for her coffee. *It's amazing, Lord, how quickly life can change. One minute we were laughing at Cary Grant, the next Irene's coffee cup dropped to the floor and she slumped over.*

The thought that she and Irene might have enjoyed their last Cary Grant movie together brought tears to Reagan's eyes. She blinked them away and focused on the road. *Help me find Noah, Lord. Use Noah and me to show Irene how much You love her. And the nurses, Lord—help them to see more than just a wrinkled old woman. She has so much life in her . . . give her back to me, God.* Reagan stopped praying. She corrected herself. No . . . *that's not what I should be asking for, is it? I should be asking for Your will. And help me to adjust to whatever it is.*

Reagan put her coffee cup back in the drink holder and gripped the steering wheel with both hands. *You know I want Irene back, Lord. I want things the way they were. But if that's not in Your plan, then help me accept it. Help me to help Irene. Thank You for the joy she has added to my life.*

As Reagan's pickup truck headed west on Interstate 80, she smiled to herself. Reading Karyn Ritter's diary had made her feel almost a part of the Ritter family. In recent months, Irene had often invited Reagan to come along when she drove out to inspect some new project of her nephew's. Reagan was almost as thrilled as Irene to see Noah's love for the past bear fruit at the old homestead.

Noah's interest in Nebraska made Reagan curious. She wondered just what it was that would motivate a man to leave a lucrative position with a computer firm for a broken-down homestead in a remote corner of Nebraska. She assumed Noah had shared his reasons with Irene. Reagan sighed. *Don't be nosy. That's family business—and you're not family.*

Reagan had to admit that Noah Ritter made her self-conscious and nervous. He refused to fit neatly into any of the slots she mentally prepared for him. He was a computer expert, but he defied every stereotype ever given the technologically gifted. No thick-framed glasses camouflaged his brilliant blue eyes. His posture never hinted of the hours he must have spent hunched over a keyboard. He might have a job that exercised only his brain, but he lifted weights. The effects showed through his cotton work shirts.

Reagan thought that hours in a computer lab appealed only to the kind of men who were ill at ease in social settings, but Noah quickly disproved that stereotype when he and Reagan went to the local diner for coffee one morning while running an errand for Irene. The moment the two strangers entered the diner, conversation at the tables halted. After a brief moment, an early morning card game among ranchers at a table in the corner resumed, and everyone took that as a cue to restart their conversations. Noah walked up to the table and asked in a friendly voice, "What's a guy got to do to get into this game?" A grizzled old man squinted up at him, noticeably inspecting the long black ponytail pulled through the back of Noah's seed cap. "About thirty years on three sections," was the curt reply.

Noah had laughed easily. "Then I don't qualify, but my dad does." He had introduced himself, and at the mention of Mason Ritter the table erupted.

"He sold out—how many years ago was it? Sure miss seeing 'Mace.' How's he doing these days?"

"I remember you when you were only this tall. You fell off your dad's tractor and scared us half to death. Thought you got run over . . . but you just had the wind knocked out of you."

Noah chuckled and pulled up a chair. You would have thought he had never been away from Custer County.

Reagan's thoughts drifted from Noah back to Irene. She drove nonstop to Grand Island, then northwest to Millersburg, and finally down the narrow gravel road that led to the deserted Ritter homestead.

There was no sign of Noah Ritter's red pickup. The farmhouse door was locked and it appeared as if no one had been there in days. Reagan made her way back into Millersburg and inquired at the diner. One of the card players at the corner table answered her question. "Noah's headed back to California. Didn't say when he'd be back."

"Irene, please," Reagan begged. "You have to try." She held up a spoonful of tapioca, but the tiny white-haired woman in the hospital bed just stared defiantly back at her.

"N-n-n-NO!" the woman squeezed out the words. "Doooo-nn wann." She turned her head away.

"All right then, here," Reagan said. Taking Irene's right hand in hers, she pried open the resistant fingers. "You can feed yourself, you know. Your therapist said so. Just don't put so much on the spoon."

Irene gripped the spoon. With excruciating slowness, she managed to put a small amount of tapioca on the spoon. It spilled on her pale blue bib before it ever reached her mouth. She let go of the spoon and turned away from Reagan. A tear trickled down her cheek.

Reagan took her hand. "It's all right, Irene. Try again in a minute. I need to run down the hall to the rest room. I'll be back." Reagan hurried out of the room. She was leaning against the wall sobbing when a nurse came down the hall.

"I can't do it," she said through her tears. "I can't get Irene to eat. What's going to happen to her if we can't get her to eat?"

"We'll think of something," the nurse assured Reagan, patting her arm. "She's made wonderful strides in every other way. And in a remarkably short time."

"But her speech just isn't coming back. She's so frustrated. And it's so hard for her to swallow. I'm afraid she's going to give up." Reagan's voice lowered. "Her family is talking about selling her house. They don't think she'll ever go back home." She bit her lip and shook her head. "If they sell her house, it will kill her." Reagan straightened up and took a deep breath. "I'm only a friend. I can't do anything to stop it but try to get her to prove them all wrong. To show them that she is going to get better. She *will* go home." She sighed. "Sorry. I didn't mean to dump all that on you."

The nurse smiled in response. "I only wish all of my patients had such devoted friends. You're doing more good than you know for Mrs. Peale. Just be patient . . . and don't give up."

Reagan didn't want to give up, but as the days passed she saw Irene growing smaller, not just physically, but in spirit. And then there was the day that Lila Ritter broached the topic of selling Irene's house. Reagan saw the effect it had on her friend. Something died in the old woman's eyes. She closed her eyes, nodded, and said, "Yessssss. I unnnerstan." Then she pretended to fall asleep.

Reagan wanted to slap the smug look off Lila's face. As Lila and Mason headed off down the corridor of the rehabilitation center, Reagan heard her say, "We won't move in right away. But we'll go ahead and have the carriage house taken down. That will make room for the new garage."

Later that night, Reagan sat in the worn recliner in her own little living room trying to concentrate on an editorial from the morning paper. She finally gave up, rolling up the paper and adding it to the others that rested in the broken water cooler that had belonged to Irene's grandmother. Looking at the crack that meandered down one side of it, Reagan smiled to herself. Who would have thought that a broken old cooler dragged out of a fallen-in dugout could change someone's life?

Leaning back in her recliner, Reagan thought about Karyn Ritter. What she knew of Irene's grandmother included a devout Christian faith. Mrs. Ritter's faith had apparently helped her through some incredibly hard times. Unfortunately, Irene seemed too depressed to respond when Reagan mentioned things like "God's will" and "trust and obey."

"What can I do for her if she can't even pray, Lord?" Reagan spoke the words aloud. The answer seemed to come: *You pray for her.* Reagan answered, *I believe, Lord, but You're going to have to help my unbelief. Things are looking pretty bleak. Mason and Lila are selling the house, and right now Irene won't even try to get better. It looks to me like we need a miracle, Lord. But I don't know if I have enough faith to ask You for that.*

The next morning Reagan's phone rang. A familiar voice said, "Reagan? Dad finally got hold of me. He said you drove all the way out to the place looking for me. Sorry to be so much trouble. I've been out of touch. I guess I should have told someone I was leaving. Tell me about Aunt Rini." Noah pronounced the nickname with long e's.

Reagan told him. As soon as they hung up, she set out for Mahoney Manor to be with Irene.

Two days later, Reagan was reading aloud to her friend when a tall young man with long black hair burst through the door pushing a wheelchair. Irene had been listening quietly, her hands at her side, her eyes closed. At the sound of Noah's voice, her eyes flitted open. But the joy in her face changed to dismay when Noah said, "Aunt Rini, I've come to take you for a ride. I have your doctor's permission, and I won't take 'no' for an answer." Gently pulling aside Irene's lap robe, he lifted her out of the hospital bed and into the wheelchair.

The old woman stiffened with protest.

"I don't want to hear it," Noah said crisply. "You need some fresh air." He turned to Reagan. "Can you come with us?" His blue eyes pleaded.

"Of course," Reagan said, closing the book and standing up. "But—where?"

Noah leaned down and whispered, "I'm taking her to the one place I think I can get through to her to stop this deathwatch nonsense. We're stopping on our way out of Lincoln to pick up a nurse to make the trip with us. But I'd like you to come if you can. It shouldn't take more than a day or two."

Noah was taking Irene to Custer County. He had rented a full-size van, and as he gently settled Irene into the plush captain's chair at his side, he said, "Don't worry about a thing, Aunt Rini. We've a nurse, and Reagan's boss said she could have a couple of days off. So relax and enjoy the drive."

From her seat behind Noah, Reagan noticed that Irene watched the familiar landscape with something approaching interest. More than once Reagan caught Noah's eye in the rearview mirror. She smiled and nodded encouragement.

Irene fell asleep long before they arrived at her grandparents' homestead. Noah carried her into the old farmhouse and upstairs to bed. As Reagan covered the frail form with a quilt, Irene sighed almost happily. The nurse was to share Irene's room, and Reagan would be across the hall.

Irene slept until mid-morning the next day. The nurse called for Noah and Reagan. At the sound of Noah's voice saying good morning, Irene opened her eyes wide and looked around her. She let out a cry of delight.

Noah asked gently, "Did I get the color right, Aunt Rini?"

Tears of joy slid down Irene's cheeks. She nodded. Then, very carefully, she formed the word "Yes." With great effort she added, "Jus—T righ-T."

After the nurse had helped Irene eat breakfast and get dressed, Noah carried her downstairs and outside. Reagan followed, but the moment she was certain Irene was secure and comfortable in her wheelchair, she headed back inside.

Irene called her back. "Ray—ray."

Reagan turned. Irene was motioning feebly. "Ray. Come."

Reagan looked doubtfully at Noah, but he nodded *yes*. "We're just going for a walk. Please come." Without another word, Noah wheeled the chair around and headed for the ridge that ran along the back of the house. He stopped at the top of the ridge where a small wrought iron fence guarded two small graves. Noah sat down beside the chair.

Reagan knelt down on the opposite side of Irene's wheelchair, smiling to herself as Irene moved her crippled hand as if to stroke Noah's long black hair.

Abruptly, Noah moved to where he could kneel directly in front of his aunt. He reached up to grip the armrests of the wheelchair and peered into Irene's face, his blue eyes brilliant with emotion. "I did what you said, Aunt Rini. I broke it off with Angela. Quit my job. Packed up." He paused, looking away briefly before adding, "And I think I've started to make things right with God, too." He cleared his throat. "It took a while to get things straight in my head . . . to know what I want. That's why I took so long to get back here. I disconnected from everything for a few days."

Noah looked soberly up at his aunt. "But I'm not disconnected anymore. I'm back to stay. And now I want you to take your own advice. You said doing what is right isn't easy. You said I shouldn't be afraid of hard work. That building a good life is always worth the work."

Noah took his aunt's aged hands in his. "Listen to yourself, Aunt Rini. You've never been afraid of hard work." He squeezed her hands, gently shaking them, "Listen to me. You can build your life again. I'll help you." He glanced at Reagan. "And from what I've seen of her, so will Reagan."

Irene took in a sharp breath. It was punctuated by something that almost sounded like sobs. Reagan put her hand on her friend's shoulder. At her touch, Irene shook her head.

Noah interrupted her thoughts. "Aunt Rini, no one—do you hear me?—no one is going to sell your home. Not now. Not ever. I don't care whether you live in it or not. If you want it to just stand there and rot, then it will stand there and rot." He raised a hand to stroke his aunt's cheek and half-whispered, "I promise."

Irene sucked in a breath. She pulled her hands from Noah's grasp, laid one palm on each of Noah's cheeks, and with great effort leaned down and kissed him on his forehead. Then, she turned to look at Reagan, her face filled with joy.

Reagan would one day look back on that moment and realize that she had witnessed the rebirth of Irene Peale's spirit. And it was all thanks to a six-foot-five-inch angel with long black hair and startlingly pale blue eyes.

"No, Reagan, no," Irene said, laughing. "Not that box."

Reagan had extracted a ridiculously large, ancient hat from the box, plopped it on her head, and posed in dramatic profile to see if she could get Irene to laugh again. It was so wonderful to hear her friend laugh.

From the overstuffed chair where she sat, Irene gestured. "The other one—the one back there—on top of that old sewing machine."

Reagan picked her way through various piles of boxes in the room and finally came to the old sewing machine, which was half hidden from view. She lifted the box Irene wanted, sneezing as a cloud of dust filled the air. Rubbing her nose, Reagan made her way back to where Irene sat and plopped the box in her lap. "Honestly, Irene," Reagan teased, "life was easier before you rehabilitated."

Irene chuckled. "Well, dearie, too bad for you. I'm back home now, and I realize that no one but me can get all of these things sorted properly. I won't have happen to my things what happened to Oma Karyn's." She paused before adding, "Someone as thoughtful about returning family heirlooms as you might not be at the next Ritter auction. There's no one much to care about these things, but the Historical Society might be interested in some of it"—Irene touched Reagan's nose lightly—"and there is a certain dark-haired friend of mine with a nose for history who might enjoy sleuthing out some of the more unusual items." Irene rattled the box, then lifted the lid and held it out for Reagan's inspection. "Like this."

Reagan looked in the box. It was nearly filled with hundreds of buttons in every imaginable size and shape. Atop the pile of loose buttons was a long strand of individual buttons threaded onto a narrow piece of frayed yellow ribbon.

"Be careful," Irene warned as Reagan reached it. "The ribbon may be rotted, and if it breaks, the mystery of the charm string will be more difficult to solve."

"Mystery?" Reagan asked. "Charm string?"

Irene nodded. "Charm strings were a passion of Victorian ladies. They traded buttons, and young men of the day gave their special friends buttons as gifts." Irene smiled. "One bit of folklore says that the goal was to get 999 buttons on a string. Then the giver of the thousandth button would be the young lady's husband." Irene ran her finger along the string of buttons. "But another story said that if the thousandth button was ever added to the string, its owner was destined to be an old maid."

"I like the first story better," Reagan said.

"Yes, I thought you might," Irene teased. "Shall I call Noah and ask him to stop at Prairie Pieceworks and buy a special button the next time he's in town? With what's in here it shouldn't take you long at all to get the other 999."

Reagan pretended to study the button string. "I don't know anything about buttons." She fingered the first one on the string, a large round button with initials engraved on its shiny gold surface.

Irene offered. "Interesting isn't it? It's from President Washington's inauguration."

Reagan looked up in amazement. "You're kidding!"

Irene shook her head from side to side. "Nope. Not kidding. I found the exact button in a book."

Reagan laid the button string back in the box. "This has to be valuable."

Irene shrugged. "It doesn't matter. I wouldn't sell it. I think the Historical Society might be interested. I've heard that complete strings are becoming more and more rare. This one belonged to a milliner who lived up in Millersburg. That's even a stronger reason for the Nebraska society to have it." Irene paused before adding, "Of course, I'm certain they would be especially delighted if the donation could be accompanied by a history of the woman who collected all these buttons."

Reagan took the bait. "I could see what I could find out."

Irene smiled. "Yes. I know." Then she added slyly, "You'll want to visit the county museum in Broken Bow. Noah might even help with some of the research. He's been trying to learn more about county history. He has some project in mind, although he won't tell me about it yet." Irene smiled slyly. "Who knows? You two might discover something else along the way."

Reagan felt herself blushing again.

Irene said, "Why don't you take it all home? All I know is that her name was Nora O'Dell. She gave the buttons and some quilts to my grandmother. Oma Karyn gave the buttons to me a few weeks before she had her stroke. She promised that the next time I came out she would tell me about Miss O'Dell. But there was no 'next time.' Oma died before I got a chance to go back."

That evening at home, Reagan set the box on her kitchen table. She brewed a fresh pot of coffee and settled into a chair. Laying the charm string aside, she began to filter through the buttons in the tin. It wasn't long before she began to sort them by color and size. She moved a desk light to the kitchen table and got a magnifying glass. The intricate designs atop some of the buttons were fascinating. There were buttons of every imaginable color. Some had scenes embossed in metals. Others seemed to be made of porcelain. There was even one that had a detailed drawing of a human eye under glass.

Reagan finally spilled all the buttons out on the tabletop.

As she leveled the colorful mound with her hand, a piece of paper fluttered to the kitchen floor. Bending to retrieve it, Reagan let out a little "oh." The paper was a business card, beautifully engraved with a line drawing of women trying on hats. The card was imprinted with Nora O'Dell's name. Reagan frowned as she read the imprint. Irene had said that Nora O'Dell was a milliner in Millersburg, but the card bore a Lincoln address.

Reagan went to get her planner. Opening it to Saturday, she added to her list, *Library-buttons* and *Hist. Soc.-Nora O'Dell, milliner, 123 N. 11th St—18??*. Beside each item, Nora printed the letter A. She would do them first. Mowing the grass had just become a C.

When Irene had mentioned Noah Ritter helping to research buttons, Reagan had smiled inwardly. Noah might be unusually interested in history, but she couldn't quite picture him bent over button books or researching a nineteenth-century hatmaker. Once again, Noah surprised her. And, while he never gave Reagan the thousandth button, which would have assured her he would be her husband, he did help her discover clues to the story of Nora O'Dell. And while they researched the story of Nora O'Dell, they began another of their own.

When I was just a little girl, my granny said to me,
"Come here, my child and sit a while upon your
granny's knee.
I'll bet you didn't know that I was once a child
like you.
I laughed and sang, and jumped and ran, and
sometimes felt sad, too."
And then my granny opened up her magic
button box,
It held more fun than dolls or tops, or wooden
building blocks.

For Granny had a story for the buttons, red and blue,
Some came from dresses, some from coats, and some
from baby shoes.
The black one was her wedding dress, the gold one
was Grandpa's,
He wore it when he went to war, to fight for
freedom's cause.
I've stored up all the stories, and I've written them
for you,
Some I made up, some Granny told, and some of
them are true.

CHAPTER 1

Remembering Mama

When my father and my mother forsake me,
then the* L*ORD* *will take me up.
Psalm 27:10

Elnora Calhoun didn't know why Pap didn't love her. Oh, it was true that Pap didn't seem to love anyone, for he snarled and snapped at her brother Will, too. Still, when he yelled at her that the biscuits were too hard or the pie tasted sour, it hurt. Elnora took the hurt deep inside herself and hid it. But it stayed there, forming a cold, hard lump that seemed to grow heavier with time. There were days when the weight of it made Elnora want to curl up around the tight ball of hurt and stay hidden in bed. But fear of Pap's buggy whip always made her get up.

Tall, fair-haired Will saw what Pap's anger was doing to his sister. He tried to comfort her, telling her that Pap hadn't always been that way. Will could remember when Pap's dark eyes still knew how to smile. He thought that maybe, if they were patient, Pap would remember the good times when Mama was still alive, would remember smiling and try it again.

Elnora couldn't remember Mama. It was Elnora's birthday that had become what the girl thought of as her mother's "death-day." And thus, Elnora reasoned, it was her coming that had taken the smile from Pap's eyes. Will said it wasn't her fault that Mama had died. He said to just forget it and ignore Pap. But Elnora couldn't forget. She couldn't ignore Pap, either.

On a clear spring morning when Elnora was nearly sixteen years old, Pap threw an entire batch of biscuits against the wall and stormed out of the kitchen, swearing. Will was in the barn milking the cow when it happened. He didn't see how Elnora's hands shook as she picked up the biscuits. He didn't see her position them carefully on the painted drop-leaf table, first making a small circle and then piling them up in layers, just like a cake.

Will knew his father was angry, but he didn't dare ask questions. He finished the milking. Uncurling his lanky body from the milking stool, he crossed the farmyard to set the pail on the back porch by the door and called good-bye to Elnora through the screen before loping back to the barn to help harness the team. He would go without breakfast, hoping that Elnora had packed unusually large portions in the lunch basket.

Elnora half-whispered her good-bye to Will. Trembling, she retrieved the broom from the corner behind the stove and swept up the pieces of the crockery bowl that had held the biscuits. She bit her lower lip, forcing back the words she wanted to shout at the walls of the kitchen. *How am I supposed to bake good biscuits without a receipt?* It was hard to know just how much saleratus to put in. And try as she might, sometimes she got confused about whether to put saleratus or soda in. You used one with sweet milk, and the other with sour . . . but Elnora couldn't always remember which went with which. *Mrs. Johnson up the road offered to teach me, but you wouldn't let me go up there. You said the Johnsons should mind their business and we'd mind ours.*

Elnora sighed and shook her head. She stopped sweeping and looked through the back door toward the barn where Will and Pap were harnessing the team. They were going to plow what Pap called the "north forty" today. At supper last night Pap had warned her to pack an extra-big lunch for the next day. He had said that he and Will would "Likely be gone till sundown tomorrow, Elnora. Pack us plenty of grub. And don't you be letting our supper get cold, no matter how late we come in."

Gone till sundown . . . the words rang in Elnora's ears. She stepped out on the back porch, taking care to avoid a loose board. Pap didn't seem to think it important to fix that board. It never got in anybody's way but hers.

To the south, Elnora could see the smoke rising from the Johnsons' chimney. Mrs. Johnson was likely cleaning off the breakfast table, sending her men out to the fields, too. But Elnora knew that at the Johnsons' breakfast table there had been no harsh words. Mrs. Johnson's biscuits had probably been perfect. *And even if they weren't,* Elnora thought bitterly, *Olli Johnson wouldn't say a word.* Everyone in the section knew that Olli Johnson worshiped his wife, loved his sons, and doted on his only daughter, Ida. Sometimes Elnora was tempted to think that the stork had dropped her at the wrong house.

Elnora shook her head. She knew storks didn't bring babies. Anyone living on a farm knew that. She just liked to pretend about it.

She passed the flat palm of her thin hand across her forehead as if to erase the beautiful specter of life at the Johnsons from her mind. Her hand dropped to her midsection, and she pushed against her stomach as if to tame the churning, hard lump that never seemed to go away these days.

Gone till sundown. Elnora went back inside. Crossing the small room that served as both parlor and kitchen, she pushed aside a frayed red gingham curtain and entered the pantry that had been her room for as long as she could remember. A narrow cot tucked beneath one window and an inverted produce box that served as a combination desk and dressing table were all the furniture she had ever known. Three hooks had been pounded into the wall at the foot of her cot to accommodate her wardrobe. Elnora pulled off her stained apron. Shivering with nervousness, she pulled her clothes down off the hooks. Then, she sat down abruptly on the edge of the cot, breathless with wondering if she had the courage to carry out what she had begun.

Finally, she stood up. On the opposite side of the kitchen was Pap's room. As Elnora crossed the kitchen she almost clung to the wall opposite the door to her father's room. Even when he was gone he left something behind that threatened to hold her back.

Elnora hurried across the kitchen, out onto the porch with the broken board, across the farmyard, and into the barn. She paused just inside the barn door, waiting for her eyes to adjust to the dusky light before climbing the ladder to the loft. In the far corner of the loft, behind a dank-smelling pile of half-rotten hay, stood a small painted trunk bearing the name *Kathleen O'Dell* and the date 1852. Elnora raised the lid and pulled out an empty sack of heavy striped fabric that had once been filled with goose down. It was one of two such pillows Kathleen had made for her marriage bed.

There wasn't much left of Kathleen O'Dell. Will had told her how Pap had built a huge bonfire in the farmyard and burned nearly everything that reminded him of Kathleen. The pillow cases and the few other things in the trunk had survived only because they were tucked in a dark corner of the barn loft. Since Will did all the chores that required ascending into the loft, the trunk had been left alone.

Will had told Elnora how Pap had refused anyone's help with his squalling, premature, infant daughter. Lining a shoe box with a fat quilt batt and setting it on the oven door to keep her warm, he had persistently fed her with an eyedropper. When he knew she was going to live he handed Elnora to nine-year-old Will. "This is your sister. Take good care of her. Anything you need to know, hightail it up to the Johnsons' and ask. She'll make us a good cook someday." Pap had left the naming of the child to Will, who pondered for days before finally deciding to call his sister Elnora after the heroine in a story his mother once told.

Will had managed to save a picture of Mama. It was hidden in the trunk. As Elnora grew, he told her everything he could remember. Mama was from a far-off place called Ireland, where the hills were green and there were crumbling castles just on the hill above her village. She called her town a village. She had a different way of talking that sounded almost like music. In the evenings, Will said, she would finish her chores and sit down by the stove and tell stories about knights and battles and someone called Saint Christopher.

Will said in those days, when Pap came in from the fields with a scowl on his face, Mama could tease him into smiling. Will said that the very air in the kitchen used to relax, just because Mama was there. It made Elnora feel terrible, knowing that if she had never been born, the magic would still be there. Somehow she knew that if it were not for her, the paint on the house would never have been allowed to peel. And the loose board on the porch would have been fixed right away.

Now, kneeling before the open trunk, Elnora held her mother's photo tenderly, trying to memorize the gentle expression, the pale eyes. Self-consciously, Elnora reached up to touch her hair. Her mother had dark hair, but Elnora's was the color of the straw in the fields. Will had told her that sometimes her hair glowed, just like the bales of hay against a dark sky when the sun made them shine brighter than ever. Peering at Kathleen's photograph,

Elnora reassured herself that while her hair might be a different color from her mama's, nearly everything else about her was an exact replica of the photograph before her.

Pap had once called Elnora's eyes "watery gray," but they were not really gray. Elnora knew that Pap's comment had just been his way of trying not to say anything nice at all. That was his way. Will had told her that Mama's eyes had flecks of blue and green so that they could be different colors, depending on the weather and the season and her mood. Will had said Elnora's eyes were exactly the same way, and that most of the time they tended toward green. If Pap thought his daughter's eyes were "watery gray," that was because Pap had never really looked at her. Elnora had always held herself away from Pap. Respectful but aloof. Gray eyes, no emotion. That seemed to work the best with Pap.

Elnora put the photo back in the trunk. As much as she wanted it, she could not bring herself to take it away from Will. She pulled a second pillow tick from the bottom of the trunk and stuffed it inside the first. Something fell out of the tick. The sound of it hitting the bottom of the trunk made Elnora jump. Laughing at herself for being so nervous, Elnora picked up the small cloth bag. Mama's mending kit. The soft bag held a useless thimble so old that it had holes worn through the top, two rusty needles . . . and one brass button.

The button was something special. Will didn't know why, but he had told Elnora that Mama had always made certain that that button was in her mending kit. He said that once, when she had dropped it and it went under the porch, she had made Pap rip up a board to retrieve it. Elnora couldn't imagine Pap taking time to do such a thing just to retrieve a button. Will shrugged. "That's the way he was with Mama. Whatever she asked, he did it. Didn't mind it, either. Just did it and smiled."

Elnora looked down at the metal button that bore the

letters *GW* in the center, encircled with the words *Long Live the President.* Interlocking ovals around the edge of the button had other initials, including *RI, NC,* and *SC.* Elnora didn't know what the letters meant, but it didn't matter. The button had meant something to her mother. Will wouldn't care about the button. Elnora held it tightly in her left hand as she descended the ladder from the loft.

Back in her room, Elnora used a safety pin to affix the *GW* button to the inside of the bag. She stuffed her clothes inside the bag and headed toward the door, where she paused momentarily to take one last look at the room that had been her universe for all of her fifteen years. She would miss Will. Swallowing hard, Elnora opened the screen door and stepped outside. She took a deep breath to reassure herself and headed up the rocky path toward the road.

Driving up the road toward Falls City, Olli Johnson couldn't resist looking up toward the Calhoun place. Thinking of Elnora and Will, Olli sighed. He shook the reins, urging his team up the incline that stretched ahead. "Get along there, Bess. Go on, there, Bones."

Bess and Bones picked up the pace, unaware that as they jerked the wagon ahead, Elnora nearly fell off the back. She clung to the edge, finally managing to pull herself up and slip beneath the tarp Olli Johnson had drawn across the load to protect his wife's eggs and butter from the sun.

Elnora remained hidden beneath the tarp for what seemed like hours. Finally, she heard the hollow sound of the horses' feet clomping across the bridge just outside of town. When the wagon cleared the boards of the bridge, Elnora squeezed between the tarp and the back of the wagon, lowered herself to the road, and skittered into the underbrush growing alongside the creek.

She waited until Mr. Johnson was well out of sight before standing up and heading across the fields toward the northwest. She doubted that Pap would look very hard for her, but he would make some effort just so the neighbors wouldn't talk. And Will—Elnora knew that Pap might try to beat something out of Will. She hoped not. She had never hinted of her plan to run off. And with her gone, he would need Will more than ever. She doubted he would use the buggy whip. Even if he did, he wouldn't hit hard.

She had biscuits to last four days, if she was careful. She would follow the creek toward the northwest, hoping to come across the old freighter's trail she had heard Pap talk about. That would take her to a better road.

Somewhere to the north and west there was a big city. If she wore the black and tan calico dress stuffed in the pillowcase and tied her hair back, she could pass for at least sixteen. Maybe older. She would hide near the train station and wait for a passenger train to arrive. Then she could mix in with the crowd. She would pretend she had just gotten off the train, head for a hotel, and ask for work. She could pretend she had left her bags at the station. Just thinking about it made Elnora shiver. Elnora told herself it was excitement.

When Will and Pap came in from the "north forty" that evening, they were greeted by the frantic bawling of the unmilked cow. Pap frowned towards the house. No lamp shown in the window. No smoke rose from the chimney. Swearing violently, Pap left Will to milk the cow and stormed toward the house. Will cringed inwardly. While he milked the cow, he strained to hear what might be happening up at the house.

The sound of the back door slamming preceded Pap's return to the barn. He grabbed an old bridle down from where it hung beside the harness. "Breakfast dishes still soaking in the washpan. Fire gone out in the stove." Pap's voice wavered a little. He thrust one dirty hand through his tangled hair, adding, "She's taken her clothes. Run off, I guess." He thrust the bridle at Will. "She's probably up at the Johnsons telling all kind of tales. Go get her. She's had the day to think it over. Likely she's ready to come back. Olli Johnson knows better than to interfere in my affairs. He won't be keeping her against my will."

Will thought it odd that Pap didn't seem to want to face the Johnsons himself. He put the bridle on old Winny and plodded across the dark fields toward where a pinprick of light shone from the Johnsons' farmhouse. Mrs. Johnson came to the door, clucking in sympathy even as she shook her head. "Why, no, Will. I haven't seen Elnora. Why?"

From his chair beside the stove, Olli Johnson listened as Will explained. He lowered his newspaper and spoke across the top of the editorial column toward the door. "You tell Eli I drove into town this morning. Couldn't have been long after you two headed for the fields. Didn't see a thing."

Olli paused and took a puff from the pipe he was smoking. His eyes narrowed as he remembered something. Something that had made him turn around just as the team pulled across the bridge and into town. Olli pondered and took another puff on his pipe. Finally, he shook his head. "Nope, can't say as I know a thing. But I'll tell you this, Will, if that girl's run off I wish her Godspeed. And I'd say the same if you was to follow." Olli looked meaningfully at Will. When the boy didn't respond, Olli raised the paper back up so that his bifocals would adjust to the tiny print on the editorial page.

Just as Will turned to go, he heard Olli Johnson's voice from behind the paper. "If you *was* to follow, Will, I'd say heading for the old freighter's trail and then northwest toward Lincoln might be the way to go."

The morning after Elnora disappeared, Pap took the road southeast to a nearby town. He returned with a wizened, stringy-haired woman in tow.

"This here's Selma," he announced curtly to Will. "She'll be cooking for us now."

Pap never said Elnora's name again. He ordered Will to "stay out of your sister's room," and made up a cot for Selma in the lean-to next to the kitchen.

CHAPTER 2

Defending Lily

Fools because of their transgression, and because of their iniquities, are afflicted.
Psalm 107:17

Three days of walking across a succession of freshly plowed fields and virgin prairie dampened Elnora's enthusiasm about her new life. One morning she had to traverse several acres that had been burned off to promote more lush spring growth. The trek left her bare feet tender from contact with blackened stubble and exposed rocks. More than once she climbed up creek banks still covered with late-melting spring snow.

Her diet of increasingly stale biscuits washed down with whatever creek water she could find left her ravenously hungry. She slept fitfully at night, terrified by the sounds of yelping coyotes. She shivered at the thought that perhaps all the Pawnee and Otoe Indians were not on the reservation, after all.

When Elnora finally came within sight of the city, it was after dark on the fourth night of her trek. She had walked nearly eighty miles. The hem of her dress was torn, her hair was tangled and dirty, and she felt shaky and weak. She dared not go into town until she could put on her clean dress. And she must try to do something with her hair. Perhaps she could simply tuck it all up under a bonnet.

In the moonlight she saw the outline of what appeared to be a barn. It proved to be more of a shed than a barn, but inside there were two stalls, one vacant. Other than to momentarily stop nibbling the top of the board that divided his stall from his former partner's, the broken-down old nag in one stall made no protest when Elnora crept in the door. She sank into the hay and fell asleep almost instantly.

"Stop that, Frank! I said I'd meet you, but I don't want any rough stuff. Hey, you heard what I—"

The sound of someone being slapped brought Elnora instantly, completely awake.

A female voice tinged with fear pleaded, "What's the matter, honey? Settle down. We're going to have plenty of fun. Just don't be so—"

This time, there was the sound of a struggle, then ripping fabric. A muffled voice was protesting, but it sounded odd. Elnora peered over the edge of the stall where she had slept. A man with his back to her was forcing a woman against the wall. Her dress was ripped, and there was a wad of cloth stuffed in her mouth.

Elnora sank back into the hay, her heart pounding, her mind racing. She had been afraid that she had been discovered. But now fear gave way to rage. There was a shovel leaning against the opposite corner of the stall. She grabbed it, peeking over the side of the stall again to get her bearings. There was no door on the stall where she had spent the night, and she reasoned that if she moved quickly enough, she could land a blow to the man's head before he had a chance to whirl around and defend himself.

Taking a deep breath, Elnora stood up. She grasped the shovel near the base and raised it over her head. It felt as if she were moving in slow motion as she lunged across the space between herself and the couple. The man barely had time to turn his head before she landed a blow on his right shoulder. He reached out to grab the shovel, but he had been caught off guard and off balance. He missed, and Elnora raised the shovel again and slammed him hard against the side of his head. He toppled over like a felled tree and lay silent in the dust. The woman pulled the wad of cloth from her mouth and scooted herself away. She sat in the dirt, trying to catch her breath, staring up at Elnora in disbelief.

Elnora was trembling all over. She gulped for air before croaking, "Do you think he's dead?" She dropped the shovel and slid down the side of the stall opposite the woman.

"Frank? Dead?" came the reply. The woman clutched at her torn dress and laughed bitterly. "Nah. Frank's too mean to die." She leaned forward and watched him for a moment. "See? He's breathing. But he's gonna have a whopper of a headache when he comes to." The woman brushed a lock of white-blonde hair back from her forehead. She raised one knee, revealing ornately ruffled and trimmed petticoats. Resting her arm on her knee she looked back at Elnora and said, "Thanks."

Elnora nodded.

"Where'd you come from?"

"I was asleep in the empty stall."

A tall black rooster strutted its way across the doorway of the shed. It paused and crowed, heartily flapping gigantic wings. Frank stirred momentarily. Elnora started to jump up, but then he moaned and sank back into unconsciousness.

Elnora remembered the outline of a small house not far from the shack. "What if the owners find us?"

The woman nodded toward Frank. "This is his place—miserable as it is." She started to stand up. When she did, the entire bodice of her dress fell down around her waist, exposing more elegant "unmentionables."

At sight of how bad the damage was to the bodice of her dress the woman moaned, "Oh, I'm in for it now. Goldie will tan my hide good when she sees this. It's brand new." She sank back to the earth in dismay.

"Goldie?" Elnora asked.

The woman looked up. With a sardonic grin she said, "Yeah, Goldie. My—uh—employer."

Elnora just stared.

The woman's expression changed. She stopped teasing. "How old are you, honey?" she asked.

"Fif—sixteen," Elnora lied.

"Where you from?"

"From somewhere I'm not going back to. Ever."

Understanding filled the woman's eyes. "Me, too." She held out her hand. "My name's Lily. Lily Langley. I was about 'fif-sixteen' myself when I decided I didn't like where I was from and I was going somewhere else. That's when I met Goldie. All her girls have flower names. There's Rose, and Pansy, and Violet, and Iris. I always liked lilies, so that's my name." Lily gathered the bodice of her dress up. "You looking for work?"

Elnora shook her head. "No—I mean, yes, but—"

Lily interrupted her. "Not my kind of work, honey. I can tell you're not ready for that. Goldie needs a cook."

"I been cleaning and cooking most all my life."

Lily smiled. "Bet you never got paid for it."

Elnora shook her head.

"Goldie pays her girls well. Even the cook. Come on. You'll like her." Lily got up and headed for the door. "What'd you say your name was?"

"Nora. Nora O'Dell." Elnora hoped it sounded natural.

"Well, Nora, pleased to make your acquaintance. I'm going to get a blanket out of Frank's house to cover myself up. Goldie won't be up yet. Maybe I can sneak in and get this mended before she finds out."

"I've got an extra dress," Nora offered. She went back to the empty stall and retrieved her pillowcase. "We're about the same size. If you've got a needle and thread, I can mend your dress for you. I've done lots of mending." As she talked, Nora pulled her black calico dress from the bag, apologizing. "It's not much, but—"

Lily reached out and grabbed the dress. "It's perfect." Lily was already pulling her torn dress down over her petticoats. She stepped out of it and then tried to pull Nora's black calico on. "Just a minute—" She wriggled out of two petticoats and handed them to Nora. Smoothing the skirt of Nora's good dress down over her petticoats, she said, "There. That's better. How do I look?"

"Plain," Nora said.

"Plain is good. I shouldn't have snuck out on Goldie like that. This way, if she catches me before we get upstairs, at least I'm not dressed for work."

Together, Lily and Nora managed to stuff the yards and yards of satin and lace that made up Lily's "work dress" into the two old pillowcases Nora had brought with her. Nora picked up two buttons that had popped off the dress and added them to the pillowcase. Finally, they stepped across Frank's motionless body and out into the sunshine.

Nora hesitated. "Do you think he'll be all right? Shouldn't we—"

Lily swore softly. "No, we shouldn't. He's a varmint. He deserves what he got." As the girls walked toward the road, Lily added, "I deserve what I got, too. I was cheating on Goldie. Trying to make some money on my own. Guess I learned my lesson." Lily shivered slightly. "I hate to think what would have happened if you hadn't been in that stall—" Lily grabbed Nora by the elbow and pulled her toward the road. "Guess you're my guardian angel, honey."

The two women headed into town. As they walked, Lily told Nora about Goldie's Garden. "Violet is Goldie's favorite. We all know that, but we don't mind. Violet's a sweetie. The professor is teaching her to sing. Ivy and Rose are best friends. They both have black, curly hair. Some people think they're sisters, but they're not. Iris is real smart. She kind of mothers us all. Then there's Fern. Stay clear of her. She's been here the longest, and the longer she's here the meaner she seems to get. Just don't get in Fern's way and you'll be all right."

They had reached the edge of Lincoln. The streets were quiet. One- and two-story buildings, some brick, some frame, stretched to the north and east. Imagining the broad, dusty streets filled with wagons and people made Nora's stomach lurch with a combination of excitement and fear.

Lily continued with her lecture on the finer points of operating Goldie's Garden. "As long as we keep things quiet, the sheriff is happy to look the other way. Goldie doesn't allow any rough stuff, and she isn't afraid to run a man off. She packs a pistol in her pocket and she gets mean real fast when anybody tries anything out of line. She pays a lady doctor to take care of us."

The girls had been making their way up an alley between two long rows of buildings. Lily paused to catch her breath. "Be straight with Goldie, and she'll make you glad you work for her. Cross her, and she'll kick you out on your ear faster than you can pack your pillowcase. Which is why I'm grateful you were there with a shovel and a dress to help me out. And why I'd appreciate your not saying anything about Frank. I learned my lesson."

"What if Frank tells?" Nora wanted to know.

Lily smiled smugly. "Frank won't say a word. If Goldie finds out he tried to rough me up he'll be banned for life. Men like Frank don't want to have to deal with women like Goldie. I don't have to worry about Frank."

CHAPTER 3

Goldie's Garden

I was envious at the foolish,
when I saw the prosperity of the wicked.
Psalm 73:3

Never in her fifteen years had Nora imagined the existence of a place as beautiful as Goldie's. When Lily led her through the back door of the two-story brick building, down a long hall paneled with dark mahogany wood and to the parlor doorway at the front of the house, Nora let out an amazed "ohhhh." Three immense cut-glass chandeliers hung from the ceiling of the parlor, which was one vast, sparkling, light-filled room with walls completely covered by floor-to-ceiling mirrors. At the east end of the parlor, an ornately carved bar was set into the wall, partitioned off from the room with heavy purple velvet draperies trimmed with wide gold fringe.

"Goldie calls this her Hall of Mirrors," Lily said proudly. "It's where we entertain." The Hall of Mirrors was furnished with several lounges upholstered in thick, deep-red velvet. Each sofa was adorned with several silk pillows, most of which had been embroidered with homey mottoes. Nora reached out to touch one that said *Remember Me* in bright yellow satin stitches made on blue silk.

"I made that one," Lily said. "I can teach you. We do a lot of handwork in our spare time. Sometimes Goldie or the professor reads to us while we sew." Lily sighed. "Goldie looks out for all of the boarders. That's a nice word, don't you think? *Boarders.* Helps us feel more respectable."

Nora bent down to run her hands over the surface of the carpet that covered the polished wood floor. It was so thick that it sunk beneath the pressure of her hand. Its surface was covered with a maze of elaborate designs in rich dark reds, blues, and golds.

"The carpets are from the Orient," Lily said. "We waited nearly a year for them to come."

Nora had no idea where the Orient was, but if the people there could create such gorgeous things as this carpet, she wanted to go there someday.

"I'll show you the dining room and the rest of the house later. We'd better scoot if we're going to get this dress fixed before Goldie gets up."

Nora followed Lily up the wide stairway, tripping as she looked about her. The same wonderful designs from the parlor carpet were repeated in a runner on the stairs. The intricately carved railing and the spindles shone with polish. Nora was loathe to touch the railing for fear of marring its shine with her handprints.

At the top of the stairs, Lily held a finger up to her lips. The two girls tiptoed down the hallway and past two heavy closed doors. Lily opened the third door and Nora followed her in.

"This—this room—this whole big room is yours?" Nora asked in wonder.

Lily shrugged. "This? Sure." She was already struggling to pull her torn dress from Nora's pillowcase. "You should see Violet's room. It's much bigger than mine."

Nora looked about her at Lily's room. A motto hanging on the wall said, *All the Comforts of Home*. There was a soft blue coverlet on the brass bed, and while no Oriental carpet covered Lily's floor, there was a small rug right where her feet would hit it when she got out of bed.

Looking at the rug, Nora remembered trying to dress under the covers at home, pulling on three pairs of stockings before reaching down for the heavy leather boots Pap gave her when Will outgrew them. The boots never fit, but of course Pap was never concerned about that. Nora thought it the supreme height of luxury to be able to actually get out of bed barefoot on a cold morning and have one's feet land on a rug.

The walls in the room were papered. Huge clusters of open pink roses danced across a background of fancy designs. A panel of exquisite lace hung from a rod at the top of the long, narrow window. The lace was gathered up the middle to give it a soft fullness. Everything in Lily's room was covered with a beautiful cloth of some kind, and the edge of each cloth was decorated with silk fringe in a rainbow of colors.

Lily said, "Goldie has the most elegant room you'll ever see. Her curtains are velvet. And she has an Oriental carpet that goes almost wall to wall. And a four-poster bed, and a lamp with beaded fringe. One of her best customers is a hunter. Goldie has bearskins and even a tiger skin high up on the walls." Lily sighed. "Wait until you see it."

Lily opened a trunk that stood in the corner of her room and pulled out a small sewing kit. She sat down on the floor next to the window to examine her torn dress and shook her head. "This is a mess. I don't know what I'm going to do. If Goldie finds out I was trying to go it on my own—"

Nora sat down beside her. "Here, let me have a look." She held the dress up, admiring the soft sheen of the fabric. Frank had popped several buttons off the front, and there was a jagged tear at the neckline near the shoulder.

"I only found these two buttons in the dirt," Nora said.

Lily knelt before the trunk and fumbled in the tray that formed the uppermost storage layer. She pulled out a small, clear jar, unscrewed the top, and spilled a pile of buttons on the floor. "They aren't very fancy. Maybe there are some that will match."

Nora found a match for the small white pearl buttons. "I don't know about this tear," she said. Then she had an idea. "Do you have any ribbon this color?"

Lily shook her head. "Why?"

"Well," Nora reasoned, "if you had ribbon, we could just sew the rip up and not worry how it looks. Then I could add the ribbon as a trim here at the neck. We could ruffle it up some and it would cover the rip. No one would ever see it." She smiled. "If I do it just right, it will look like the dress came that way. Goldie might not even notice."

Lily removed the top tray from the trunk. Reaching into the depths of the bottom section, she pulled out a pair of elaborately trimmed drawers. She pointed to the rows of peach-colored trim along the bottom edges. "Is there enough of this?"

Nora examined the undergarment. It would take only a few moments to take the trim off. She nodded. Turning the garment wrong side out, she began to snip away at the threads holding the ribbon in place.

"Here," Lily said, reaching for the drawers, "let me do that. You start mending the rip."

The two girls worked for nearly an hour, during which Lily learned that Nora was quite innocent regarding the ways of the world and took it upon herself to initiate her protégé. "Goldie doesn't usually entertain the gentlemen. But she does just about everything else, from ordering the groceries to buying our clothes to arranging the doctor's visits. She lets us keep half of what we make and she pays the bills with the rest. There are six of us. I already told you we're called boarders." She jumped up. "Some of us even have our own business cards."

Lily went to the nightstand beside her bed where a few small cards were stacked next to a vase of flowers. She held out a card to Nora, who took it and read, "Miss Lily Langley, Gent's Furnishings, 134 South Ninth Street—All the Comforts of Home."

She sat down next to Nora again and took up the mending. "I get lots of business because of the name Lily." At Nora's noncommittal nod, Lily sighed. "My, my, dearie . . . you really do come from the back forty, don't you? Miss Lilie Langtry is an actress. She's very famous, and everyone loves her." Lily reached up and twined a finger through a long curl just in front of one ear. "That's why I did the peroxide job on my hair. I'm not a natural blonde like *the* Miss Langtry, but it helps the image."

Nora had just secured the last ruffle to the neckline of Lily's when footsteps sounded in the hall. Someone knocked at the door, and a mellow voice said, "Lily, darlin', breakfas' is suhved."

Lily grabbed the sewing kit and the untrimmed lingerie and tossed them into the trunk. Quickly closing the lid, she hung the dress on a hook behind the door just as the woman knocked again. "Lily. Is ev-uh-ry-thin' all right?"

Lily ran to the door and opened it. "Everything's fine. I've been out for a walk already and—and—I've brought you a surprise." She stepped back to allow the tallest woman Nora had ever seen into the room.

Nora jumped up quickly, managing to cover the pile of buttons on Lily's floor with her skirt as she reached down to grab her nearly empty pillowcase.

"This is Nora O'Dell," Lily said. "She needs a job. I told her you've been looking for a cook, and she thought she'd come talk to you about it."

"Aftuh breakfas', honey," Goldie said. Her voice was mellow, calm, gentle. She looked at Nora and laughed. "Y'all bringin' that bag to thuh table with yuh?"

Nora looked down at the pillowcase and blushed. "No, ma'am." She set the bag down on the floor. Goldie winked at her and left the room, continuing on down the hallway knocking at doors.

"Thanks for remembering the buttons," Lily whispered as she led Nora down the back stairs to the kitchen. Nora marveled at the reality of a house that actually had two stairways, but her wonder at the food piled on the breakfast table was even greater. Her stomach growled and her mouth began to water as she anticipated the feast. Lily poured them each a cup of coffee. "I know you're near starved, but we should wait for the others. It won't be long." She sat down and pulled Nora down beside her. "Goldie was born in the South. Way South. She doesn't usually talk with that accent, but sometimes it comes back. Especially early in the morning and if she's tired. Most of the time she tries not to talk like a southerner."

Nora just nodded. She was longing to grab the platter of sausage—or potatoes—or eggs—or gravy . . .

Lily continued. "Her voice is mellow, but whooo-*eee*—she's got a temper. Cross her and she turns cold as ice." Lily shivered. "Trust me, honey, you do *not* want to see that side of Goldie."

To keep herself from stuffing an entire biscuit into her mouth, Nora grasped her coffee cup with both hands and took a huge gulp. It was too strong and too hot. Coughing and sputtering, Nora set the cup down. She reached for the milk and sugar and doctored the coffee liberally with both, good-naturedly enduring Lily's comments about her being a babe-in-the-woods.

Nora drank coffee while Lily talked and talked. The liquid helped her stomach stop churning so violently. When were the others going to come down, anyway? Nora looked hopefully toward the stairs.

"Violet told me Goldie's family was real wealthy. She learned to sing and dance. She's smart, too. But they wanted her to marry someone she hated, so she ran off. She worked in New Orleans and learned the ropes from one of the best madames. Then she quit for a while. She moved north and set up a dressmaking business, but it wasn't two years before she moved again and opened this parlor. Nothing but the best of everything. The prettiest girls, the best professors, the finest wines—"

The concept of a professor in a brothel confused Nora, but she had no time to ask Lily to explain. At last, footsteps sounded on the stairs. Goldie was scolding someone, but when she came into the kitchen Nora saw that her arm was about the waist of the girl she was scolding. She gave the girl a friendly shake and then shoved her into a chair.

"Well, girls," Goldie said. "If we're lucky, Lily has brought us a cook." While the other girls pulled their chairs up to the table, Goldie seated herself opposite Nora. Finally, the platters of food were passed. She tried, but Nora could not concentrate on what Goldie was saying. All Nora was to remember of that meal was the food—that, and the sudden realization that she had found a place where Pap's anger could not reach her, and that she would do whatever it took to make certain that she could stay.

CHAPTER 4

Firing the Cook

For the love of money is the root of all evil.
1 Timothy 6:10

"Face it, honey," Goldie said. "You can't cook." As she spoke, the older woman was inserting a knife into what was supposed to be gravy and spreading it on a piece of bread. It was early evening. A gray sky had forced Nora to light the gas lamps in the kitchen. She had set the table for supper between bursts of activity at the kitchen counter, but as Goldie inspected the gravy, Nora realized her first day in the city was about to end in disaster.

Nora had spent the afternoon in the back parlor, listening while Lily and the other girls bantered back and forth about past conquests and future plans. It was Sunday, and Goldie dared not risk ignoring the social taboo of doing business on the Sabbath. Rose, Fern, and Ivy had dressed modestly and gone out for a carriage ride, accompanied by a fully bearded pencil-thin man Goldie introduced as "Shep, the Professor."

Lily said, "I don't know why they call themselves professors . . . unless it's because they have to know so much about everything. But every parlor house has a professor. They usually travel around quite a bit, but Shep's been here ever since I can remember. Goldie depends on him a lot. He knows how to fix just about anything. Wherever we go, Shep goes. That way we have an escort, just like all the respectable ladies in town.

"Shep comes from back east somewhere. He plays the piano and the violin. He even acted on the stage for a while. We're lucky to have someone like Shep around. Violet says the professor before Shep was a low-life drunk, plain and simple. Shep never gets drunk. Except maybe on Sunday once in a while. Even then, he's never mean. When Shep gets drunk he just crashes to the floor wherever he is." Lily giggled. "We all drag him off to bed to sleep it off."

While Lily talked Nora was sewing beautiful flower-shaped buttons on one of Iris's new dresses. Lily, Violet, and Pansy boasted freely about their earnings from the past week. Nora was flabbergasted to hear Iris complain she would get only about ninety dollars when Goldie "settled up" after supper.

Lily and the other girls had introduced Nora to many new realities of life in the city before Goldie interrupted them. "It's time for Nora to really earn her keep." Goldie had hustled Nora down the hall and into the kitchen, pulled an apron off a hook by the back door, and then presented her with three freshly plucked chickens and a myriad of instructions regarding supper. Nora's head was swimming when Goldie finally departed to spend the next few hours in her room "settling up with the girls."

Nora had done her best, but, remembering the luncheon earlier in the day, she knew the results of her hours in the kitchen fell woefully short of Goldie's expectations. When she heard Goldie's steps coming down the back stairs, Nora was filled with dread. Visions of Pap throwing her last batch of biscuits against the kitchen wall resurfaced. Remembering Lily's warning, "Whooo—she's got a temper," Nora was tempted to pull off the apron and run out the back door. But the four-day trek from home had worn her out. Unwilling to face the thought of running away again, she prepared to endure Goldie's temper.

Nora watched Goldie spread the congealed gravy on the piece of white bread and hand it to the small black poodle that sat waiting expectantly at her feet. The little black dog took the bread in its mouth and carried it to a rag rug next to the kitchen door, where it lay down and began daintily licking the gravy from the bread with its pink tongue.

Lifting the lid of another pan on the stove, Goldie wrinkled up her nose.

Nora twisted her apron nervously. "I—I—*can* cook," she said firmly. "I just don't know how to make fancy dishes, that's all. My Pap and my brother ate plain. Fried eggs and corn bread and stew, mostly. We never in our life roasted a whole bird. And Pap never wanted gravy." She turned the heat down under the gravy and tried to stir it. It had congealed into something resembling a light brown mass of glue. "'Ceptin' maybe milk gravy from the bacon grease in the mornings."

Goldie shuddered and held up her hand. "I get the general idea." She sat down at the kitchen table. Nora was still standing by the stove, alternately rolling and smoothing the edge of her apron. Her hands shook as she reached up to tuck a few strands of blonde hair behind her ears.

Goldie pulled another chair out from the table. "Sit down, Nora. We need to talk." She leaned back in her chair. Reaching into the pocket of her silk robe, she withdrew a small black cigar and lit it.

Nora perched on the edge of the chair opposite Goldie, fidgeting with the hem of her apron and trying not to appear surprised at the sight of a woman smoking.

After taking a few long drags on the cigar, Goldie said, "Two days ago my cook ran off with a boy from across town. I really was hoping you were the answer to that problem." Goldie sighed and looked sadly toward the stove. "But I just don't think this is going to work out."

"I didn't mean to lie." It was all Nora could do to hold back the tears. Already she was wondering which of the dozen city streets she should walk up first, which doors she should knock on looking for a place to stay. She wondered if Goldie would let her sleep in the kitchen until she found another job.

"Why, honey," Goldie was saying. "You didn't lie." She chuckled. "You just didn't know what I meant when I said I needed a cook." She patted Nora's hand. "I'm a good judge of people, and I knew from the minute I saw you that we'd get on. I can hire another cook." She laughed. "But what I can't do is ask my girls to eat *that*." She nodded toward the stove. "So, what we have to do is decide what we're going to do with you."

Nora studied the floor of the kitchen intensely. The poodle had finished its bread and gravy. It padded across the floor to where the women sat and shoved its head under Nora's hand, demanding to be petted.

Finally, Goldie broke the silence. "Lily told me how the two of you really met." When Nora looked up, startled, Goldie was smiling. "The girls can't keep secrets from me. Sooner or later I find out." She puffed on the cigar a few more times before adding, "I admire your gumption, girl. I don't know many girls who'd take Frank Albers on like that."

"I didn't really take him on," Nora said. "I snuck up from behind. He never knew what hit him."

Goldie threw back her head and laughed. "So you did, so you did. And it's a good thing, too." Suddenly, she grew very serious. "Frank's a mean so-and-so when he's drunk. When you get a little older, you'll understand men better. And you'll stay away from the ones like Frank."

Goldie took another drag on her cigar, blowing little circles of smoke toward the ceiling. She shook her head. "That Lily. Someday she's going to get herself into real trouble. It's lucky for her you were in that barn. Lucky for her you found that shovel in the hay."

Goldie smoked quietly for a few more moments while Nora concentrated on petting the poodle, who had succeeded in begging its way into her lap.

"But we were talking about you," Goldie said quietly. She tilted her head while she smoked, inspecting Nora. "You're going to be what we call a 'real looker' before long, Nora." She took another drag on her cigar, then put it out on a saucer before asking, "Can you keep house any better than you cook?"

Nora nodded.

Goldie warned, "You have no idea what a mess this place can be after a busy evening."

"I don't care about that. I'll work hard." Nora gulped. "I've never been around fancy carpet and things like that. You might have to show me how you want it."

"Lily showed me what you did to cover up that tear on her gown," Goldie said. "Some of the girls aren't as careful about their clothes as they should be. If you can sew, that'll help me out, too."

Nora nodded. "I did all the sewing at home. Pap didn't like my cooking, but he never complained about my sewing or keeping house. I made his shirts and everything."

Goldie laughed again, reaching up to touch Nora's golden hair. "You wouldn't believe it now, but my hair used to be just this color. I got my name because of my hair." She reminisced. "There was a gambler used to call on me in New Orleans. 'Goldie,' he'd say, 'your hair would assay as nearly pure gold ore, the way it shines in the lamplight.'"

Goldie reached out and patted Nora on the head. "You have potential, and I'd like to keep you around. What do you say to five dollars a week, room and board included?"

"You mean,"—Nora took in a deep breath—"you mean I don't have to leave?"

"Why on earth would you think I wanted you to leave? I just don't want you to cook anymore, that's all!" Goldie laughed. "Now get upstairs. Iris still needs help with some sewing. She's got some new idea for a costume."

She turned towards the stove. "Send Violet down to me. Maybe we can resurrect something edible from this mess." She said it with mock anger, snapping a kitchen towel at Nora's posterior as the young girl bent to set the poodle down.

The setting sun was just beginning to peek through gray clouds and light the back alley with an uncanny brightness when Nora, up to her elbows in dishwater, saw a woman driving a carriage pulled by a rangy white gelding arrive at Goldie's back door. The woman didn't come right in. Instead, she sat, her head bowed, almost as if she were half asleep. With her head bowed, her entire face and shoulder were obscured from view by the brim of the largest, most elaborate hat Nora had ever seen.

Nora smiled to herself when the gelding cranked its thin neck around and eyed the driver. She could see the horse's muzzle vibrate gently, and although she could not hear the soft whicker, she knew the sound.

The woman dozing in the carriage seat started awake. Nora saw her arch her back and rub her neck wearily before climbing down from the carriage. Not wanting to be seen spying on the visitor, Nora bent her head and gave renewed energy to scraping the last bit of burned chicken from the bottom of the roasting pot before her.

The visitor clomped up the back steps. Nora waited for her to knock, but instead of knocking the woman came in.

"Where's Olga?" she asked abruptly.

"If Olga was the cook, Goldie said she ran off with a boy from across town."

Nora's announcement regarding Olga's defection had an odd effect on the visitor. Closing her eyes, she pressed her lips together and said quietly, "Hallelujah."

Suddenly infused with a burst of energy, the woman set a large black bag on the table and removed her hat. Her hair had once been black. Now it was graying, white streaks sweeping up from her temples and back from the left side of her forehead.

As the visitor looked her over, Nora began to feel self-conscious. "I'll get Goldie," she said.

"There's no hurry about that," the woman said crisply. She removed her wrapper and tossed it on a chair. "I'm Maude Allbright. Dr. Maude Allbright."

The doctor held out her hand. Nora hastened to dry her hands on her apron before returning the woman's firm handshake, all the while wondering why meeting a doctor should make her blush. "I'm Nora," she said.

Maude Allbright did not beat about any bushes getting to her point. "Well, Nora, you are probably thinking that I am going to pull a long face and ask a million questions and then read you a tract and preach a little to try to talk you out of the error of your ways." Dr. Allbright snapped open her medical bag as she talked. "But the truth is I am going to do nothing of the sort. I don't pull long faces and I hate tracts and lectures. And I don't ask questions because I already know the answers. Every one of you girls probably makes more in a week than I do." The doctor removed a stethoscope from her bag and put it around her neck.

Dr. Allbright's voice was sad. "You don't know me and I don't know you, young lady, but I know who you will be in a few years. You'll be Fern, knowing you don't have much longer before Goldie will pass you over for a younger girl, mixing potions and pots to try to cover the wrinkles and bring a youthful blush back to your faded cheeks, desperate because you squandered all that money you made instead of saving up for a good retirement."

Dr. Allbright snapped the medical bag shut and headed for the back steps. She stopped abruptly and turned around. "What did you say your name was?"

Nora answered, "Nora O'Dell." She lifted her chin before adding, "And I'm not one of Goldie's girls. Not the way you think. I'm the new housekeeper."

Dr. Allbright smiled. "How long have you been in Lincoln?"

"Just since this morning."

"And your family?" Dr. Allbright raised her hand. "Never mind. I know better than to ask that." She looked Nora over, taking in the golden blonde hair, the wide-set green eyes set off by beautifully arched eyebrows, the tiny dark brown mole just above one corner of the girl's full mouth. "You may be the housekeeper today, dear, but I can assure you Goldie has other plans for you in the very near future."

The older woman pointed upstairs. "Goldie would try to laugh it off if she heard me say this, Miss O'Dell, but I want you to know something. This is not the place to realize your dreams. You're very young and you'll get on quite well for a while. But when you've scratched through the veneer of beautiful furnishings and fancy dresses, you're not going to like what you see."

Nora heard Goldie call from the upstairs hall. Dr. Allbright leaned over and whispered to her, "We'll talk again." Then she tripped up the stairs, calling out to Goldie in a cheery voice that belied the weariness Nora could see in every line of her face.

Nora returned her attention to the kitchen. She might not know how to cook, and she might be ignorant of caring for fine things, but she was going to clean the kitchen until it shone. She dismissed the doctor's harangue as the tired blatherings of an eccentric old woman. It seemed to Nora that a lot of dreams could be realized with ninety dollars a week.

CHAPTER 5

Thornhill Dressers

To him that is afflicted pity should be shewed from his friend.
Job 6:14

A week after her arrival in the big city of Lincoln, Nebraska, Nora still had not ventured beyond the back stoop of the two-story brick building on the edge of town. Goldie and the girls kept her busy cleaning, dusting, sewing, mending, combing hair, ironing ruffles, sweeping stairs. Chores were as endless as they had been at home, with one all-important difference: No one yelled or threw things at her. She actually felt welcome. For Nora, Goldie's was a haven. If she did not feel loved, she did feel liked, and that was enough.

Nora's happiness went undisturbed for two weeks, until one Monday morning when Goldie rose from the breakfast table and headed upstairs to change. "I'm going to do some marketing, Nora," she said. "It would save me a lot of time if you learned how. Why don't you come along. Meet me at the front door in an hour."

Goldie retreated upstairs to dress, unaware that her simple invitation had wreaked havoc with Nora's newfound peace of mind.

Lily and Iris exchanged knowing glances. The effect of Goldie's invitation on Nora had not been lost on them.

"You can borrow my blue calico," Lily offered.

"Come on, honey," Iris said, taking Nora's hand. "I'll help you with your hair."

An hour later Nora, primly dressed in indigo calico, her hair completely hidden beneath a huge bonnet, met Goldie as ordered by the front door. Goldie wore a simple dark blue morning dress with linen collar and cuffs and matching hat. Nora thought that together they looked like a mother and daughter going out to do the marketing.

Once in the carriage, Nora shifted nervously in her seat. Lily and Iris appeared at an upstairs window, laughing and making faces at her as she did her best to pretend that a carriage ride to town was nothing out of the ordinary. She watched Goldie, trying to imitate the older woman's proud carriage, hoping no one could see how terrified she was.

On the handful of times Pap had allowed her to ride with him to town, they had encountered only a few other wagons. This morning, dozens of carriages filled the wide streets of Lincoln. Streams of farm wagons flowed down the street toward what Shep called Haymarket Square.

Just as they rounded the corner of Ninth and O Streets, a runaway came charging down the road. The horse nearly grazed the side of the carriage where Nora sat. While Shep did his best to control his own terrified horse, the runaway reared, flailing the air with its hooves. Nora squeezed her eyes shut against a shower of foam from the runaway's bit. She ducked toward Goldie, who laid a protective hand on her shoulder. In a moment, the runaway was off in the opposite direction from them, finally disappearing to the north where Nora could see the tower of a building Goldie said was the university.

People were everywhere—on the boardwalks, entering stores, exiting stores, riding in carriages, climbing into wagons, perched on the rafters of buildings under construction. A throng of people exited the train station, flocking about carriages waiting to take them home or to local hotels. From her vantage point in Goldie's carriage, Nora could see more people than she had seen in fifteen years of living in Hickory Grove.

She pointed out a strange sort of iron wheeled wagon being pulled along a metal track by a team of mules. Nora thought it looked like a cheese box with windows cut out. Shep explained that the Lincoln Cable Car Company operated a line of horse- and mule-drawn taxis that, for the reasonable fare of only five cents, could transport more than a dozen people to various destinations throughout the growing city.

"You should ride out to Wyuka some afternoon," Shep said. "It's a cemetery, but it's in a kind of garden setting. Nice place to walk."

"Sounds like fun," Nora lied, already wondering when Goldie would be finished with her shopping so that they could return to the familiar quiet of the house.

Finally, Shep pulled the carriage up to the doorway of a store. Gazing down the half-block-long row of display windows, Nora thought of the little general store in Hickory Grove, one corner dedicated to checkers by the stove, and another corner serving as the post office. She could have spent the remainder of the day simply gazing at the array of merchandise in the windows of the gargantuan store.

The entrance to the store was a double-wide wonder with leaded glass transoms and fancy woodwork. Above the street level, a rounded turret soared upward from the entrance for two full stories. Nora thought Herpolsheimer's must look like one of the castles in her mother's stories about knights and fair ladies.

While Goldie swept through the door without a glance at the dozens of display cases they passed, Nora gawked openly, her head turning from side to side. There were linen collars, and silver spoons, and kid gloves in every hue of the rainbow. Nora wondered how anyone could turn a calf's skin to such glorious shades of lavender and red, yellow and blue. Her eye sockets ached with the effort of taking everything in.

Goldie finally paused at a counter near the back of the store to inspect a newly arrived assortment of ribbons and laces. Initially she was assisted by a sallow-complexioned girl with a space between her front teeth and a slight lisp when she spoke.

"You'll like these." The girl laid an assortment of black laces on a tray.

Goldie picked up a piece of lace and fingered it. Frowning slightly, she laid the first sample aside and examined another. Finally, she put it down and looked sharply at the girl. "You are new here, I believe?" she asked with the tone of a queen requesting the history of a servant. When the girl nodded, Goldie said abruptly, "I believe I made it clear that I was interested in authentic Egyptian lace, young lady. I have no interest in these cheap imitations."

The sallow-faced girl looked surprised. She opened her mouth to reply just as another shop girl strode up. "Thank you, Liza, I'll take over. I believe Mr. Herbert was looking for you."

The girl with the space between her front teeth disappeared into the nether regions of the store. Her replacement looked down at the tray of lace with distaste and pushed it away. "I'm sorry, Miss Meyer," she apologized. "Liza is new, and she doesn't know the merchandise very well." Pulling a second tray of lace from a huge drawer behind her, the girl said, "I believe this is more what you want."

Nora found herself wondering how this girl had managed to arrange her hair in the elaborate updo that made her appear even taller and more elegant than she was. Then she remembered a trick with hair that Fern had shown her. *Rats.* Fern had called the extra pieces of human hair that she used to expand her coiffure "rats." Nora decided that this girl probably had several "rats" tucked beneath the layers of her own hair. No one could have that much hair.

The girl lowered her voice and asked, "Do you have any openings yet, Miss Meyer?"

Goldie shook her head. "I'll take fifteen yards of this." She pointed to a roll of wide black lace. Then, pointing out three other rolls, she said quickly, "Twenty of that, thirty of that, fifteen of that. Have it sent to Elise Thornhill, and put it on my tab." Goldie turned briskly away from the counter, ignoring the disappointed expression on the young girl's face.

It did not take many more stops before Nora began to notice that while gentlemen who walked alone surreptitiously nodded and tipped their hats to Goldie, those who walked with ladies on their arm pretended not to see her. All women looked away half-frowning as if an invisible string holding the corners of their mouths upturned had suddenly broken. Goldie made eye contact with only a few of the men and pretended to ignore everyone else.

The noise and bustle so foreign to her soon began to grate on Nora's already frazzled nerves. While Goldie explained her preferences in everything from flour to feathers and wine to cigars, Nora listened with growing dismay, wondering how she would ever manage to remember any of it. She realized that she had lost track of where they were in the city. With her sense of direction confused, she grew even more uneasy. Everything in her yearned for the familiar interior of the establishment on Ninth Street.

Just when Nora thought they might actually be headed back, Goldie shouldered her way through a group of women clustered around a sale table and Nora lost sight of her. Trying not to show her sense of panic, she made her way to the front of the store and out onto the boardwalk. The carriage was nowhere in sight. Her heart pounding, she stepped toward the street, craning her neck to look for Shep. Someone shoved her from behind, and she stumbled into the street, mortified when one foot landed in a steaming pile left by one of the city's four-legged citizens.

Someone laughed derisively. Nora looked up and into the eyes of an ill-kempt man with an equally-disheveled woman on his arm. The couple clung to one another, weaving back and forth as they howled with laughter. "Looks like Goldie's new filly just made a little mess."

Passersby hurried away, almost pressing themselves against the building to create a wide berth between themselves and Nora. The expressions of disgust on their faces filled her with dismay.

Suddenly, Shep appeared. He grabbed the drunken man by the shoulder with one huge hand and spun him around. "Be on your way, Frank."

The drunken man stumbled backward. He would have fallen, save for being propped up by the equally inebriated but more balanced woman clinging to his arm. Hearing his name helped Nora remember. This was the man she had slugged with a shovel. What if he somehow recognized her?

Shep helped Nora back up on the boardwalk. He led her around the corner of the store and into the back alley, where he had taken the team to rest in the shade. He directed her to sit down and remove her shoes. While he wiped them clean with an old newspaper he found in a trash barrel he said quietly, "Frank Albers is a bad 'un. Stay clear of him."

Nora bit her lip and nodded obediently.

He squinted up at the sky, then back at Nora. "Guess now is as good a time as any to tell you how it is. The storeowners are glad to take Goldie's money, but they have to maintain their respectability. Which means they won't be overly friendly and they expect you to conduct your business and get out."

Nora nodded again. "Are we finished shopping yet?"

"Not yet," Shep shook his head. "One more stop." He helped Nora into the carriage and headed the team toward the front of the store just as Goldie came outside.

Thornhill Dressers Established 1880. The sign was painted with gold letters on a black background, one word centered above each of the four display windows that fronted the store. Bonnets and trims, dresses and capes, and other related merchandise, filled the windows.

Shep helped Nora and Goldie down. "I'll get the horses a drink," he said, "then I'll drive around back and wait." Climbing back aboard, he headed the team in the direction of a huge square fountain and watering trough in the center of the intersection at the end of the street.

Nora followed Goldie inside.

While other establishments they had been in that day were so full of merchandise it was hard to navigate the aisles, this shop exuded order and calm. Directly opposite the door was a massive table. At the moment it was bare, but Nora was soon to see that it was used for spreading out lengths of fabric for inspection. Beyond the table on the far wall was a beautiful oil painting and below it, a narrow piece of furniture consisting of several dozen small drawers, each with a glass front. Each drawer held a different ribbon or trim. A doorway to the right led to what Nora assumed must be a workroom at the back of the shop.

A fireplace surrounded with ceramic blue- and white-painted tiles was centered on the wall to the left. It boasted a massive oak mantle with another oil painting above it. Before the fireplace a large overstuffed chair had been positioned on an Oriental carpet to face the back corner and three huge dressing mirrors. A woman standing before the mirrors could get a full view of the front, sides, and back of a dress. To the right of the mirrors, standing away from the wall, were floor-to-ceiling shelves filled with every imaginable kind of cloth.

Just as Nora's eye was drawn to a deep green bolt of fabric on the top shelf, a middle-aged woman stepped out from behind the shelves and stood before the dressing mirrors, eyeing her profile critically. Nora realized that the shelving must have been built away from the back wall to create space for a dressing room. Another woman she assumed was the dressmaker stepped out from behind the shelves and joined her customer in front of the mirrors. She nodded at Goldie before turning her attention to her customer.

"Elise is busy," Goldie whispered. "Follow me into the back room. We'll help ourselves to coffee until she's free."

Goldie led Nora past the beautifully carved table toward the doorway to the workroom. The wall to the right boasted more small drawers and a long, narrow table displaying several different styles of hats on stands of varying heights. Behind the display table was a broader worktable where two partially finished hats sat on forms clamped to the edge of the table.

Going through the door, Nora and Goldie entered the workroom. It was just as long, but narrower than Miss Thornhill's studio. Where the studio exuded order and peace, the workroom was a jumble of activity. Boxes were stacked nearly to the ceiling, their contents scribbled in pencil on the flaps. At the far end of the room, a narrow stairway leading up to a second floor was also cluttered with boxes, some so full their contents spilled onto the stairs.

A row of tall windows on the rear wall of the building bathed the workroom in natural light. Beneath these windows sat two young women, each one pedaling furiously as they maneuvered yards of fabric beneath the racing needle of a treadle sewing machine.

Both girls glanced up when Goldie and Nora appeared. They smiled and nodded a greeting, but didn't stop working. Above the noise of the machines, Goldie explained, "The redhead is Hannah. The fat one is Lucy. Nice girls."

Goldie made herself at home in Elise Thornhill's workshop. A small stove in the corner was still warm. Opening a cupboard on the wall to the right of the stove, she withdrew two coffee cups. Motioning for Nora to sit down at the small table opposite the back door, she poured them each a cup of coffee and sat down opposite Nora.

Lucy finished and stood up. "Hello, Miss Meyer. Sorry we couldn't stop, but Miss Thornhill is about to have our hide today. These dresses are supposed to be packed in a trunk at the rail station even as we speak." Lucy leaned forward and whispered, "That's Mrs. Judge Cranston out there right now, and she expected to try both these on yesterday." Lucy rolled her eyes. "Of course Mrs. Judge doesn't care that the lace came late and the buttons—" Lucy reached behind her. She showed them a huge black button painted with a grotesque white face. "Can you believe she insisted we put *these* on *this*?" She laid one of the buttons against the soft yellow plaid and shuddered. "Of course she wouldn't believe us that they weren't quite right . . . until we had thirty-five of them sewn on!"

Elise appeared at the doorway to the studio. She called in a stage whisper, "Lucy! We're ready for the next gown."

Lucy draped the gown over her arm and headed for the studio. As she did, Hannah lifted her head. "Just one last hem, Miss Thornhill."

Elise gave Goldie an apologetic look.

Goldie shooed her toward the studio. "Go. We can wait."

With a sigh, Elise headed back into the studio.

Goldie said, "I keep telling her she needs more help, but Elise is too tight with a dollar to want to hire anyone else." She got up and walked to where the boxes were piled haphazardly along the far wall. "She probably had the exact lace she needed in one of these boxes . . . but how could she know with everything in such a mess."

Hannah finally stopped pedaling her machine. "Whew," she breathed. Jumping up, she spread the skirt of the dress along the length of the pressing table behind her. Then, she crossed the room to where two flatirons waited on the stove. Hannah wielded one flatiron expertly, then plopped it back onto the stove, grabbed up the dress, and hurried into the studio.

Finally, Nora heard someone she assumed was Elise bidding Mrs. Judge Cranston good-bye. Goldie got up and Nora followed her into the studio where Miss Thornhill was leaning against the door. At the sight of Goldie she exclaimed, "Honestly, that woman!" Then she held out her hand to Nora. "Goldie didn't tell me she had a new boarder."

"Nora's not a boarder," Goldie said. "She's my housekeeper. As it turns out, she's also quite good with a needle and thread."

"Really?" Elise asked, eyeing Nora with curiosity.

"I can read your mind, Elise Thornhill, and forget it. You're not taking any more of my girls out from under my nose." Goldie walked across the studio to the shelves filled with bolts of cloth. She pointed to a soft yellow and blue plaid silk. "This is new."

"I thought you'd like that," Elise said. "Let me get the sample book the salesman left. It comes in several different color-ways."

The two women were soon lost in sample books and fashion magazines. Lucy peeked in from the storeroom. Catching Nora's eye, she motioned for the newcomer to join her. Once back in the storeroom, Lucy and Hannah introduced themselves while they unrolled several yards of a fabric they called foulard on the workroom table.

"Sit down and relax," Hannah urged Nora. "They'll be a while. They always are."

Just then someone knocked at the back door. Lucy hurried to open the door to a young man with a thin auburn mustache. He smiled shyly. "Hey, Luce," he pronounced it "loose." "Want to go for a walk?"

Lucy grinned at him before looking doubtfully over her shoulder at Hannah. "We didn't get lunch yet. Do you think Miss Thornhill would mind?"

Hannah smiled. "Just don't be gone too long. We have to get this gown cut out today, and it's that new pattern."

Lucy grabbed her bonnet from its hook by the door and the two left. Nora saw the young man slip his arm around Lucy's broad waist as they walked off. Lucy pushed him away, but it was a playful refusal.

Nora turned toward Hannah, "Can I help?"

"Sure," Hannah said. She pointed to a wrinkle in the foulard. "Smooth that out. Then lay this—" she handed Nora an oddly shaped piece of paper—"along the folded edge and pin it down." Hannah opened a notebook and ran her finger down a row of penciled notes. "Oh, wait a minute," she said, taking the pattern piece back. "We have to lengthen the sleeve at least an inch. Here—" She cut the pattern piece in two. "Now when you lay it along the fold, put this bottom piece one inch away from the top piece. Like this." She demonstrated what Nora should do before handing her a measuring tape. "Measure exactly. Miss Thornhill is very, very exacting. Which, I suppose," Hannah said, sighing, "is why she is so successful, although it can be a trial at times."

While Nora laid the pattern piece in place on the fabric, Hannah referred again to her notes. "You one of Goldie's boarders?" Hannah asked.

Nora bristled. "No. I'm the housekeeper."

"You from Lincoln?" Hannah wanted to know.

"No." Nora didn't offer any more information.

"Hey," Hannah said. "I'm just trying to be friendly. You don't have to talk if you don't want to. I just wondered how you knew Goldie, that's all. If you're not a boarder I thought you might be family. Goldie's Miss Thornhill's sister, you know."

Nora had never imagined that women like Goldie had families. She was clearly surprised. Hannah smiled and nodded. "Yup. Sisters. Funny, ain't it? Word is, they were both dressmakers at first. Then Miss Thornhill fell in love and ran off. All the way to Paris, France. She learned a lot about dressmaking from the high-fashion people over there. I don't know what happened. When she came back, she had a different last name but no husband. By then, Goldie was already set up in the house over on Ninth Street. Miss Thornhill threw a fit. She told me that herself. But Goldie didn't want to come back to the old life."

"Thank you for the history lesson, Hannah." Goldie was standing in the doorway.

"Oh, Miss Meyer—I didn't mean to—" Hannah's freckled face flushed crimson. She swallowed hard and took a deep breath. "I'm sorry, ma'am. Guess I can't resist gossip."

"It wasn't really gossip. Every word I heard was the truth. And there wasn't a drop of ill will in it, either. Thank you for that."

Hannah was flustered. She had obviously expected a full "dressing-down." But Goldie didn't seem bothered. Instead, Goldie said, "I suppose I should add that since then Elise and I agreed to disagree about our career choices and declared a truce, it's worked out very well. My girls enjoy having their own dressmaker, and my business has helped Elise make ends meet through some lean times. We get along very well, as long as Elise doesn't steal my girls."

"Where's Lucy?" Miss Thornhill peeked into the workroom just as the front bell rang.

"I told her to go ahead and get some lunch," Hannah said.

"I don't suppose lunch included a Mr. Fielding?" Elise asked.

Hannah blushed again. "I told her not to be gone too long. I didn't think you'd mind after she worked so late last night."

Elise sighed. "No, of course I don't mind." She retreated back into the studio.

Nora heard her say, "Good afternoon, Mrs. Gilbert. What can I do for you?"

"We'll be going," Goldie said. "Elise is coming to do a fitting later this evening after she closes the shop."

Shep pulled up to the back door. Nora followed Goldie outside and climbed into the carriage. As they pulled away from the shop, Lucy and Mr. Fielding came around the corner of the building, arm in arm. Lucy waved happily to Nora, who waved back. It was an odd sensation, having someone in the crowded city recognize her. Nora liked it.

CHAPTER 6

Hopes and Dreams

Wine is a mocker, strong drink is raging: and whosoever is deceived thereby is not wise.
Proverbs 20:1

Nora had been a housekeeper for only a few weeks when Goldie suggested she help serve "the guests." Taking Nora behind the ornately carved bar that stretched nearly the full length of one end of the front parlor, Goldie explained, "If Shep hits a sour note on the piano when a customer steps up to the bar, pour the drink out of these bottles." Goldie reached for some beautiful wine bottles under the counter. "Be certain you use the good crystal glasses and pour it like you're measuring every drop carefully. If Shep just plays on, you'll know to give the customer the really good stuff from here—" Goldie indicated another rack of wine bottles. She explained, "I buy the best, but I'd be stupid to waste it on men who don't know the difference." She patted Nora's shoulder. "If you're not sure what to do, ask Iris—but be discreet. She'll be working with you tonight."

When Nora only nodded, Goldie asked, "Something wrong, honey?"

Nora shook her head. "I'm just nervous."

"Nothing to be nervous about. A big city's just like a small town—full of both varmints and nice folks. There's just a few more of each, that's the only difference. Working the bar is easy. Just smile and be polite and the nice folks will love you. Shep and I take care of the varmints." Goldie paused before adding, "I never rush anyone to the next level before they're ready, honey. Now, get on upstairs and help the girls get dressed."

Nora hustled upstairs. The door to Iris's room was open. Nora peeked in. "You need any help?"

Iris was sitting at her dressing table, trying to decide exactly how to place a comb in her curly black hair. Watching her, Nora marveled at the absolute perfection of her coffee-colored skin. Iris smiled at her in the mirror and nodded. "Come on in. Help me decide how to wear this comb." Iris positioned the comb in various ways before deciding to secure it behind one ear.

Nora rubbed one forearm nervously. "Goldie said I should help you at the bar tonight."

Iris turned around. "Don't let that scare you. You'll do fine. Just smile and be friendly." She picked up another comb from her dressing table. "Maybe we can wear our hair the same way. Let's see if my other comb will stay in your hair."

Nora sat down at Iris's dressing table. Just as Iris took the last pin out of her blonde hair, Nora blurted out, "I don't know if I want to be a boarder."

Iris looked at her in the mirror. She began to brush Nora's hair. "You happy making five dollars a week?"

"I didn't get anything for doing the same work—and more—not so long ago," Nora said.

Iris sat down on the bed next to the dressing table. "I read an ad in the paper today," she said. "There's a man hiring strawberry pickers out east of the statehouse. Pays three dollars a week." She snorted. "That same man thinks nothing of handing Goldie twenty-five dollars for an hour of my time on Saturday night. Now which pay would you rather collect?"

Nora shook her head and bit her lip.

"Don't you have any plans, Nora? Any dreams?"

The girl shrugged. "Sure. To get away from being yelled at and hit when Pap didn't like my cooking or the way I walked or the way I sat at the table or—"

"—I get the picture." Iris stood up and began to brush Nora's hair again. In a maternal tone of voice, she said, "Listen, honey. No woman plans this career. But life has a way of crushing dreams. That's how Goldie stays in business." She waved her brush in the air as she added, "That, and the fact that most men are low-life good-for-nothings who talk out of both sides of their mouths and are totally dominated by one thing."

She was quiet for a moment, then said abruptly, "I was a teacher before I came to Goldie's." At Nora's look of amazement she smiled. "Surprised you, didn't I? Of course I could only teach black children. But I loved it." She sighed. "Then I made a big, big mistake. I trusted someone I shouldn't have. When I found myself *enceinte*, that was the end of teaching. And the end of the relationship." Iris swallowed before continuing. "It was almost the end of me." Her eyes filled with tears. "My little darling died when she was only three days old. I buried her under a big oak tree in the woods, and said a prayer over her. And then I headed for New Orleans. I was a mess when Goldie took me in. I've been with her ever since."

Iris opened the trunk against the far wall and pulled out a pale green silk dress. She held it out to Nora. "Put this on. It will bring out the color of your eyes." Nora stepped behind the folding screen in the corner of the room and began to unbutton the bodice of her work dress while Iris talked.

"I'm not like the other girls, wasting every dollar that comes my way on baubles and candy. I've been saving up for a long time. One day very soon I'm heading out west to Denver. I'm going to buy a little house and take in every unloved black child that comes my way. I'll teach them to read. Give them a dream." Iris sighed. "The day I die, I'm going to be able to look back and know I did something with my life."

Nora stepped out from behind the screen.

"I knew that green would make your eyes shine. Come see." Iris directed Nora to the full-length mirror in the corner of the room.

"Well now, ain't that just touchin'?" Fern was standing in the doorway, her thin arms folded across her flat chest. Fern's abundant hair had probably once been beautiful, but time was not being kind to the color, which was fading to a mousy light brown. Fortunately, it was not thinning. Fern spent hours doing it up. She was knowledgeable about fashion and meticulous about having the latest styles in the finest fabrics. Her hazel eyes were streaked with gold.

She peered at Nora, her voice dripping with sarcasm as she said, "So Iris is gonna teach all the little 'chillen' to read. I thought I heard Goldie send you upstairs to help us all. You gonna' help anybody besides her?"

"Of course," Nora answered quickly.

"Come on, then."

Nora followed Fern to her room at the far end of the hall. It was the smallest room on the floor, and when Nora followed her in she wrinkled her nose with distaste. The stale air smelled of powders, heavy perfume, and a chamber pot.

Every surface in Fern's room assaulted the eye with a different garish pattern. Fringed runners and cloths adorned every piece of furniture. Even the top of Fern's mirror and folding screen were laden with fringe and tassels. Her dressing table was cluttered with an array of bottles and powder puffs.

Fern shed her duster. Grasping the edge of the bed with

both hands, she braced herself and ordered, "Lace me up. Tight."

Nora pulled and tugged on the laces of Fern's elaborate corset in vain. She could not pull the waist in far enough to please. Fern sucked in air, thrusting her bosom forward and holding her breath. Nora tugged harder, and suddenly Fern lunged across the room and gave lunch to her chamber pot. She paused to rinse her mouth and then returned to grab the bed. "Again."

Nora protested, "You'll hurt yourself."

"Don't you tell me what to do, little miss," Fern snapped angrily. "I've been at this long enough to know what I'm doing. Now lace it tighter."

Finally, Fern nodded at Nora, gasping, "Okay. That's good." She nearly collapsed on the bed struggling to catch her breath. When she finally recovered, she directed Nora to help her position her bustle, a spring-loaded affair designed to ride low over the hips until the wearer needed to sit down. Then, the bustle lifted to allow its wearer's posterior to come in contact with a chair. The moment the wearer stood up, the bustle sprang back into position. Nora nearly shook with laughter at the ridiculous contraption. But she had to admit that when Fern was completely dressed, the bustle gave a pleasing line to her elaborate gown.

Nora was turning to go when Fern said abruptly, "You and Iris had a nice talk, did you?" When Nora didn't speak, Fern answered for her. "She told you about her little plan for a house in Denver, and all that. Well, let me tell you something, Nora. Hopes like that are what destroy women like you and me. Take my advice. Forget hope. Just take today. That's all you have. It's when hopes are disappointed that life gets dreary. So don't hope. I once read a description of a house like Goldie's that stuck with me. 'Bounded on the north by stumbling virtue, on the south by wrecked hopes, on the east by a miserably gray dawn of shame, and on the west by the sunset of dissipation'." Fern laughed sadly. "Once I realized how true that description was, I gave up hoping for anything different. This life is as regular as sunrise, and that's what gets me through the day. It ain't much, but lying about the future is worse. Don't think for a moment that some strong, classy rich man is going to come along and whisk you away from Goldie's. There's no grand mansion or vine-covered cottage with big roses growing all over it for Goldie's girls."

"I don't want any cottage with roses," Nora blurted out.

Fern nodded approvingly. "You remember what I said. Don't get false hopes. They'll kill you in the end. And don't bother with religion, either."

"My family didn't have any religion," Nora said.

"Good. Religion kills more good livin' than anything." Fern adjusted her bosom. While she talked, she leaned over to inspect her teeth in the mirror. She rubbed across them with her finger, then reapplied color to her lips. "I went to a meetin' once. Man got up and starts to tell us all that there's only one faith, and his is it. Next time I went to a meetin' there was another man telling me the same thing. Only his faith was different from the first. Now, tell me, what good is that?"

Fern turned around to face Nora. "Worst of it was, both those preachers who claimed theirs was 'the only way' checked in at Goldie's the night after their meetin's was over. That was it for me. I say forget religion. Pay your way and don't be a hypocrite."

Nora nodded. "Yes, ma'am."

"Has Dr. Allbright given you her speech yet?"

"What speech?"

"Oh, the one about how this is no way for a woman to live and how she'll help you get out whenever you want."

Something kept Nora from confiding in Fern.

Seeing Nora's hesitation, Fern said, "That's all right, girlie. You don't have to say anything. If she hasn't gotten to you yet, she will. She says the same to all the girls. *Humph*. Self-righteous old bag. Ought to mind her own business."

Fern turned to examine herself in the mirror again. She reached for another pot on the dressing table and dabbed herself with powder. "Well, that's it for me I guess. You can see if the other girls need anything. Check with Pansy first. She's practically a half-wit, you know. I don't understand why Goldie keeps her around." Fern shoved past Nora and headed downstairs.

Nora could hear the tinkling of the piano as Shep warmed up his fingers. There was no particular melody to what he was playing, he simply progressed up and down the keyboard, going faster and faster. Nora moved on to Pansy's room.

"Oh, Nora," the girl panted. "I'll never be ready in time. And Lars said he would come tonight. I must look my best for Lars." Pansy stared into her dressing mirror. She had a dress in each hand and kept holding one up and then the other. "I can't decide. I can't decide." She seemed on the verge of tears.

Nora walked up behind Pansy and looked in the mirror. "Wear the red one. It makes your dark hair glow with red highlights."

"Really? Will Lars think I look beautiful in the red dress?"

Fern was right. Pansy was slow-witted. But she had maintained a sweetness that amazed Nora, considering her surroundings. Nora smiled at Pansy and patted her on the shoulder. "Here, Pansy, I'll put a red ribbon in your hair, too. And maybe this flower." Nora reached into the lid of Pansy's trunk for a ribbon rose. She held it up to Pansy's hair. "See? Won't that look nice?"

Pansy giggled. "Lars is going to propose to me tonight. He told me last week that the next time he came, he would ask me to be his wife. He's going up to Dakota Territory to homestead, and he's going to take me with him." Pansy whirled happily. "No more Goldie's for Pansy. Just a home and a husband." Her voice softened. "And maybe a baby. Dr. Allbright said it could happen. She said I'm healthy." Pansy's cheeks colored. "Lars said he wants lots of sons."

Nora's heart ached for the plump, simple-minded girl, who trusted a man's word and believed his promises for the future. *Maybe I'm more like Fern than I thought.*

By eleven o'clock, Goldie's girls had all descended to the Hall of Mirrors and another evening was in full swing. Nora worked behind the bar, grateful for the physical barrier between herself and Goldie's clientele. She did her best to smile and be nice, but she never stopped longing for the quiet of her little room off the kitchen.

Near midnight, Nora noticed Pansy casting nervous glances toward the front door. As it grew later and later, Pansy drooped visibly. By midnight, she was sitting in a corner by herself, her chin trembling with the effort of keeping back a flood of tears.

Goldie finally went to her, and laid a hand on her shoulder, and whispered something. Pansy shook her head and protested, but whatever Goldie had said finally resulted in the baby-faced girl rising and heading up the stairs.

Just as Pansy reached the landing, the doorbell rang. When Goldie opened the door, there was a shout of joy as Pansy rushed down the stairs and into the arms of a gigantic, blonde-haired man. He put his arm about Pansy's shoulder and held her close while he whispered something to Goldie. The trio disappeared down the back hall in the direction of the kitchen. When they emerged, Pansy's face was shining with joy. The man leaned over and kissed her on the cheek, then left. Pansy fairly bounced up the stairs.

It was nearly dawn when Nora was awakened by the sound of footsteps in the front hall. Her heart pounding, she tiptoed through the kitchen and peeked into the parlor. Fern stood at the bar, guzzling down whiskey. Nora cleared her throat. "Fern, is something wrong?"

Fern sneered at her. "What are you looking at?"

"I just heard something and came to check."

"Well, you've checked. Now get back to your little room. Or would you rather just move on in to my room right now? That's where you're headed, you know. Right up the ladder into my room. And out I go."

"Fern." Goldie stood on the front stairs. She spoke calmly, but the coldness in her voice frightened Nora. "I warned you before about your drinking. I won't have any boarders who can't hold their liquor. Get back to bed."

Fern grasped the whiskey bottle by the neck and waved it at Goldie. "Get yourself back to bed, Madame Meyer. I know what the score is around here. I know."

"You don't know anything. I don't have any plans to ditch you. Unless you start drinking again. Then you've done it to yourself. You know I won't have a drunk in my establishment."

Goldie came all the way down the stairs and stood, her arms folded. There was no hint of the warm southern accent that usually surfaced when Goldie was tired. Her eyes were cold, her face expressionless as she said, "Make up your mind, Fern. Put down the bottle or get out."

Fern wavered. "Oh, all right. Have it your way." She set the bottle down on the bar, threw back her shoulders, and started across the room. She stumbled and Nora went to help her, but Fern shoved her away. "I don't want your help, thank you very much." She drew herself up and said with drunken dignity, "I can take care of myself."

She made her way past Goldie and slowly up the stairs.

"Should I check on her?" Nora asked Goldie.

Goldie shook her head. "No. Let her take care of herself. If she can." Goldie turned to go back upstairs, then stopped and called to Nora, "Pansy is leaving this morning. Believe it or not, that big lummox Lars really does want to marry her. Would you set the table with the good dishes? I'm making a special farewell meal for her."

Nora hesitated before asking, "Do you think Pansy and Lars will—I mean, does Lars know—"

"—that she's simpleminded?" Goldie finished Nora's sentence. "Yes. And he seems to love her anyway." Goldie chuckled.

"I hope she's happy," Nora said.

Goldie smiled. "Yes. So do I. It happens rarely enough. It would be nice to see one of the girls truly happy." She hastened to add, "If one can call living in a shack on the prairie having babies happiness." She laughed nervously. "That certainly wouldn't be my definition of happiness. But it seems to suit poor, simpleminded Pansy."

Nora nodded and headed back to her room. Lying in bed, she was suddenly overwhelmed by a great feeling of sadness. The veneer Dr. Allbright had spoken of had been scratched, and Nora did not like what lurked beneath the surface.

CHAPTER 7

Life Goes On

There is no hope: no; for I have loved strangers, and after them will I go.
Jeremiah 2:25

Nora had never had difficulty sleeping—until the night Goldie ordered Fern to "sober up or leave." That night, Nora tossed and turned through dreams where she alternately played the roles of Dr. Allbright, a madame, and a boarder. Frank Albers was there, too, fighting with Shep. There was no logical sequence of events. Instead, short bursts of bizarre activity played themselves out and then melded into other scenes. Even though she was asleep, Nora felt she were watching rather than participating in the events. *This is really stupid, I wish I'd wake up.* The thought would occur, and then another sequence of dreams would begin.

Nothing was frightening until the last dream, which seemed very real. Someone was shrieking so loudly that Nora jerked awake, terrified, only to realize the shrieks were filling the house, echoing from the upstairs hall down both stairways.

Nora stumbled out of bed and lunged up the back stairs. At the end of the hallway she stopped abruptly, panting. Near the front of the house, Goldie's girls were clustered in a little knot of humanity. They clung to one another, whispering just outside Fern's door.

Nora padded barefoot down the hallway. She intended to walk by them and go into Fern's room, but Iris reached out and tugged on the sleeve of her nightgown. "Don't, honey. There's no need for you to see what's in there."

Just then Goldie came out of the room, practically supporting a shaking, deathly white Lily. Nora reached out, wrapping her arm around Lily's waist.

Goldie turned to the clutch of girls and said, "You can all go downstairs and make some coffee. Shep's gone for the sheriff and Dr. Allbright. You can't do Fern any good standing up here in the hall shivering."

When no one moved, Goldie repeated herself. "Go on, now. Downstairs."

Iris pulled Ivy after her, holding the trembling girl's hand. The others followed, filing down the front stairs.

Lily began to sob violently. In spite of the support of Goldie and Nora, she sank to the floor. Goldie sat down next to her. Lily laid her head on Goldie's shoulder and reached for Nora, who took her hand.

"We had a fight," Lily sobbed. "An awful fight. I shouldn't have said those things." She moaned softly, pulling her hand away from Nora's covering her face. "I shouldn't have said those things." Lily dissolved in tears.

Nora patted Lily's shoulder while Goldie gathered the girl into her arms. "Don't do this to yourself, Lily. You didn't know Fern was over the edge." Goldie's voice mellowed, and her southern accent crept in. "We all know that Fern had seen bettuh days. She knew it was jus' a matter o' time. It wasn't your fault she hadn' saved up an' prepared. Fern made thousands o' dolluhs in her day. She could o' retired comfortably. But she let drinkin' get the best o' her. None o' that's yo' fault."

Lily shook her head. "But I made it worse. I just wanted to borrow that pink chiffon gown of hers for one night.

She was so nasty about it. She called me terrible names, raged on and on about how we were all just counting the days, hoping she'd kick the bucket so we could divide all her things. I got so mad." Lily shuddered. In a hoarse half-whisper she said, "I told her if she was going to be so mean all the time, I hoped she did kick the bucket. I told her she was getting old and it wouldn't be long before you'd tell her to go anyway." Lily looked up at Goldie, tears streaming down her face. "I said I'd be glad when she was gone. That maybe we'd get someone nice in her place."

Goldie's expression hardened. "You didn' say anythin' Fern didn' already know. Fact is, I prob'ly woulda made Fern leave before too much longuh."

Goldie gently shook Lily by the shoulders. "And she was mean to y'all. She had no call to treat you bad. Fern was havin' hard times. So what? Ever'body has hard times."

Goldie nodded toward Nora, who noticed that the accent was fading as Goldie reasoned, "Look at Nora, here. She's had hard times. But she didn' get mean. She got out. She's making somethin' of herself. Fern had the chance to do the same thing. It's a shame she hung herself, but *she* did it. Not you. It's not your fault. People make all kinds of sloppy excuses for what they do. It just shows their weakness. I've never stood for excuses, and I won't make any excuses for Fern. I'm just glad she didn't shoot herself. That's an ugly way to die. And it sticks somebody else with a mess."

Goldie's final remark shocked Nora. She had never felt any particular affection for Fern, but it seemed incredibly sad for them to be sitting in the hallway just outside her room talking this way.

Goldie began to talk about who might be taking Fern's room. "Of course, I'll have it redone first."

Lily stopped crying and said that the least she could do was take care of Fern's things.

As Lily and Goldie talked, Nora looked over her shoulder toward Fern's little room. Morning light spilled through the doorway, leaving a small dapple of gold on the hallway floor. The aroma of coffee floated up the stairs. Nora thought about how all across town, people were climbing out of bed, getting dressed, and beginning a new day. Their lives would go on unaffected by the fact that at Goldie's Garden, Fern was dead.

Nora shivered thinking of the body that was still in that room. Was it still hanging there? Murmuring an excuse, she got up and went downstairs. The other girls were sitting around the table sipping coffee. Nora walked past them and into her little room off the kitchen. She closed the door and sat down on her bed. Burying her face in her pillow, she cried.

"You don't belong here."

Nora was standing in the alley behind Goldie's patting the neck of Dr. Allbright's horse when she heard the doctor's voice. She leaned her head against Casey's thin neck.

Dr. Allbright repeated. "I said, you don't belong here."

"I heard you." Nora patted the horse's neck again before turning around. Picking up her skirts, she climbed up on the stoop and sat down. She leaned over, putting her chin on her knees as she scratched meaninglessly in the dirt with a stick.

Dr. Allbright sat down beside her. "The undertaker's on his way," she said matter-of-factly. "He'll be coming through the back."

"I can handle that," Nora said.

"That's not what I meant when I said you don't belong here."

Nora twisted her neck and looked up at Dr. Allbright. "I know." She sighed and straightened up, arching her back and moving her feet back and forth in the gravel. "Is Lily all right?"

"She will be. Iris made her some tea. I gave her something to help her sleep."

"The others?" Nora asked.

"They're all in shock, like you. I think Goldie has them all gathered in the parlor, trying to come up with a service of some kind." The doctor shook her head sadly. "Shep will serve as the minister, I suppose. I think the sheriff has finally found a place for the burial."

Seeing Nora's puzzled expression, Dr. Allbright said quietly, "You don't think all the good Christians in Lincoln are going to want someone like Fern buried in their cemetery, do you?"

"Oh," Nora said. "I hadn't thought."

"Yes," Dr. Allbright said crisply. "I believe that's a good summary of your life in this city to date." She barely paused before saying, "May I suggest that you do some very thorough thinking now?"

Nora protested. "I'll never end up like Fern."

Dr. Allbright sighed deeply. "I pray to God not. And I'm not a praying woman." She reached over and patted the back of Nora's hand. "Do you think Fern expected her life to end this way when she was fifteen or sixteen?"

A wagon rounded the corner at the end of the block and headed up the alley. Dr. Allbright stood up. She went down the two back porch steps and led her horse up the alley a few feet, making room for the undertaker to pull his wagon up to the back door.

Nora stood up just as the sheriff stepped out the door. "Sam," he said, nodding to the driver of the wagon.

"Henry." The undertaker nodded back.

Goldie came out on the porch and handed Sam an envelope. "This should be enough for a respectable coffin," she said. "Red velvet for the lining. If you don't have red, send to Thornhill Dressers for a bolt. Elise will take care of it." Goldie motioned to Nora. "Come inside. The other girls are in the parlor. Stay there until I come for you."

The rest of the day was a blur of activity. The girls gathered for a melancholy farewell breakfast for Pansy. The minute the undertaker's wagon pulled away from the back door, they were all sent to get dressed. Lars arrived to claim his bride just as Shep pulled up at the back door driving Goldie's carriage. Behind him was a rented phaeton driven by a stranger. Goldie insisted that Pansy go with her fiancé, while the rest of the girls all piled into the two other vehicles. They drove off toward the south, waving good-bye to Pansy and Lars who headed north.

At the edge of town, the mourners were met by the undertaker, who now drove a team of four black horses pulling a hearse. A dark wooden coffin could be seen through the windows of the hearse. The three vehicles made their way south of Lincoln, to a small cemetery on the side of a hill. Someone had already dug a grave. While the girls stood by, Fern's casket was lowered into the grave. There were no flowers, and there was no minister. Shep read two verses of a song he knew Fern liked. That was all. The girls filed by the open grave, each one taking a handful of earth to sprinkle on the casket. They rode back to town in silence.

The girls ate an early supper. After the meal, Goldie stood up at the end of the table and said, "We all feel bad that Fern had to go out the way she did. But we did right by her. She had a respectable funeral. I've sent Shep to the florist for a mourning wreath, and he's going to hang it on the front door in Fern's memory. We won't be open tonight." Goldie paused for a moment, clearing her throat before she continued. "I'll not have you all tiptoeing past the door to Fern's room like it was some sort of shrine. I've been thinking how I can help you all get past this, and I've decided it would be fitting if you girls were the ones to take care of Fern's things. I'm putting Lily in charge and I want you all to go up there together and get the job done. It's not meant to disrespect Fern, but life goes on. So, go on up there and get started."

Violet asked, "You want us to go do it *now*?"

Even Lily protested. "But, Goldie—she's just in her grave. Don't you think we ought to wait at least a couple of days?"

Goldie shook her head. "No. I want it done right now. You girls just need to trust me that I know what's best. I don't want you haunted by this. We need to close the books on Fern and let her rest in peace."

Nora simply could not just "close the books on Fern." And she didn't think Fern could rest in peace, either. The way Goldie had handled things wasn't right. Nora had no particular creed from which to draw that conclusion, and yet something deep inside her knew that even Fern deserved something better than a hastily dug, unmarked grave.

A week after Fern's death, Nora decided that she was going to do something more. When she ran errands for Goldie on Saturday, she stopped at the undertaker's and made certain she knew the way to the cemetery where Fern was buried. At Herpolsheimer's she bought a length of the most beautiful red ribbon she could find. On Sunday, Nora went to the livery and rented a farm wagon. Climbing up onto the wagon seat, she couldn't help smiling to herself. Being raised on a farm was finally doing her some good. She could drive a wagon.

When Nora finally reached the little country cemetery, it was late afternoon. She spent nearly an hour walking along the field that joined the cemetery, collecting stones, each one about the size of a potato. When she had a pile of stones by Fern's grave, she collected a huge bouquet of wildflowers, tying it with the red ribbon.

To complete her task, Nora knelt beside the fresh grave and used stones to spell the name F-E-R-N. Once the name was spelled, Nora laid the bouquet above it. She stood up, brushing the dirt off her skirt, wishing she knew something appropriate to say.

Swallowing hard, she finally spoke aloud. "I hope you're in a better place, Fern. I know it was hard for you down here. I'm sorry for the way things ended up." Looking up, Nora said, "God, you and I don't know each other much. But I thought you'd want to know about Fern. I marked her resting place. So now I guess she's all yours." Nora paused uncertainly. Something was missing. She remembered hearing her neighbor Mrs. Johnson pray at a church picnic once. What had she said when she was finished? "Oh," Nora said. "And hay-men."

She lingered for a little while in the cemetery, reading headstones, wishing she could have done better for Fern. Finally, she climbed back up into the wagon seat and headed for Lincoln. The setting sun shed a rosy glow on everything in sight. Nora wondered if the sunset meant that God thought that she had done a good thing.

It was dark when Nora finally returned the horse and wagon to the livery. She hurried up the block and ducked into the alley that ran just east of the row of buildings where Goldie's was located. She was humming to herself when someone stumbled out of the shadows and grabbed her. A gritty hand clamped over her mouth as a man threw his weight at her and pinned her against a brick wall.

In spite of the dark, Nora recognized Frank Albers. His breath testified to the fact that he had spent far too much time in a saloon, but he sounded frighteningly sober as he leaned close to Nora and said, "Thought you got away with it, didn't you?"

"What?" Nora gasped. "What are you talking about?"

"You know what I'm talking about," he sneered. "I heard Lily laughing about it. She was uptown today. Telling some friend of hers the whole story about how she and a friend of hers made a fool of Frank Albers." He belched before continuing, "As long as she kept quiet, I was ready to forget it. But I won't have anyone spreading garbage about me to anyone." He slammed Nora's head against the wall. "Anyone. You hear?"

"I wouldn't," Nora gasped. "I didn't. Please. I won't ever say—"

"You got that right," Frank said. There was the glint of steel as Frank laid the blade of a huge knife against Nora's throat.

At the touch of the cold steel against her neck, Nora gathered all her strength and brought up one knee as hard as she could. She didn't quite hit her target, but Frank was caught off guard enough that he let go of her momentarily. In an instant, Nora pulled away from him and was running up the alley. She let out one desperate cry for help before Frank caught her from behind, dragging her down to the ground by her skirt.

Nora heard tearing fabric and felt him kick her before a voice called out of the darkness. "Let her go." Frank refused to relent. The voice in the darkness spat out the order. "I said, let her go. I have a gun and I know how to use it."

Rage and intent to do evil deafened Frank to the warning in the voice. He slapped Nora across the face. She felt searing pain across her left side as he punched her midsection. She nearly fainted, but not before she heard the other voice shout again. There was a loud sound and then, suddenly, Frank was no longer sitting on her legs. Dr. Allbright was kneeling by her, laying two fingers on her neck, asking, "Nora, can you hear me?"

"Yes," Nora gasped. She tried to sit up, but excruciating pain prevented it.

Dr. Allbright pushed her gently back to the earth. "Lay still. I can't tell a thing in the dark. Wait until I get some help to get you inside."

"Frank? What—"

Dr. Allbright stood up. "Henry," she said firmly, "I've

killed Frank Albers. I'm not sorry and I'd do it again in similar circumstances. Here's my gun. Can you wait to arrest me until I tend to this poor girl? Help me carry her up to Goldie's, will you?"

Nora closed her eyes and tried to keep from fainting. She pulled air into her lungs in short bursts, struggling against the pain that accompanied each tiny gasp. She realized the sheriff must be examining Frank's body.

"Well, well, Maude," he said, clucking his tongue. "See that? It's loaded. Appears to me this is a case of self-defense, pure and simple. I don't think I'll be hauling you off to jail."

The sheriff crouched down next to Nora. "Now, miss, I've got to carry you up to Goldie's where Dr. Allbright can tend to you. I'm sorry to have to hurt you."

It really didn't hurt much. In fact, it was the next morning before Nora knew it hurt at all, because she passed out the minute the sheriff bent to help her up.

CHAPTER 8

Bombazine and Black Jet

Hath God forgotten to be gracious?
hath he in anger shut up his tender mercies?
Psalm 77:9

"I'm sorry this has to be so painful," Dr. Allbright was saying, "but I don't want to run the risk of your becoming dependent on morphine."

"It's all right," Nora mumbled through her swollen lips. She wondered how long she had been drifting in and out of sleep. Was it just hours, or days? She didn't have the energy to ask.

Dr. Allbright seemed to sense the question. "It's Tuesday morning. You got hurt Sunday night. Don't be frightened if you don't remember. That's normal. You're going to feel awful for quite a few days to come. Don't fight it. Let your body rest and heal. You endured quite a beating, but you're going to be fine."

Nora had already drifted off to sleep before Dr. Allbright finished her reassurance. The next time she opened her eyes, Lily and Iris were standing over her, concern etched into their faces. Nora tried to smile, wondering if both sides of her mouth were even moving.

Iris pulled up a chair and sat down next to the bed. "Where'd you go so late, Nora?"

Closing her eyes and frowning she thought back. "Fern. Took Fern some flowers."

"Oh, honey, that was nice. Real nice."

Lily spoke up. "Guess you wonder what really happened. It was Frank. He must have been laying for us both. We don't have to worry about him anymore."

Nora raised her hand to her face, laying her open palm against her swollen cheek. Iris nodded. "Several shades of purple. And your eye's swollen shut. Dr. Allbright had to take a few stitches, but they're right along your hairline and I don't think the scar will show much at all." Iris barely touched Nora's hair along her left temple. "She left it open to the air. Said it would heal better that way."

Nora reached up and carefully felt for the stitches. It was numb along the line her finger traced. She hoped Iris was being truthful, that it wasn't a very long row of thread.

"Dr. Allbright said none of the bones in your face are broken," Lily offered. "But you're going to be a walking rainbow for a while." Lily paused awkwardly. "I'm going to get you some tea, Nora. You want some?"

Nora shook her head, but Lily was already gone. Iris sat holding her hand, and Nora could not bear the compassion on her face. It made her cry again. What was wrong with her anyway? It seemed like everything made her cry. She hated being a crybaby. And besides, the broken ribs made it hurt.

As Nora's tears slid out the corners of her eyes and into the hair at her temples, Iris took up one of her hands, squeezing it affectionately. "It's all right. Go ahead and cry. It must have been awful."

Nora winced against the pain in her midsection as she tried to control her sobs. Through swollen lips she managed to whisper, "Hurts terrible."

"I know it does. I had broken ribs once."

Nora opened her eyes, blinking to clear her vision. Iris nodded her head. "You know how it is. The men are the masters. We do what they say. Period. Well, one time—and only one—I made the mistake of refusing." She called the man a name. "He broke two of my ribs."

The thought of Iris being hurt made Nora start to cry again.

Lily came back in with tea, but Nora only shook her head.

"Why don't you leave the two of us alone for a few minutes?" Iris said to Lily. "I want to have a little talk with Nora."

Lily left, visibly relieved to have an excuse to escape.

Iris got up and closed Nora's door. Sitting down again, she began, "This thing with Fern, and now you, has got me thinking. I don't have quite as much saved up as I would like, but there's enough for a start out in Denver. I can take in laundry or do whatever else I have to do to make ends meet. I'm finished with this life."

She put her hand on Nora's shoulder. "Don't answer right now. But think on it. If you decide you want to come with me, I'll wait until you're better."

Iris stroked Nora's forehead tenderly. Nora took a breath and let it out slowly. She wanted to whisper her thanks, but she didn't have the energy. Iris kissed her on the cheek and left the room.

Dr. Allbright came daily for the first week, urging Nora to get up and move around as soon as she could bear it. "The longer you stay in bed, the weaker you'll become and the longer it will take you to fight your way back."

At each visit, Nora struggled to keep from crying. She felt as if she had done nothing since that dreadful night but cry and wince from pain. The girls took turns helping her drink soup and tea. Every kindness brought more tears. Unexpected noises made her jump with fright. She braced a broom handle in the window sashing, but it wasn't enough. She could not sleep at night until she had braced a chair beneath the doorknob on her side of the door.

When Nora made her first efforts to shuffle out of her room, Goldie saw it as a triumph. She sent Shep to the store for a luxurious treat. "You ever had fresh orange juice, honey? No? Well, just wait until you taste it. It's a little bit of heaven."

Nora nodded. She had bitten her tongue in the struggle with Frank, and the orange juice made it sting. Still, she had to agree with Goldie that orange juice tasted good.

Days passed. Nora wanted to sleep late, but found that she couldn't. She developed the routine of making herself breakfast while the house was quiet. By the time the girls awoke, Nora was ready for a nap. In the afternoon, she took a walk. At first, the walk was simply to the back porch and then to the kitchen table where, trembling with weakness, she would manage to gulp a cup of coffee before creeping back to bed.

The evenings were the worst. When the girls were busy at work, the house echoed with noise. Shep played the piano by the hour; there was laughter and the sound of footsteps clomping up and down the stairs. One day, Goldie asked Nora what her favorite color was. Having heard that Fern's room was being redone, Nora wondered if Goldie was going to invite her to move upstairs. The thought made her ill.

Nora floated from day to day, making progress physically, but in suspended animation emotionally. Every time she saw Goldie coming her way, a sense of dread loomed up. She began to feel the same way about Iris. Some days, she thought she would simply resign herself to life as a boarder and get it over with. Then, she would think about Denver. Sometimes she even wished she was back on the farm with Pap and Will.

Goldie assured Nora she would "cheer up directly." Dr. Allbright said that healing would take time. But as the days passed, and her sense of confusion and despair grew, Nora began to doubt that she would ever feel better.

When Nora finally felt well enough to get dressed and take a carriage ride, Goldie had Shep drive her to Thornhill Dressers. "Pick out something for a new dress, Nora. Something that'll cheer you up."

Nora nodded and mumbled a thank-you. Although she was no longer frightened by Lincoln's busy streets, Nora still spent the ride to the dressmaker's fighting back tears. Goldie's idea that a new dress could fix what was wrong inside of her only made her sadness worse.

When Shep lifted her down from the carriage and deposited her on the boardwalk, Nora stumbled against him, gasping for breath. She reached for him and put a hand on his shoulder to steady herself.

"Hey," Shep said tenderly. "If this is too much for you—"

"No," Nora said. "I'm all right. It just hurt a little more than I expected. I'll be fine. I'm not going to miss a chance to get a new dress."

Shep chuckled. "That's my girl."

Nora looked up at him sharply. Was Shep actually blushing? He was looking down at her with an odd expression on his face. Nora realized that beneath his beard, Shep wasn't all that old. She had never noticed.

Shep cleared his throat nervously. "You've been through some bad business, Nora. I guess I know that getting a new dress isn't going to fix things." He put his hand on the side of the carriage and, removing his hat, took a deep breath. "What I wanted to say was, Goldie expects me to keep an eye on things. I wish I would have been there when that happened. I wish I could have stopped it."

Nora felt herself blushing. She blinked back the tears that were welling up in her eyes and managed to croak, "Thank you." Then, she headed inside Thornhill Dressers.

Miss Thornhill directed Nora to the corner of the studio where the three-way mirrors stood. It was the first time Nora had looked in a mirror since that awful night. Dr. Allbright had taken the stitches out, but turning her head Nora saw that an angry red line ran nearly the entire length of the left side of her hairline and then to her cheekbone. Iris had been wrong. There would be a scar, and it would show. She reached up to touch the welt. Her eye was no longer swollen shut, but the skin on the left side of her face was still a sickly greenish-yellow color with some rings of darker red still apparent around her eye.

Miss Thornhill cleared her throat. "My sister said you were to have anything you wanted, Miss O'Dell. From what I can see, you should spend her money liberally."

Nora cupped her hand over the injured side of her face. "It wasn't her fault," she said loyally.

"I didn't say it was," Miss Thornhill snapped back. "But I know my sister's affairs pretty well, and I also know she isn't given to fits of generosity often. So let's get you something really wonderful while Goldie's in a spending mood. She can afford it and you deserve it. What's your favorite color?"

"I don't—know," Nora said. After a moment's hesitation, she replied, "Green, I guess."

Elise pulled down three bolts of green fabric, each one a different shade. Holding the fabric up to Nora's face, she shook her head. "I'm afraid green isn't the right color. At least not right now. It makes your face look like death."

Nora looked in the mirror. Miss Thornhill was right. One of the bolts of fabric matched her bruised skin almost perfectly. "I look like a pickle—bumps and lumps included," she said.

Miss Thornhill chuckled. "A good analogy. However," she said, grabbing another bolt of cloth, "if we ignore your pickled skin and concentrate on your eyes, I can see why you like green."

"I guess I hadn't really thought about that," Nora said. "I just like green." She was beginning to feel weak. "Would you mind if I sit down for just a minute?" She apologized. "I haven't been out much, and—"

Miss Thornhill's voice was warm with kindness. "I'm sorry. I should have thought about that. I'm going to get you some tea. You sit right there." She directed Nora to the plush chair beside the fireplace and disappeared into the workroom.

Once again, Nora fought against the tears that seemed to flow so freely.

Nora was wiping her eyes when Miss Thornhill returned with tea. True concern sounded in her voice as she asked, "Is there anything I can do for you, Miss O'Dell?"

Nora took the tea and shrugged, embarrassed. "Not unless you can come up with a cure for being a crybaby. I can't seem to do anything lately but cry. I don't know what's wrong with me. It isn't like me. I'm usually pretty tough. But not lately. I cry when I hurt. I cry when I go to sleep. Now, it seems, I cry when someone is nice to me, too." She set the cup of tea down and bent her head, rubbing her forehead with the tips of her fingers.

Miss Thornhill said gently, "Don't be so demanding of yourself." She hesitated before saying, "There's a promise that I return to often that says, 'Wait on the LORD: be of good courage, and he shall strengthen thine heart.' Have you tried asking the Lord for strength? It always helps me."

Nora frowned slightly. "You mean, like he was a real person or something?"

"Of course," Miss Thornhill said with a smile. "He *is* a real person. Maybe not flesh and blood like you and me, but He certainly cares about our problems. And He listens when we talk to Him."

Nora shook her head doubtfully. "Maybe he cares about you, but he sure doesn't spend much time worrying about the likes of me."

Miss Thornhill replied, "I understand why you would feel that way. I don't know why you've had such a hard time, but I know God does love you." She guided the conversation back to Nora's new dress. "You know, I think I have something you'll like in the back. If you'll just relax and enjoy your tea, I'll bring it out." She went back to the workroom.

Just as Miss Thornhill disappeared through the doorway the bell on the back door rang. Nora heard Lucy and Hannah chattering and laughing. They came into the studio together and greeted Nora.

Lucy spoke first. "Heard about what happened. I'm awful sorry."

"Me, too," Hannah agreed. Then she said quickly, "You don't look half as bad as I expected."

Nora smiled weakly. "Thank you. I think."

Miss Thornhill came out of the workroom with a bolt of cloth in her arms. "Hannah. Lucy. Pull out my box of special buttons."

Nora's eyes grew wide as Miss Thornhill spread out a length of fabric. "Oh," she said softly. She reached out to touch it. "It's so soft." She gathered some of it up in her hands. Looking at Elise, she said, "It makes a real pretty bustle, I bet."

"Yes," Miss Thornhill agreed. "You're quite right. This manufacturer has a special way with the weaving process. This is called bombazine. Most are cotton and worsted, and have a dull surface. But this manufacturer combines silk and wool. That's what gives it the twilled surface. And it does drape more gracefully."

Nora shook her head. "It's far too nice for me. Where would I ever wear it?"

"'Get the gown and the occasion will present itself,'" Miss Thornhill said. She winked. "Don't you think that's a good motto for a dressmaker?"

Nora smiled. "Yes, I suppose it is. But I don't think—"

"I'll tell you what," Miss Thornhill said. "Let's go ahead and get you measured. You can be thinking about it while I do your fitting."

In the end, Nora could not resist the bombazine. She selected black corded silk trim. When Miss Thornhill insisted that Nora sort through her personal "stash," of buttons, she selected a set of tiny jet buttons.

"Those will be just perfect," Miss Thornhill said. "I insist you take them. As a gift from me." She smiled. "I won't even charge Goldie for them."

"What about a hat?" Lucy wanted to know.

"Oh, no," Nora protested. "Goldie didn't say anything about a hat."

"There'll be enough left from cutting out the dress to make something nice," Lucy said convincingly. "It really won't cost that much more."

"I'm certain Goldie expected we'd make a hat," Miss Thornhill agreed, pulling out a lightweight buckram frame. "I think this base would be perfect. It really does compliment an oval face. Here, try it."

"How do you turn this little thing into a hat?" Nora wanted to know. She put the frame on her head, wincing a little as she stretched her arms upward. The hat frame featured a short, squarish crown. The brim was narrower at the back to allow for an abundance of curls in the wearer's coiffure, then the brim curved around the side of the head and grew wider over the forehead.

"Here, I'll show you," Lucy said. "We cover the frame with fabric—in your case the bombazine. With a black velvet bow on this side, and a black ostrich feather curving up across the top, it'll be stunning." She indicated the underside of the front brim. "I'll gather some dark purple moiré here."

Nora shook her head. "It's too much."

"Perhaps you're right," Miss Thornhill interrupted. "Simpler is sometimes better." She handed the hat frame to Lucy and returned her attention to the dress fabric. "You know, Miss O'Dell, you have a good fashion sense. You were right about that one trim I pulled out. What you selected is much more in keeping with the feel of the bombazine. And you knew the moment you saw them that those jet buttons were right."

The bell on the shop door rang. Nora started and turned away from the door, hoping to hide the bruised side of her face.

"Oh," the gentleman said. "I see you're busy. I can come back."

"No, no, Mr. Chandler. It's quite all right. Please. Come in," Miss Thornhill insisted.

Nora had learned a great deal about judging men from behind the bar at Goldie's. Viewing Mr. Chandler in the dressing mirrors, she thought that here was one who was very well aware of the effect he had on women. He was clean shaven except for a thick, blonde mustache. Almost a goatee, the mustache drooped down both sides of his mouth, framing a well-formed chin. Nora took note of brilliant blue eyes and an aristocratic nose. And, when he removed his hat, thick, curly blonde hair.

The man glanced her way. Quickly, Nora lifted a gloved hand to hide her cheek. Hoping her demeanor was realistic, she said, "Miss Thornhill, if you don't mind, I'll have a cup of tea with Lucy and Hannah before we proceed with my fitting." She kept her face turned away from the stranger as she got up. Brushing her hand across the bombazine, she said, "This will be lovely."

Miss Thornhill rose to the occasion. "Thank you, Miss O'Dell. I appreciate your patience. Mr. Chandler did have an appointment. Are you certain you can wait?"

"Of course," Nora said. Making her way across the shop, she nodded at Mr. Chandler. Back in the workroom, she sank gratefully into a chair.

Hannah and Lucy were beside themselves. "Is it really Mr. Chandler? Did you see him?"

"Miss Thornhill called him Mr. Chandler. Why?"

"Oh," Lucy said, "I wish I had some excuse to go out there. To see for myself."

"Well," Nora said, "I suppose you could make a case for getting the cloth for my dress."

Lucy smiled in triumph. "Of course!" She patted Nora on the shoulder. "Perfect." Lucy took a deep breath. She looked at herself in the mirror, smoothing her hair, pinching her cheeks. She clasped her hands before her, closed her eyes, and took a few deep breaths. Then, she went into the studio.

She was back in a moment, flushed with excitement. Clutching Nora's bolt of cloth in her arms, she whirled happily about the room. "It *is* him! It is! He's talking to Miss Thornhill about making a special costume for the theatrical troupe. That means he'll have to come back. Oh, wait until the girls at meeting hear about this. They'll just die from envy. They'll just die."

"And wait until Mr. Fielding hears about it," Hannah teased.

"Oh, Hannah, you wouldn't!" Lucy exclaimed.

Hannah shook her head. "Of course not. Unless I need to blackmail you sometime."

"Oh, you!" Lucy shot back. "You know I like Adam Fielding better than anything. But, Hannah," she sighed. "Greyson *Chandler*, for heaven's sake! And in the *next room!*"

Nora was beginning to feel shaky. When was Shep coming for her? Listening to Lucy and Hannah chatter taught her more about Greyson Chandler than she ever wanted to know. Apparently this was an important person who came to Lincoln infrequently. He was an actor. A famous one. Everyone knew that he and Mamie Patterson were lovers. That's how they could play their love scenes so convincingly.

Nora's back was beginning to hurt, she was hungry, and she needed a nap. Neither Lucy nor Hannah showed much inclination to get on with her dress fitting. She wanted to leave, but she didn't want to go through the studio to look for Shep. She might not be a fan of Greyson Chandler, but she didn't want any stranger staring at her green and yellow face.

Finally, she heard the bell on the front door ring. Shep. She practically sighed with relief. Making her way to the studio, she was dismayed to see a stranger closing the shop door and heading across the street. Nora's knees were wobbly. She began shaking. She was too afraid of fainting now to worry about hiding her face. It took all her concentration to keep her head erect and take another step toward the workroom. *Oh, Lord, am I going to faint?* Suddenly, someone was at her side, taking her arm, helping her to a chair. Nora closed her eyes and took a deep breath. When she opened them, a very handsome man with incredibly blue eyes was offering her a glass of water.

"Thank you." She closed her eyes as she drank the water, feeling her cheeks go crimson. Had she believed in the power of prayer at that moment, she would have prayed fervently for Miss Thornhill's floor to open up and swallow her.

Miss Thornhill was there, too, patting her shoulder. "I've sent Hannah for Mr. Roberts, Miss O'Dell. We can do the fitting another day. I'll reserve that bolt of cloth for you."

"Please accept my apologies for making you wait so long," Chandler said. "I feel responsible for the delay. You've obviously been convalescing. I should have waited."

Nora wasn't certain what "convalescing" meant, but she knew that Chandler had seen her bruised face. Unconsciously she lifted her gloved hand to her cheek. "I'm better now."

Shep drove up. Nora pushed herself up from the chair, only to find her head swimming again. Greyson Chandler took the opportunity to live up to his reputation as a dashing rescuer of distressed damsels. With a quick apology for "taking the liberty," he swept Nora up in his arms just as Shep was opening the door. The two men's eyes met. Shep laughed. "Still up to your old tricks, I see," he said.

"This one's yours?" Chandler asked. In spite of Nora's weak protests, Chandler carried her out the door and deposited her in the carriage.

Then he turned toward Shep, slapping him on the back and shaking his hand. "Well, you old scalawag. What are you doing all the way up here? I thought you were never leaving New Orleans."

"And I thought you were going to be a famous symphony conductor," Shep retorted, shoving his hat back on his head.

"Just goes to show," Chandler said, laughing, "what fools we both were a few years back."

The two men arranged to have a drink together later that evening. Chandler turned toward Nora. "Are you all right, Miss O'Dell?" When Nora nodded, he directed one last jab at Shep. "I'd say she's a 'keeper.'"

He turned quickly back to Nora. "No disrespect intended, ma'am."

Nora couldn't be certain, but she thought Chandler winked at her.

CHAPTER 9

A Lost Lamb

A man's heart deviseth his way: but the LORD directeth his steps.
Proverbs 16:9

When Dr. Maude Allbright pulled her white gelding up to the back door of Thornhill Dressers and knocked at the workroom door, Lucy and Hannah were still in a state of profound excitement over Greyson Chandler's visit. Lucy blurted out the story of Nora O'Dell's encounter with the famous actor. "Can you believe it? He actually picked her up and carried her. Oh," Lucy sighed, "isn't that *romantic?*"

Dr. Allbright removed her hat and plunked it down on the workroom table. "I suppose so. If you like blond-haired fops who masquerade as talented actors and think they can have the world because they can spout a few lines of Shakespeare."

Dr. Allbright marched into Miss Thornhill's studio.

"The girls said that Nora O'Dell was here. How is she doing? I mean to call on her later."

Miss Thornhill shook her head. "She had a little fainting spell."

Dr. Allbright asked, "Did she seem melancholy to you? I know she's going to be fine physically. But I'm concerned about her in other ways."

"I know what you mean. There is something—something that a new dress isn't going to heal," Miss Thornhill said. She sighed. "She does *not* belong at Goldie's. I wish my sister would admit that. If ever I saw a little lost lamb, that girl is one. She makes you just want to put your arms around her and mother her."

"*Humph,*" Dr. Allbright replied. "That's where you and I are different. You want to mother everyone and introduce them to the Almighty. I want to give them a shake and tell them to get on with life."

"But I don't think Nora is pretending so we'll feel sorry for her."

Dr. Allbright grimaced. "I didn't mean Nora." She sighed. "But it is getting so I see so many pampered, hysterical women, I hardly know what to do when I encounter one who is honestly traumatized."

Miss Thornhill said, "I know you won't approve, Dr. Allbright, but I'm thinking of inviting Nora to go to church with me. She needs to know that God loves her."

Maude replied testily, "And if God loves her so much, where was He that night Frank Albers was beating the tar out of her?"

Miss Thornhill smiled. "I've wondered about that. Didn't you tell me there was something odd about that night?"

Maude frowned slightly. "Yes. There was. It wasn't my usual night to call at Goldie's. Something—" She stopped and held up her hand. "Don't start."

Miss Thornhill nodded. "Yes. That's what you said. Something just seemed to head you over that way. And you'd taken Casey to be shod, and had to walk, so you tucked the gun in your bag—at the last minute—almost as an afterthought."

"Are you trying to tell me that my being in that alley with a gun was an act of God?"

Miss Thornhill smiled.

"That's drivel," Maude said. "It was just a fortunate

coincidence. If there *were* a God involved in people's affairs, surely he would have intervened before that poor girl got hurt."

Elise said quietly, "Perhaps Nora needed something shocking to happen to move her in a different direction." She looked at Dr. Allbright. "Some people are uniquely stubborn, you know—present company excluded, of course."

While they talked, Miss Thornhill had been pulling bolts of cloth down from the shelf.

"Well," Dr. Allbright interjected, "I'll agree with you that it was fortunate for Nora that I was in that alley. But as to it being God who put me there, don't you think he would have used one of his own instead of an old infidel like me?"

Miss Thornhill turned to the fabric on the table. "See anything you like?"

Dr. Allbright thumped three bolts. "Brown. Gray. Black. One of each."

"Do you want me to use the same pattern?" Miss Thornhill asked. "*Peterson's* is showing a return of the high bustle for next year."

"I doubt a single fashion editor of *Peterson's* has ever had to drive a rig twenty miles at breakneck speed in the dead of Nebraska winter," Dr. Allbright said. "If they had, they wouldn't be trying to resurrect anything so ridiculous as that. I declare, I saw a bustle yesterday a person could set a tea tray on." She shook her head. "I'm not objecting to a little feminine fullness at the back, you understand, but let's do be sensible."

"What about the sleeves?" Miss Thornhill wanted to know. "They're more puffed this season . . . and the cuffs can be quite exaggerated."

"Oh, good," Dr. Allbright said dryly. "Bigger cuffs. Just the thing for facilitating an appendectomy." She chuckled. "No. Just cut three of the same old thing, and never mind *The Delineator*, or *Peterson's*." Dr. Allbright headed for the opposite corner of the shop. "Now," she said, briskly rubbing her hands together, "let's talk hats."

She may not have been a slave to fashion, but Dr. Maude Allbright was definitely a slave to hats. She could order three new suits in less than ten minutes, but she spent the next two hours looking over sketches and selecting fabric and trims for three new hats.

"Every red-tailed hawk in the county will be dive-bombing me if I wear that," she scoffed, pointing to a French creation sporting three gray birds perched on the crown. "I like the shape, though. Can you make a tower of posies or something at the front instead of the dead birds?"

"What color?"

"How about something salmony-pink—with brown trim to go with the brown suit?" Turning the pages of Miss Thornhill's *Fashion Guide*, Dr. Allbright pointed to a large-brimmed hat entirely camouflaged in felt-gray plumes and curled blue and yellow striped ribbon. "Make this one to go with the gray suit. And that"—Dr. Allbright pointed to another gigantic hat—"that to go with the black."

She finished her order and said abruptly, "Now. What do you think might be done to help Miss Nora O'Dell?"

An hour later, Elise Thornhill walked Dr. Allbright to her carriage behind the shop. As Dr. Allbright took up the reins, she nodded. "Thank you, Elise, talking with you always renews my hope in humanity. Now, if the humanity in question will only do what we say, I think we'll have done some good."

"Let's pray that she listens," Miss Thornhill said, stepping away from the carriage.

"I'll leave the praying to you," Dr. Allbright said. "I think God hung up on me long, long ago." She slapped the reins across her gelding's flanks and set off up the alley.

Nora was attempting to sweep the kitchen floor at Goldie's when Miss Thornhill came to the back door.

"Goldie's not here right now," Nora said. "But if you want to wait, I can make you some coffee."

Miss Thornhill replied, "Thank you, but I just had lunch. I don't need any coffee. Actually, I came to see you." She reached into her bag and withdrew a measuring tape, notebook, and pencil. "I'm glad to see you're feeling better. If I can take a few measurements, Hannah and Lucy can get started cutting out your new gown."

"I've been thinking about that," Nora said doubtfully. "I really shouldn't be getting anything so fancy."

"Are we back to that again?" Miss Thornhill asked. While she talked, she draped the measuring tape about her shoulders. "Well, I'll tell you what. I need the same measurements whether I'm making a dress from a potato sack or bombazine, so let's get started anyway."

Smiling softly, Nora set the broom aside. "All right."

"I don't use ready-made patterns, and with today's styles, the measurements have to be very exact. Shall we remove to your room?"

In her room, Nora stripped down to only three petticoats and her chemise. Miss Thornhill began to take measurements. "With all those numbers you'll be able to build an entire new me."

Finally, Miss Thornhill wrote the last measurement in her notebook. Snapping it shut, she headed for the kitchen. "I'll make coffee. I believe I would like some now."

Nora winced as she pulled her dress over her head. She was buttoning the last button at her neckline when Miss Thornhill called from the stove, "It's good to see you feeling so much better. We've been worried about you."

"Worried? About me?"

"Lucy and Hannah both took a liking to you," Miss Thornhill said matter-of-factly.

"They were nice to me, even if I was out of sorts." Nora tied her apron about her waist and joined Elise in the kitchen. "I bet they have some good times together."

Elise thought Nora sounded like a child standing outside a store window wishing for a piece of candy she knew she could not have. She poured two cups of coffee and settled into a chair at the kitchen table. "Yes, they do. They share a room at a boardinghouse a few blocks from the shop. Most of the time, they are inseparable. They attend the same church, too. Perhaps you'd like to go with them sometime." Elise didn't wait for Nora to react to the mention of church. "They can be a bit much at times—especially when Greyson Chandler *himself* comes into the shop!" Miss Thornhill imitated Lucy, clasping her hands before her and sighing.

Nora said, "I wanted to roll up into a ball and die from embarrassment." She smiled faintly. "It helped a little that Shep knows him." She set down her coffee and said abruptly. "I'm feeling better. At least I'm not such a crybaby."

Elise asked, "Is that because you really *are* better? Or because you're getting better at hiding your true feelings?"

Nora shrugged. "Nobody wants to be around a crybaby all the time."

"Are you happy here at Goldie's?"

Nora looked away. "It's all right."

Miss Thornhill cleared her throat. She lifted her eyebrows toward the second floor. "Do you see yourself up there?"

"Lily and Iris have done all right."

"What about Fern?"

"Fern was stupid. She didn't plan ahead."

"Are you planning ahead? Is this where you want to be when you get old?"

Nora sounded defensive. "Up 'til now, I never planned anything—except getting away from my pap. But I'm learning fast." She reached up to touch her bruised face.

Miss Thornhill set down her coffee cup. "Perhaps you

could make some plans of your own before Goldie does it for you." She paused, pointing a finger to the ceiling and asked again, "Is that where you want to end up?"

Goldie's steps sounded in the front hall. Miss Thornhill called out a greeting, and Goldie joined them in the kitchen, pouring herself a cup of coffee, and joining Nora and Elise at the table.

Nora was amazed when Miss Thornhill said, "Goldie knows that I love her. She also knows I hate what she does. And I hate what becomes of most of the girls who stay with her."

Goldie interrupted. "And Elise knows that I see no particular value in becoming a poor drudge just to gain the respect of people I don't give a hoot for."

Miss Thornhill didn't seem to mind Goldie's comparing dressmaking to drudgery. She continued talking to Nora, "Not a day goes by that I don't pray that God will reach out and grab Goldie—by the throat, if necessary—and turn her life back around."

Goldie interrupted dryly, "I'll be certain to tell Reverend you-know-who that you shared the faith with me when he stops in next time."

"Oh, Goldie," Miss Thornhill sighed. "You keep making the same mistake over and over again. You know there are snake oil salesmen, but you still trust Dr. Allbright to care for the girls. So why does Reverend Cooper's hypocrisy make you deny Christ? The existence of men like him doesn't mean that what Christ said and what He did have no meaning, any more than quacks negate the good of true medicine."

Goldie waved her hand in the air. "All right, Elise. All right. Point taken. But, let's finish up here. I know you're trying to talk Nora into leaving behind this dreaded life of sin and woe." Goldie mocked her sister without bitterness or anger.

Miss Thornhill removed the measuring tape that was still draped about her neck and began to fold it up. She waited until the tape was tucked back into her bag before looking at Nora. "Do you remember what I said the other day about your having a knack for fashion?" She pulled the drawstring on her bag tight as she said, "Would you be interested in coming to work for me?"

"At the Dressers?"

Miss Thornhill nodded. "After you left, Mr. Chandler presented me with the opportunity to do some regular work for his theatrical troupe. When I realized how large the troupe is, I also realized that I will need more help if I accept his proposal. Even before that, I was considering expanding the millinery part of my business."

"But I don't know very much about sewing."

"Goldie told me you've been helping the girls with their mending."

Nora shrugged. "That's just poke in the needle and take a few stitches. What you do is—art—compared to that."

"Everyone has to start some place," Miss Thornhill said. "All it takes is enthusiasm and interest. I can teach you the rest. My old apartment over the shop is empty. It was too small for both Lucy and Hannah. But I'd like knowing there was someone on the premises. It's not fancy, but it's available."

"You'd trust me to live upstairs? You barely know me."

Goldie interrupted. "We know you well enough."

"Yes." Miss Thornhill nodded. "You didn't take the pennies."

"What?"

Goldie explained. "Do you remember when I told you I'm a good judge of character? Well, I don't just trust my instincts with new girls. Sometimes I give them a little test to find out if I'm going to have to worry about them stealing me blind behind my back. Remember that day when we talked about you being a housekeeper instead of a cook?"

Nora nodded.

"Do you remember your first assignment?"

"You had me clean Ivy's room to see if I could clean better than I cooked." Nora smiled.

Goldie nodded. "Right. And when you did, what did you find under Ivy's bed?"

"Some pennies."

"And what did you do with them?" Goldie asked.

"Put them on top of Ivy's bed."

"Why didn't you take them?" Goldie asked. "Most girls would have. It was only four pennies."

"It wouldn't have been right," Nora said. "They weren't mine. My pap might not have taught me much, but he taught me to be honest. Tanned my hide good once for hiding an apple under my pillow and then lying about it."

Miss Thornhill spoke up. "So there you have it, Nora. Most girls would have thought, 'No one's going to miss four pennies.' But you did the right thing."

Goldie cut the final threads tying Nora to her. "Go, Nora. The truth is, you don't have the temperament for this kind of work. And while I was tempted to make an exception on account of those green eyes and that blonde hair, I usually don't hire girls without experience. I think I've known for a while it wasn't going to work out for you to stay here. Elise's proposal solves it for everyone. And no hard feelings."

Goldie turned to Elise. "I'll send Shep by later today to help get Nora's apartment ready. Dr. Allbright is stopping by to check her over. I suspect she'll agree that Nora is about ready to get back to work."

Goldie stood up. Laying a hand on Nora's shoulder, she said, "As for you, Miss O'Dell, I know what you're thinking. You'll accept the bombazine, and I'll not hear another word about it." She winked. "You *could* clean better than you cook, dearie. You earned your way. Now it's time you moved on."

CHAPTER 10

More Than Cloth and Cutting

Whatsoever thy hand findeth to do, do it with thy might.
Ecclesiastes 9:10

The first day Nora came to Thornhill Dressers for training, she worked with Lucy and Hannah. "You'll grow to love Miss Thornhill," Hannah said. "She's truly an angel. You wouldn't believe how some of the dressmakers treat their back room girls. We used to work for Madame Hart over on N Street."

"You mean Madame Heartless," Lucy corrected her. She had been rummaging through some boxes along one wall. She finally found what she needed and turned around, a length of lace in one hand. "You won't catch *her* customers confiding in *her*." She looked at Nora. "Miss Thornhill's patrons tell her everything. Sometimes I think she knows more about what really goes on in Lincoln than anyone."

"But she never gossips," Hannah said. "She just listens."

Lucy giggled. "I heard Dr. Allbright tell her once that she was tempted to start prescribing a visit to Thornhill Dressers for all her hysterical and melancholy patients."

The day after Lucy and Hannah's comments, Mrs. Sadie Hawks came in the shop to order a new walking dress and Nora had the opportunity to see what Lucy and Hannah had been talking about. As Nora jotted down measurements for Miss Thornhill, the portly older woman launched into a discussion of family events that ended in her mentioning several recent financial setbacks in her husband's business. She sighed. "I told Phillip I didn't need to order this dress, but he insists I can't be seen walking about town with a frayed hem. He says it gives the wrong impression."

"Well," Miss Thornhill offered, "perhaps we can come up with an alternative." She reached for a bolt of cloth. "I could insert a panel of this as a contrast near the bottom of the skirt. Then we could salvage a good piece and lower it to the hemline. We could also make new cuffs and a new collar to match the insert."

When Mrs. Hawks hesitated, Nora retrieved a copy of *The Delineator* from the workroom. Opening it to a page of illustrations, she pointed out a dress with a contrasting fabric set into the skirt.

Mrs. Hawks was thrilled. "Phillip is always so concerned about appearances. Now if he says I look like I've been trying to 'make-do', I can tell him I saw the idea in the latest fashion magazine. That should hush him up." She went on, "And that provides the solution to another difficulty. Philip is taking our Martha to visit a girl's school in St. Louis next week. I simply cannot send her in last year's dress, but our clothing budget is only forty dollars a month." She smiled with satisfaction, "Now I can do everything without having to bother Philip about money."

Nora could barely hide her amazement. Here was a woman who could spend the equivalent of two *months* of Nora's salary on clothing every month, and yet she was not happy. Nora thought back to Iris's complaint that she made "only" ninety dollars a week at Goldie's. It made one wonder about the notion that money and happiness were connected.

After Mrs. Hawks left, Miss Thornhill took Nora aside, "Now you see that there is more to dressmaking than cloth and cutting. A dressmaker's most valuable asset is often the ability to lend a sympathetic ear." She explained. "A woman can purchase a hat or a new dress any number of places in Lincoln. But God seems to have made me a good listener. They know that they can pour out their troubles to me, and I will never breathe a word of it to anyone but the Lord. It seems to mean something to them." She sighed. "You'd never guess that Mrs. Hawks has money troubles, would you? And hers is not a unique position. The finest gown in the city is sometimes only a thin disguise, hiding heart-breaking circumstances. You'd be surprised how many of my patrons are wrestling with very real problems, and all they have at home is an uncaring man who pats them on the shoulder and says, 'there, there, it will be all right' over his newspaper."

Nora shared what Lucy had said about Dr. Allbright's prescribing Thornhill Dressers as a cure for hysteria.

Elise smiled and shook her head. "I don't think I'm all *that* important. It is good, though, to end the day knowing that I've made someone else feel better."

When Mrs. Hawks brought "our Martha" in to order her new travelling ensemble, Nora learned that tact and patience were not always easily practiced. The girl bore absolutely no resemblance to her kind-hearted, well-intentioned mother. She simpered over every decision and grew positively hostile when her mother hesitated regarding a high-priced trim. Nora wondered if the girl didn't know about her father's precarious finances, or if she simply didn't care.

Trying her best to learn from Miss Thornhill's example, Nora said, "Well of course, Miss Hawks. Whatever you think. Just this morning I saw this very trim on a bonnet in the most recent issue of *Peterson's*. But if you don't care that the more expensive one is a bit outdated—"

Miss Hawks quickly changed her mind. Nora appreciated the grateful nod of Mrs. Hawks' head as the two left the shop. Miss Thornhill's praise made her blush with pleasure. "Very good, Miss O'Dell. Very good indeed."

Nora was thankful to know that her handling of Martha Hawks pleased Miss Thornhill. She was less certain of her ability to please when it came to the technical aspects of the trade. At times she felt that she was wallowing in an endless sea of new words and terms. Miss Thornhill spoke of morning dresses for street and home, for welcoming visitors, or for housekeeping. There were carriage dresses and riding dresses, dinner dresses and ordinary evening dresses. Church, theater, and the opera, each had its own etiquette. Miss Thornhill sometimes made a "yachting dress" or a "bathing dress" for wealthy clients' outings to Capitol Beach just west of the city.

Bustles and silks, which had been "out," were coming back "in." Satins were going "out," but Scotch plaids were all the furor. The homeless girl who owned only two garments of her own struggled to learn the advantages of bombazine over broadcloth and cambric over chintz. A dress with a natural waistline had a "bodice," but if it extended below the waistline, it was called a "basque." Miss Thornhill called trims "garniture," and a glove a "gauntlet." Nora's head swam with so much to learn.

And then there were the nearly endless rules connected to mourning. "We don't observe strict time periods," Miss Thornhill said. "The change from full- to half-mourning garments is dictated more by the wearer's feelings. Toward the end of mourning, ladies add white, purple, and gray to their black ensembles. Children under twelve wear white in summer and gray in winter, with black trims."

"How do you remember it all?" Nora wanted to know. "Do things change quickly? How do you know what's fashionable and what isn't?"

Miss Thornhill smiled. "I'm constantly perusing the fashion magazines—as should you. It helps that my average customer really only has a simple calico wrapper for housekeeping, one or two silk dresses for making and receiving calls, and a silk gown for special occasions. Some of my more thrifty patrons even like to make their own clothing. They have me do the fitting and the cutting, then they take the project home to finish."

When it came time to make Nora's work clothes, Miss Thornhill cautioned, "Businesswomen must take care not to overdress. Superfluous trim must be avoided, although a watch and chain are certainly acceptable. I would suggest gray and brown as the best colors to wear."

Nora knew without asking which buttons to choose for her work dresses. Dull. Boring. Boring. Dull. She made a mental note to begin saving for a watch and chain, thinking longingly of the green bombazine that hung inside a dustcover on a hook upstairs.

Miss Thornhill seemed to read her mind. She patted Nora's hand. "Don't worry, Miss O'Dell. We can make an exception for the green bombazine. It is, after all, a more conservative shade of green."

It was not long before Nora met someone who paid no heed to the "rule" that dictated dull colors and understated styles for businesswomen. Mrs. Augusta Hathaway, a local hotel owner known for her philanthropy, entered the shop one day dressed in a bright purple walking dress with wide lace cuffs and a shamelessly huge opal brooch. She was a large woman who sported stylish clothing and a broad smile. It was not long before Nora realized that Mrs. Hathaway knew the "rules." She simply didn't care to obey them. Nora liked her.

"Well, Elise," Mrs. Hathaway inquired. "Who's this?"

"My new associate, Miss O'Dell," was the answer. "She's just learning the trade, and if you have no objection, I'd like yours to be the first fitting she conducts—with my supervision, of course."

Mrs. Hathaway nodded. "Mind? Of course not. Why would I mind?" She headed for the dressing room. Pausing in front of the mirror, she shook her finger at Nora as a mock threat. "However, young lady, if you ever breathe a word of my relentlessly increasing measurements, I shall have you summarily dispatched!"

From the dressing room, Mrs. Hathaway kept up a running monologue that required little response from either Nora or Miss Thornhill. When she was finally ready for her fitting, she flung open the door. "All right then, let's get this disagreeable business over with."

Miss Thornhill talked to Nora as she worked. "I used to follow S.T. Taylor's system for cutting, but that requires ten measurements for the basque alone. Now I use a system developed by Elizabeth Gartland—"

"Leave it to a woman to improve upon things," Mrs. Hathaway interjected. Nora decided she liked Augusta Hathaway very much.

Miss Thornhill continued, "With the Gartland System we only need thirteen measurements for the entire garment. It's much more efficient."

"Of course it is," Mrs. Hathaway added. "A woman developed it with women in mind."

Miss Thornhill showed Nora how to take the final measurement and then sent Nora to the workroom. "Give your figures to Lucy and Hannah. They will demonstrate the rest of the process for you. You'll be doing it yourself in no time."

Taking her leave of Mrs. Hathaway, Nora made her way back to the workroom where she gave Lucy the measurements and prepared to watch while Lucy and Hannah created a pattern for Mrs. Hathaway's new wrapper.

Hannah spread out a huge piece of plain brown paper on the worktable. Referring to a chart on the wall labeled *The Gartland System for Cutting Women's Clothing,* she began to draw as Lucy read step-by-step instructions.

"'Draw line 1 ten inches above the bottom of the paper, the entire length of the square, for waistline.'"

Wielding a ruler and a freshly sharpened pencil, Hannah drew.

"All right," Lucy said, "'Step two: Draw line 2 from center of line 1, according to length of back. Step three: On line 2 make a dot above the waistline for the underarm measure. Draw a line parallel to line 1, for line 3.'"

Nora gave up trying to follow exactly what the girls were doing. Lucy and Hannah finally completed step number 40 and held up the completed pattern. "There," Hannah said. "That's all there is to it. Simple, huh?" She started to laugh. "Don't worry. It won't seem like Greek to you for long."

Nora spent her evenings restoring order to Miss Thornhill's workroom. She eliminated the clutter on the stairs to her apartment and devised an inventory method so that there would be no last-minute telegrams to suppliers for items that lay forgotten in the bottom of a box in the workroom. In less than a month, Miss Thornhill grew to depend on Nora's organizational skills.

Nora began to learn proper grammar by imitating Miss Thornhill and Dr. Allbright. She became more at ease with patrons, although she doubted she would ever have the patience Miss Thornhill exhibited with her more difficult ones.

"I know," Miss Thornhill said one day. "Mrs. Judge Cranston has never really considered the possibility that a mere dressmaker might be intelligent. But I'm not too proud to adopt a servile stance when it's good business. I have enough Augusta Hathaways that I don't mind the few Mrs. Judge Cranstons. If she needs to treat me like a servant to assure her superior place in society, I don't mind. Especially when it brings me business."

"If you pay attention," Miss Thornhill said, "you can learn nearly all you need to know to get along in society by observing and imitating our patrons. You have already improved your grammar tenfold. The next time Mrs. Judge Bryan stops in, observe her ease of manner and the way she carries herself. The mannerisms of a lady are easily learned. Just look around you."

Lucy interrupted, giggling. "Just remember that if you take to imitating Mrs. Judge Cranston, we'll kick you out the back door."

During the day, Nora concentrated on the craft of dressmaking and the art of being a lady. In the evenings, Dr. Allbright stopped by and helped Nora develop her mind. She began to move toward answering the questions she had been asked about her dreams and plans for the future.

Her days settled into a routine. Every evening, she said good night to Lucy and Hannah and locked up. She ate a cold supper while poring over the newspaper or some book supplied by Dr. Allbright. Shortly after dark, she mounted the stairs to her apartment, where she quickly fell asleep. On the evenings when she was tempted to wish for more, she reminded herself of the half-starved, shabbily dressed girl who had stood in the kitchen of a run-down farmhouse less than six months ago and determined to make a change.

Perhaps she did not have a family or a home, but no one was yelling at her, and the fear of moving upstairs at Goldie's was gone. She had a regular income, two new friends, and a kind employer. She began to think that millinery might be her niche at the Thornhill Dressers.

For now, it was enough.

CHAPTER 11

Nature's Limit

For what hath man of all his labour, and of the vexation of his heart, wherein he hath labored under the sun? For all his days are sorrows, and his travail grief; yea, his heart taketh not rest in the night. This is also vanity.
Ecclesiastes 2:22–23

"This simply will not do, Miss O'Dell." Mrs. Judge Cranston clicked her tongue against the roof of her mouth as she inspected herself in the mirror. "It doesn't look a bit like the drawing I brought you." As she turned her head from side to side, her small dark eyes flickered angrily. Finally, she jerked the hat off her head and nearly slammed it down on Nora's work counter.

Nora drew a deep breath and tried to calm herself. She had remade the hat in question three times in as many days. "If you'll excuse me for a moment," Nora said, "I'll just get the drawing and you can point out the deficiencies."

"I'd prefer to take the matter up with Miss Thornhill," Mrs. Cranston said. She reached up to smooth her auburn hair. From where she stood by Nora's work counter she screeched toward the workroom, "Miss Thornhill, are you *there*?"

Nora went into the workroom where a page from *Demorest's* was tacked up on the wall. It pictured several beautiful models wearing elegant hats, one of which was circled. Mrs. Cranston had selected the hat and then spoken the fateful words, "Of course, I'll want a few changes. I don't want to simply copy the picture." *No woman wants a hat like any other hat that has ever been made.* Nora had read that warning in the *Milliner's Guide*, and now she was about to enter millinery hell with a customer who expected her to realize that dream.

Mrs. Cranston had selected a hat that featured huge ridges of embroidered yellow taffeta anchored on a high-crowned base covered with folded black satin and a towering black ostrich feather. Nora had contacted several wholesalers before finding just the right shade of taffeta for the project, when Mrs. Cranston announced that she thought perhaps a pale aquamarine would be better with the tone of her skin.

When Lucy and Hannah overheard the request, Lucy mumbled under her breath, "Tone? What tone? Is *sallow* a tone?"

For one moment, Nora had wished it was seven months earlier when she was still a "back room girl," so that she could say what she was thinking. But she couldn't. She had worked through the fall and winter learning dressmaking and millinery, and begun to think she wanted her own shop someday. Miss Thornhill was gone on her annual spring buying trip, and it was time she, Nora, learned to deal with irascible customers on her own.

Snatching the drawing that inspired Mrs. Cranston's hat down from the wall in the workroom, Nora went back into the studio. "I'm sorry, Mrs. Cranston, but Miss Thornhill isn't here. She's in St. Louis, combining a holiday with visits to some of the more important designer showrooms in the city." Nora picked up the hat and set it on a stand. Spreading the illustration out before her, she asked, "Now then, perhaps you could show me where I've gone wrong."

Mrs. Cranston wore reading glasses about her neck on a long gold chain. She unfolded them and put them on the bridge of her nose. Her eyes went from the drawing to the hat and back again. "This—" She waggled her index finger at the taffeta. "It just isn't right. It makes my head look—well—pointed."

"I believe, if you'll recall, madame," Nora said quietly, "we discussed the possibility that that might happen. Your face is much narrower than the model's. But we tried to accommodate that with a little more fullness along the sides."

"Well, I don't like it. I want it to look like the picture."

No, Nora thought, *you want to look like the picture*. "I have honestly done my best, Mrs. Cranston. I don't know what else to do. There are limitations. I can't make you look like the model."

"Well." Mrs. Cranston drew herself up and crossed her scarecrow-thin arms. "I guess I know that. There's no need to be impertinent."

"I don't mean to be impertinent," Nora said as evenly as possible.

"I've been a good customer of Elise Thornhill's for more years than you've been alive, young lady," Mrs. Cranston said imperiously, "and I won't be spoken to in that tone by the hired help. There are plenty of other hat shops in Lincoln, you know. I don't have to tolerate impertinence from some little snippet who, less than a year ago, was residing over on South Ninth Street."

It took a moment for Nora to understand exactly what Mrs. Judge Cranston was saying. At first, she wanted to cry. But she wouldn't give Mrs. Cranston the satisfaction of seeing the hurt. Instead of crying, she got angry. Grabbing the edge of her work counter, she retorted, "Yes ma'am, I *do* know there are many other millinery establishments in the city. And not a single one of *them* can make you look like the model in the magazine, either."

Mrs. Judge Cranston removed her glasses from her nose and folded them so they would lie flat on her flat chest. Pressing her lips together, she wheeled about and made for the door.

Nora controlled her tears until the door closed. Trembling all over, she crossed the studio and put the "Closed" sign in the window. She drew the blinds before walking to the back of the studio where Lucy and Hannah were working, pretending they had not heard the exchange.

It began to rain. *At least I know why my side has been aching all day*, Nora thought. Frank Albers had given her an internal weather-minder when he broke her ribs.

"Lucy, Hannah," Nora said. "Why don't you two take the afternoon off. I'm going upstairs to lie down." Nora headed for the stairs.

"Nora," Lucy said softly, "don't let it bother you. Miss Thornhill never even *liked* Mrs. Cranston."

"Thank you, Lucy. It's kind of you to say that." Wearily, Nora climbed the stairs. She heard the door to the workroom close as Lucy and Hannah left. The rain beat steadily down on the roof over her bed.

What's wrong *with me? I made the break with Goldie's. I have my own corner at Thornhill Dressers. Only last week, Elise said I should begin to order in and keep my own stock of supplies instead of sending customers shopping for their own. She's even having business cards printed for me. I'm making ten dollars a week. More than I ever expected.*

Nora found herself wondering if anyone had ever gone back to Fern's grave. Perhaps she would go out there on Decoration Day. She wondered if Will was all right. If Pap had changed. She thought that if Lucy and Hannah asked her one more time to go to church with them, she just might go. Nora began to cry tears that had nothing to do with Mrs. Judge Cranston's hat.

Silence woke Nora early in the evening. It had stopped raining. She sat up and looked out the small window on the wall opposite her bed. The sky was clear. The sun was beginning to go down. Her stomach rumbled. Sighing, Nora got up and went downstairs. Her favorite time of day was approaching, the brief moment when the sun had barely dipped behind the horizon, and the world was bathed in a light that was at once bright and mellow. Nora stepped outside on the back stoop, leaning back against the wall of the building. Closing her eyes, she inhaled deeply. The air smelled of damp earth and wet brick. A ray of sunshine dappled the brick of the building across the alley with spots of gold. Someone had set a blooming geranium on a windowsill up on the second level. It glowed scarlet in the dusky light.

Just as Nora bent to retrieve a small bundle of firewood from the stack by the back door, she heard a now-familiar cadence, and she looked up just in time to see Casey, Dr. Allbright's rangy white gelding, come into view around the corner at the end of the block.

Nora waved and headed inside, leaving the door open for Dr. Allbright. Maude came in just as Nora bent to stoke the fire in the little woodstove in the workroom corner.

"I'm just making some supper. Have you eaten?"

Dr. Allbright climbed down from her carriage and grabbed her medical bag. "I haven't had a minute since early this morning. That seems a long, long time ago." She followed Nora inside, set the medical bag on a table, and pulled an apron off its hook. "Why don't you go over there and read the newspaper and let me cook something?"

"You?" Nora made no attempt to hide her surprise.

"Yes, *me*. I can tell you aren't feeling well." She shook her finger at Nora. "Now listen, you. I *can* cook. I just don't generally *choose* to." She teased, "As I recall, you're not known for your cuisine, either." She opened her medical bag and withdrew a quart-size canning jar filled with white liquid. "Cream of potato soup. I stopped at the hotel and ordered some." She headed for the stove. "I'll heat this up. There are rolls and butter in there, too."

Nora looked inside Maude's bag, smiling at the sight of four huge dinner rolls wrapped in a linen napkin.

Maude wasted no time getting to the point. "I was surprised to see Lucy and Hannah downtown this afternoon." She slathered a roll with butter and handed it to Nora. "Don't let Mrs. Judge Cranston get your goat, Nora. She's a difficult old broad. If it's any comfort to you, she doesn't treat her physician"—she pointed to herself—"any better than she treats her milliner."

"Well," Nora said, "I don't think I'm her milliner anymore."

"I guarantee you she will be back in less than a week with some excuse as to why she behaved so badly. She'll want the hat and she'll probably pay you more than you initially agreed upon. She never, *ever* apologizes with words, but she always apologizes."

Nora swallowed a tablespoonful of soup. "The business with the hat didn't bother me so much. It's part of being a milliner. They expect us to remake them in spite of nature." She hesitated. "It was her reference to Goldie's that hurt. The way she said it made me feel—" Nora thought for a moment. "Oh, I don't know. I probably made more of it than it was. I've been out of sorts all week. I overreacted."

"Perhaps it's the weather," Dr. Allbright said. "I haven't had the best week, either." She went on. "But I'm old and allowed to be cranky. You have your life ahead of you, my dear, hopes and dreams, dreams and hopes . . ."

Nora replied, "I do appreciate your taking time for me this way. I told Lucy and Hannah that our talks take the place of all the education I missed. You always make me feel better. Like I'm—important."

Dr. Allbright leaned forward. "You *are* important. It's very gratifying for a sour old bird like me to have a lovely young lady like you interested in spending time with her." She smiled gently. "I've never regretted not being married, but at times I do regret not having had children. I could have a daughter about your age, you know."

Nora's face flushed with pleasure as she got up and cleared the table. "I want to show you something," she said. Opening a large brown envelope that lay on the table, she handed Dr. Allbright a sheet of paper, before sitting down. "Miss Thornhill said I should write it myself. It goes in the paper next week."

Dr. Allbright read, *Miss Elise Thornhill announces that Thornhill Dressers has employed a first-rate milliner and invites those who desire the finest in hats, flowers, hair, and fancy goods to stop by and make the acquaintance of Miss Nora O'Dell.*

"Good work. I like the way you've worded it."

Smiling shyly, Nora held out a small card for Dr. Allbright's inspection. "She had these printed up for me. Surprised me with them before she left for St. Louis." The card featured a black-and-white engraving of a millinery shop. A table took up the left lower corner, and the side of the table provided space for printing. *Miss Nora O'Dell, Fashionable Millinery, Thornhill Dressers, 123 N. 11th Street, Lincoln. Mode de Paris Straws, Ribbons, Feathers, Flowers &c.* Atop the table on the card was an array of hats on ornate stands of various heights. Behind the table stood a fashionably dressed milliner, handing a hat to a female customer while her two young daughters looked on. The scene suggested wealthy patrons and a thriving business.

"Congratulations," Dr. Allbright said. "I know that Elise is very, very happy to have you as a part of her business.

You've enabled her to expand, and your talent with hats has brought her new business."

"I felt a little odd about getting my own card, so soon," Nora said. "But Lucy and Hannah don't seem to mind. They seem happy just being the 'back room girls.'"

Dr. Allbright nodded. "Lucy and Hannah are good girls, but they have neither your drive nor your potential. Both are content being barely literate, and they'll probably work for Elise the rest of their lives—unless Lucy marries young Fielding, which is highly likely from what I can tell. And you know what I think of that."

Nora knew. Dr. Allbright made no secret of her opinions about women and marriage, which she tended to call legalized slavery.

"Hannah will, I dare say, be a common seamstress for the rest of her days," Dr. Allbright continued. "Not that that's anything to be ashamed of, mind you. She's content and that's more than you or I can say." She held out her hand. "May I take a few cards with me? I'll send some home with the other physicians after our next Medical Society meeting."

Nora handed Dr. Allbright a half-dozen cards, then turned to the newspaper. "Have you seen this?" She pointed to an article titled "The Color of the Eyes. Shades of Character Indicated by the Shades of Color."

Dr. Allbright scanned the article. "Well, it isn't very complimentary to me, is it? 'In women, brown eyes mean jealousy and cruelty.'" Dr. Allbright sipped her tea. "What does it say about you?" She handed the paper to Nora.

Nora read aloud, "'Self-satisfaction and conceit are commonly the characteristic traits represented by the green eye.'" She frowned. "What is *conceit*?"

"It means you think you're absolutely wonderful just the way you are. A little better than everyone else, in fact."

"Well," Nora said, grinning, "I do think I know more than Mrs. Judge Cranston about fashion."

"That's not conceit, my dear. That's a fact," Dr. Allbright shot back.

"Listen to this," Nora said, turning back to the paper. "'The main characteristic of the violet eye, which is called the woman's eye, is affection and purity'—now get this," she said, "'affection and purity . . . and limited or deficient intellectuality.'"

Dr. Allbright snorted. "Let me see that." She grabbed the paper.

Nora baited her. "It's written by one of your colleagues."

Maude read through the article. "Humph. Dr. John Gannon. I should have known." She rattled the paper.

"Well, what do you think? Can you tell what someone is like by the color of their eyes?"

"I think," Dr. Allbright said, "this makes just about as much sense as shaving your head so some idiot can inspect the bumps on your head and tell you what career you should follow."

"What?"

"It's called phrenology," Dr. Allbright explained. "When I went to Chicago a few years ago, Dr. Gannon was espousing some new version of a practice that was popular earlier in this century. It seems he has expanded his repertoire. Interesting, don't you think, that he says it's the *woman's* eye that's connected with *limited* intellectuality . . ."

"He's lecturing at the GAR hall this Friday evening at eight o'clock." Nora said quietly. "Want to go with me to hear what he has to say?"

"Absolutely," Dr. Allbright said. "I'll pick you up at seven-thirty."

CHAPTER 12

Shades of Character

I am not alone, because the Father is with me.
John 16:32

Nora's interest in Dr. Gannon's theories had resulted in her overlooking another announcement in the *Daily State Journal*. Funke's Opera House had engaged the Daniel Frost Theatrical Troupe, and from the moment they arrived at work the next morning, Lucy and Hannah talked of little else. They spoke of Greyson Chandler as Hamlet, Greyson Chandler as the lead in a comedic farce, Greyson Chandler at Thornhill Dressers. They planned to join the crowd expected to greet the troupe at the railroad station Friday afternoon and invited Nora to go along.

Nora shook her head. "I promised Mrs. Cranston I'd have her hat ready on Friday, and I don't want to risk missing the lecture that evening with Dr. Allbright." (Just as the doctor had predicted, the "old bat" had come in the day after Miss Thornhill returned from St. Louis. She had explained that she and Nora had had a "slight disagreement," but she hoped that the hat could be salvaged, and she would be willing to pay an additional three dollars if it could be ready in time for the opening of the next production at Funke's Opera House.)

Lucy and Hannah exchanged glances. They were not quite certain it was good for Nora to be spending so much time with Dr. Allbright. Nora said it was her way of getting an education instead of going to school, and that she was very grateful that Dr. Allbright considered her worth the trouble. Miss Thornhill said she feared Nora's spending so much time with an atheist would put an obstacle between Nora and God, and that she wished Dr. Allbright would get called away on more emergencies.

Nora finished Mrs. Judge Cranston's hat early on Friday and proceeded to her next project—adjusting the trim on a mourning hat to signify the next "stage of mourning." Miss Thornhill had explained, "Mrs. Hogsdon is from the old school. She is new to Lincoln and she doesn't care much for our relaxed ways. The more rigorous law requires the veil be worn for three months. Mr. Hogsdon passed away just over three months ago, so now we can remove the crape in the front and replace it with Brussels net. Shorten the knee-length crape at the back so that it merely covers the shoulders. The hem should remain quite deep. In three months we will replace the crape entirely."

Nora smiled to herself, realizing that "city folks" mourning could result in a good income for a skilled milliner. She was just removing the crape from the front of the bonnet when the studio door rattled.

The gentleman did not just come through the door of Thornhill's. He made an entrance, pausing momentarily before giving the door a good shake to make certain the bell rang loudly. After he stepped across the threshold and closed the door behind him, he removed his fedora with a flourish, and waited. From their brief encounter the previous fall, Nora had a vague memory of blue eyes and blonde hair. She had been feeling too ill to notice much else. But she still recognized Greyson Chandler. He was tall, with a wavy lock of blond hair that spilled over his high forehead and softened his classic profile. A thick mustache drooped around the corners of his mouth. He wore an impeccably tailored suit fashioned to make the most of his broad shoulders and small waist.

Nora stood up. Just as she opened her mouth to greet Chandler, Elise appeared at the workroom door. Behind Elise, Nora could see Lucy's and Hannah's eyes grow wide. They nudged one another and quickly disappeared into the workroom.

Nora bit her lower lip, trying to squelch a smile. She pretended to work while Chandler spoke with Elise. At Goldie's Nora had met men with an intangible something that caught women's attention and pulled the unwary in. Chandler had it. Nora reminded herself that Lily and Iris had both warned her about men like that. Drawing her brows together in a scowl, Nora forced herself to concentrate on Widow Hogsdon's hat.

Miss Thornhill was spreading an impressive number of fabric samples out for Chandler's inspection. Nora turned to the pressing board behind her. She reached for a box of black scraps, selecting a few large pieces to press. She hummed softly to herself to close out the sound of Chandler's voice, trying her best not to eavesdrop while he concluded his business with Miss Thornhill. But as Chandler made his way to the door, Nora could not resist the temptation to look up. When she did, Chandler smiled and tipped his hat. "Glad to see you feeling better, Miss O'Dell. May I greet Shep for you? We're having a drink together this evening."

He didn't wait for her to reply. If she hadn't known better, Nora would have thought Greyson Chandler was flirting with her.

Chandler had requested that Miss Thornhill construct an elaborate robe for one of Mamie Patterson's costumes. It was needed for the following Wednesday's performance of *Hamlet*, and it presented one of the greater challenges of Miss Thornhill's designing career.

She personally supervised as Lucy and Hannah cut and stitched, filling the hours with talk of the famous actor. As soon as the basic cape was constructed, Miss Thornhill took over the intricate finish work, which including beading and quillwork.

"Mr. Chandler remembered Nora," Lucy said for what seemed like the tenth time.

"And he knew her given name. Did you tell him, Miss Thornhill?" Hannah asked.

"No," Elise replied. "He didn't speak of Nora to me."

"That means he asked someone else," Lucy teased, casting a glance toward where Nora stood by the stove sipping tea.

"Honestly, girls," Nora exclaimed. "You've been over and over this. Did life as we know it suddenly stop with Greyson Chandler's arrival in Lincoln? Can't you find something else to talk about?"

Lucy and Hannah found something else to talk about—when Nora was within earshot.

Nora finished Widow Hogsdon's bonnet and began working on a ready-made sample to put in the shop window. Even without Lucy and Hannah's constant chatter, she remained short-tempered. She winced inwardly at the mental image of Shep sharing stories with Greyson Chandler. Was her association with Goldie's to haunt her forever?

On Friday evening, Dr. Allbright was called out on an emergency, forcing her to cancel the planned attendance at Dr. Gannon's lecture on "The Color of the Eyes. Shades of Character Indicated by the Shades of Color." Lucy and Hannah already had plans involving a Mr. Fielding and Friend, and Elise had developed a raging headache after hours of eyestrain bent over the intricate beading on Mamie Patterson's costume.

Nora had a flickering thought of attending Dr. Gannon's lecture alone, but she knew that being seen without an escort would only invite raised eyebrows and perhaps a whisper or two about Goldie's, especially if one or two certain gentlemen happened to be present. When intermittent showers became a downpour, Nora determined to spend another Friday evening alone.

After Elise and the girls left, Nora made herself a cup of tea and sat down at the downstairs worktable with a cold supper before her. She got up and retrieved the newspaper from where she had laid it on the stairway that led up to her apartment and prepared to reread Dr. Gannon's proposal about eye color and character. What was it he had said about blue eyes in a man? *In a man it denotes a phlegmatic disposition.* She would have to look the word *phlegmatic* up in the dictionary. She leaned back in her chair. Goodness, but she was weary of encountering words she did not understand.

Darkness came prematurely as the storm outside continued unabated. Sitting alone in the darkened workroom, Nora sighed. Rain always seemed to make her feel out of sorts, and this evening was no exception. She really had been looking forward to attending the lecture with Dr. Allbright. She wondered how young women her age managed to make friends in the city. Miss Thornhill had suggested church several times. She had been tempted to try it, but then reconsidered, thinking she probably wouldn't fit in. What if most of the churchgoing women were like Mrs. Judge Cranston?

She longed for the camaraderie of Goldie's, without the attached reputation. Goldie herself had told Nora that since she had chosen "another life," it would be best if she didn't come back to the house. "It's kind of a black-and-white thing," Goldie had explained. "Either you're one of the girls or you're not. You can't walk a line between both worlds."

Nora missed Iris the most. She wanted to know why Iris was still at Goldie's, after all her talk of leaving. And Lily. She worried about Lily's lack of common sense.

A huge clap of thunder brought Nora back to reality. Looking about her, she sighed again. Leaving her dinner on the table, she climbed the stairs to her tiny apartment and lit a gas light. Another evening alone, reading. Ah, well. At least her education was progressing. Nora reached for the dictionary. What was that word . . . phleg-something. She couldn't remember how to spell it. She would have to go downstairs and get the newspaper. Funny how you had to know how to spell something before you could look it up to see how to spell it.

Nora was halfway down the stairs when someone pounded on the back door yelling, "Hello, hello, is anyone there?" The voice sounded vaguely familiar. She hurried down the stairs and flung the door open.

Greyson Chandler was standing in the rain, his felt hat wilted into a shapeless mess, the ends of his mustache dripping. Mud had totally obliterated any view of what Nora knew to be fine kid boots. Mud was splattered halfway to his knees. In his left hand he held a crushed hatbox.

"Miss Thornhill isn't here," Nora said.

"Yes, I know. She pleaded a headache and went home. And Lucy and Hannah are out with two young gentlemen. I saw them earlier. They mentioned that you were attending a lecture with Dr. Allbright." The blue eyes looked steadily at Nora. "But I happen to know that Dr. Allbright is tending a case. Miss Patterson has a toothache. And I have an emergency that requires a skilled milliner." Chandler held up the crushed hatbox. "At least in theatrical circles, it's an emergency."

Just then, a cloudburst sent torrents of rain, completely drenching Chandler's hat and sending a gush of water down the back of his neck. Nora stepped back from the door. "Come in out of the rain."

Chandler stepped across the threshold and set the hatbox on the table. As he did, Nora grabbed up the newspaper, which she had folded around Dr. Gannon's article. Wondering why her cheeks were growing hot, she hugged the newspaper to herself so that Chandler could not see it.

Chandler removed his dripping coat, hanging it on the hook by the door. He tried to reshape his drenched hat.

"Here," Nora said. "Let me see to that." Plunking the newspaper down on the seat of the chair and shoving it quickly beneath the table, she retrieved a soft cloth from a bin by the worktable and began to dab moisture out of the felt.

Chandler reached up to push a lock of blond hair off his forehead. Then, taking up the crumpled hatbox, he said, "I hope you can do something with this. Some of our more ornate costumes just arrived this morning. Unfortunately this box fell off the carriage on the way from the station. The costume matron didn't miss it right away. By the time she realized it was missing and we found it, it had been run over by a wagon and drenched in the rain."

He opened the box and extracted something that used to be some sort of crown. The metal was intact, but the supporting structure was nearly destroyed.

"Oh, my," Nora said, setting Chandler's hat down on the worktable and taking the headpiece in her hands.

"Yes," Chandler agreed. "Exactly." He sighed. "I've just escaped from a tantrum performed by my leading lady over this fiasco." He grinned at Nora. "And believe me, she throws a magnificent tantrum." He looked at the headdress, shaking his head. "While I admit to being able to handle just about anything that comes my way from the fair sex, I really do *not* want to face Miss Patterson again unless I can tell her that this monstrosity will be complete for the opening."

"What's it supposed to look like?" Nora asked.

"We're doing *Hamlet*," Chandler said.

"Yes?" Nora asked, with the tone of, is that supposed to mean something to me?

"I apologize," Chandler said quickly. "I know it isn't really correct for the time period, but Miss Patterson firmly refused a Queen Gertrude with a head rail and a veil. This was the compromise." He cupped both his hands and covered the back of his head. "That finer brocade fabric is supposed to form a sort of cup here. It completely covers the hair—and Miss Patterson has a *lot* of hair, so it had to be quite full. Obviously the part that looks like a crown sits atop the head, but there was something underneath that"—he pointed to a completely ruined band of fabric—"to frame her face. Sort of like a nun would wear. Have you seen a nun's habit?" He apologized, "I know this is completely outside your area of expertise, but would you try?"

"Let's go into the studio where I can get a better look at it," Nora said. Chandler followed her into the darkened room and waited while she fumbled with the gas lights. When her work area was finally illuminated, Nora placed the headpiece on one of her stands and sat down on a stool to inspect it.

"This is wonderfully made," she murmured almost to herself.

Chandler was standing so close she could feel his breath on the back of her neck. She got up. "Excuse me," she said, indicating one of the drawers built into the wall behind him. He stepped aside so that Nora could open a drawer. She pretended to look through the contents before saying, "I don't have anything like this." She ran her finger along the edge of the headpiece. "This piece that you said frames Miss Patterson's face has to be completely replaced. I can't match it."

Chandler seemed to be watching her instead of looking at the subject of their discussion.

Nora felt herself blushing again and took a step backward. "Don't you have anyone in the troupe who does this sort of thing? Lucy and Hannah said they counted twenty people getting off the train when the troupe arrived."

Chandler smiled. "You didn't come to the station to meet the famous actors?"

Nora felt herself blushing again. "I had work to do. Actually," she said, "I had planned to attend a lecture, but then Dr. Allbright had to cancel." Nora thought, *Why on earth am I telling him this?* Nora asked again, "Doesn't a troupe your size have someone who oversees the costumes?"

"Of course," Chandler said. "The costume matron. She's the one who finally discovered this was missing. She's superb at the day-to-day mending and minor, last-minute changes, but she doesn't have the skill to re-create something like this."

Nora said, "It needs to be completely rebuilt. The bracing that supports the coronet has been broken. I may need to construct an entirely new frame." She bent over to inspect the piece more closely. "If I can let it dry naturally, most of this fabric can be cleaned and reused—except for that piece around the face."

Chandler said, "Miss Patterson was personally involved in its design. Any change would have to be just exactly right. She'd need to see it."

"You said there was a matching cloak. What if I add a border along the cloak to match the new border on this?"

"How long would it take?" Chandler wanted to know.

"I can probably get the framework rebuilt over the weekend," Nora said. "I don't stock anything appropriate, but Herpolsheimer's just got in a new shipment of trims. Would Miss Patterson want to meet me there? If she could bring the cloak, it would make things easier. They open at nine o'clock."

Chandler asked, "Can your schedule accommodate this?"

Nora smiled. "I think I can manage to rearrange my hectic social calendar."

"Were you planning to attend the opening?"

She shook her head. "No. I don't usually go to the theater."

He was amazed. "Why on earth not?"

Nora shrugged. "I want to open my own shop someday. I can't waste money on the theater." She put her hand to her mouth. "Oops. Sorry. I didn't mean—"

Chandler didn't take offense. He simply said, "Well then, you must be my guest. I insist." He headed to the workroom, where he flung his damp coat over his shoulders and clapped the half-ruined fedora on his head. "Nine o'clock tomorrow morning?"

"Right," Nora said from the doorway to the studio. "It's right on the corner of Tenth and O Streets. You can't miss it."

Not long after Greyson Chandler left, Nora went upstairs and retrieved the dictionary. Settling at the workroom table, she searched until she found and read, *Phlegmatic: Not easily aroused. Composed. Apathetic.* Nora closed the dictionary. Crossing the workroom, she lifted the lid of the little woodstove and fed Dr. Gannon's article to the flames.

CHAPTER 13

A Good Friend

Therefore all things whatsoever ye would that men should do to you, do ye even so to them.
Matthew 7:12

"Well, if it isn't Nora O'Dell. Hey, Nora!"

Nora was on her way to meet Mr. Chandler and Miss Patterson and had just crossed O Street on Saturday morning when a drunken female voice called her name. Nora turned around, horrified to see Lily stumbling across the street toward her, obviously at the end of a long, long night. She was dressed in an electric purple satin gown, and she had dyed her hair an unbelievable shade of red.

Nora shrank inwardly from the expressions on the faces of several passersby. Her first instinct was to turn away, hurry into Herpolsheimer's, and hope that Lily was sober enough to know she shouldn't follow, and drunk enough to forget the snub. But her second instinct to be a loyal friend won out. Just as Lily arrived at the boardwalk, Nora held out one arm to steady the girl and asked, "Lily, what's happened? What's the matter?"

"Nothin's the matter, Nora. Nothin' a-tall," Lily said, weaving uncertainly and looking up at the sky. "Everthin's jus' fine." A little "Uh-oh," was followed by a gigantic hiccup. Lily giggled then squinted, as if the bright morning sun hurt her eyes. "Nothin' 'cept I did a little business on the side and Goldie kicked me out. Tha's all." She puckered up her face and began to cry. "Oh, Nora, what'm I gonna do *now*?"

People walking by were glowering at the drunken girl sobbing loudly into a none-too-clean handkerchief. Just as Lily said, "Oh, Nora, what'm I gonna do *now*?" Greyson Chandler walked up with Mamie Patterson on his arm.

She took one look at Lily and sniffed audibly.

"Good morning, Miss O'Dell," Chandler said. "Is there some trouble?"

Lily looked up at him. "Hey! I know you. Yer that actor Shep was drinkin' with las' night." She nodded and patted Chandler on the chest. "How are ya?"

Chandler smiled. "I'm fine, miss. But I think you may need some assistance. Can I be of help?"

"Not unless you need a live-in, sweetie," Lily said. She looked at Miss Patterson and covered her mouth with her hand in an exaggerated pose. "Oops. Sorry. Now I've gotten you in trouble."

The long feathers on Miss Patterson's hat waved furiously as she hissed, "Greyson. People are beginning to stare."

"It's all right, Mr. Chandler," Nora said quickly. She linked her arm through Lily's. "I'll take care of Lily."

"Good ol' Nora," Lily sighed, patting Nora's shoulder. "Always takes care of her frens." She turned and looked at Nora. "Don' ya, Nora? Jus' like when you saved my behind that morning when Frank was punchin' on me . . ." She began to tear up again. "You always been a good fren', Nora," she added, drunkenly nodding and beginning to alternately hiccup and sob.

"Nora?" Miss Patterson said in disbelief. She looked at Chandler. "Oh, Grey. What were you thinking? We can't possibly deal with—"

"Miss O'Dell is a first-rate milliner," Chandler said. "She works at Thornhill Dressers. We need her if you want to appear on stage Wednesday evening in that costume. Now behave yourself and go inside. Miss O'Dell and I will be along directly."

"Greyson Chandler," Miss Patterson said firmly. "I am not about to be ordered about by you or anyone else. And certainly not so you can assist some drunken trollop."

Clasping her gloved hands in front of her, she said to Nora, "I am much too busy to wait while you tend to this *person*, Miss O'Dell."

Nora held fast. "I'm sorry you feel that way, Miss Patterson. Are you certain you cannot meet me later this morning? This really shouldn't take long."

"No," Mamie said firmly.

"It's all right, Nora," Lily said. She pulled away, weaving uncertainly. "You go on. I'll be all right."

"Miss O'Dell." Miss Patterson actually stamped her neatly booted not-so-little foot. "We have an appointment."

"Which, you can see, I cannot keep," Nora said. She reached for Lily and held on to her arm.

Miss Patterson threatened, "We shall take our business elsewhere."

"Do what you must, Miss Patterson." Nora wrapped her arm through Lily's and began to guide her around the corner, thinking to get her to a more inconspicuous spot while she decided what to do.

Miss Patterson thrust her nose high in the air, whirled about, and stormed into Herpolsheimer's.

Greyson Chandler hurried after Nora. "What can I do?"

"You'd better tend to your own troubles," Nora said, nodding toward the store. "Lily can sleep it off in my apartment. Then I'll take her to talk to Goldie."

Lily stirred. "You think if I apologize, she might take me back?"

"Well," Nora said, smiling, "we'll see what we can do." They rounded the corner and were nearing the alley when Lily stumbled.

"Do you think she can walk to Thornhill's?" Chandler asked.

"I doubt it," Nora said truthfully.

"Well then," Chandler said, "wait here and I'll get a carriage."

"You don't have to—"

"I know that. I want to help." He was already hurrying up the street toward the livery stable in the next block.

Nora put her arm around Lily, wrinkling her nose in distaste at the strong smell of whiskey on Lily's breath. She pulled Lily to sit down beside her on the steps of a boarded-up warehouse. "Now, tell me what happened," she said quietly.

"You know me," Lily said, sighing heavily. "Never learn from the first mistake. I told Goldie that Shep was taking me shopping, but I went somewhere else instead." She giggled, then began to cry again.

"Never mind," Nora said quietly. "We'll talk later."

"She'll sleep for hours," Nora said. She was descending the stairs from her apartment over Thornhill Dressers, surprised that Greyson Chandler was still there.

"I imagine so. And have a terrible hangover." He asked abruptly, "Do you think Goldie will take her back?"

"I don't know. Goldie can be—"

"—unbending," Chandler said. At Nora's look of surprise, he smiled. "You can't exactly keep in touch with an old friend like Shep without encountering Goldie." Chandler shook his head. "I wish Shep did something else for a living. He really had a lot of promise."

"What happened?" Nora asked.

"The bottle," Chandler said, shaking his head.

Nora sighed. "I don't know why they can't see it's ruining their lives."

"You're a good friend."

"Well, I owe Lily. She helped me out when I first came to Lincoln."

"I would think broken ribs and not a few stitches had already paid that debt in full," Chandler said. At Nora's look of surprise, he said, "Shep likes to tell stories."

"Yes," Nora said, half whispering. "I imagine he does."

"Don't worry," Chandler said suddenly, "his stories about you haven't damaged your reputation. Quite the contrary."

Nora shook her head. "I can't imagine anything connecting me to Goldie's could help my reputation."

"Actually," Chandler said, "Shep speaks very highly of you. Loyal, true—"

Nora held up her hand, blushing and laughing. "Enough. You make me sound like a prize hunting dog."

Chandler smiled back at her. "Only half right, Miss O'Dell."

"Which half—the head or the tail?" Nora wanted to know.

"The prize." Chandler turned to go. "If you think you can endure another session with Miss Patterson, I'll have her at Herpolsheimer's in an hour."

Nora raised her eyebrows. "Are you certain? She was really angry."

"Haven't you heard about me?" Chandler grinned. "The powers of Svengali. Beware." He closed the door behind him.

Herpolsheimer's "Parade of Parasols" stopped Nora short when she entered the store an hour after putting Lily to bed in her apartment. Every counter sported at least one open parasol, and sunshades and umbrellas had been suspended from the ceiling by thin wire so that it appeared to be raining parasols inside the store. Nora saw samples of the eccentric shapes one of her trade publications had predicted: triangles, pentagons, hexagons, and octagons. Handles ranged from common wood in crooks and loops, to carved pheasants' heads and German porcelain balls. Nora noted that apples, pears, and oranges seemed popular, as did ducks, owls, and swans. She would have to remember those trends for hat trims.

She made one quick trip around the store looking for Chandler and Miss Patterson. When it appeared they had not yet arrived, she indulged herself the opportunity to inspect a few parasols. Her eye was drawn to a white satin one painted in the Japanese style with butterflies. It boasted a chiffon ruffle and a porcelain handle. Nora opened it and looked at herself in the mirror. There was a shade of green in some of the larger butterflies that exactly matched the green bombazine gown hanging in her apartment. Nora glanced at the price. Ah, well. As if she ever had need to dress like a well-to-do lady, anyway.

Apparently Mamie Patterson really had decided to take her business to someone else. Looking at her watch, Nora decided she should check on Lily. She circled round the store once more, enjoying the display overhead, when she was stopped dead in her tracks at the sight of the most elegant parasol she had ever seen. Its ivory handle was carved as a girl in a classical costume picking roses. The entire cover was made of unbelievably intricate, handmade lace over lilac silk. A dark green tassel dangled from the carved ivory tip. Nora dared not touch it, but she stopped, and bent down to look underneath at the lilac silk.

"Something has caught the fair Irish lass's fancy," someone said.

Nora stood up abruptly.

Greyson Chandler was standing on the opposite side of the island of counters, watching her.

Nora blushed. "I—uh—I have to keep up with what's being shown in accessories. It helps me know trends."

"Of course," Chandler said quietly, nodding toward the parasol. "Why don't you pick it up and see how it looks?"

Nora shook her head. "No. That's not necessary." She had seen the price tag. Mrs. Judge Cranston herself would have to save quite a while to afford this treasure. Nora had no intention of touching it.

Chandler made his way around the counter, took the parasol down, closed it, and handed it to Nora. "Really. I insist. Miss Patterson said she'd come, but she's always late. It will give us something to do."

Nora marveled at the intricate workmanship in the parasol's handle.

"There's a mirror over there." Chandler motioned to the back of the store. Then, he touched her arm. Not wanting to appear rude, Nora allowed herself to be led to the mirrors. Mr. Herpolsheimer himself appeared. "May I help you, Mr. Chandler?"

"We're just enjoying your display," Chandler said easily. He turned to Nora. "Go on, Miss O'Dell. See how you like it."

Nora shook her head and held the parasol out to Mr. Herpolsheimer. "No, that's all right. I can't begin to afford it. It is exquisite, though."

The store owner smiled kindly. "Please, Miss O'Dell. One need not be buying to enjoy the Parade of Parasols. Perhaps if you like my things, you will mention me to your millinery customers." He nodded toward the mirror.

Carefully, Nora opened the parasol. She set it over her shoulder.

Mr. Herpolsheimer smiled with approval. "You see, Miss O'Dell, how elegant a lady feels with the right accessories. But that is probably why you enjoy your art so well, eh?"

Mamie Patterson strode up.

Quickly, Nora lowered the parasol and handed it to Mr. Herpolsheimer. "Thank you, sir. It's lovely." She nodded upward. "And that is truly an inspired way to display your wares."

"Well?" Miss Patterson said. "Can we get on with it?"

Greyson Chandler took Nora's arm. "Lead the way, Miss O'Dell. And please rescue Miss Patterson's costume for us." He took Miss Patterson's arm as well, and the three walked to a counter closer to the front of the store.

Miss Patterson was dour and determined not to be pleasant, but in the wake of Greyson Chandler's attentions and Mr. Herpolsheimer's kindness, Nora was just as determined to appear professional.

Several trays of wide ribbon had been laid out and inspected before Chandler saved the day by lifting a piece of ribbon and saying casually, "Look at this one, Mamie. It's very nearly the exact color of your eyes." The ribbon was violet. Mamie had gray eyes.

"Why, Grey," she purred. "How sweet of you to think of that."

"What about this, Miss O'Dell," Grey said. "Will this work?" His eyes pleaded with her.

Nora examined the ribbon. "Well, it could be stiffer. But if I line it—"

"Perfect," Miss Patterson said, snatching up the ribbon and holding it to her face.

Chandler and Miss Patterson left the store after arranging to try on the completed headdress on Monday. Nora waited for the ribbon to be cut. Tucking it in her bag, she went back to take one last admiring look at the lace parasol before returning home to check on Lily.

On Monday morning, a completely restored headpiece stood at Nora's workstation. Miss Thornhill inspected it and nodded with satisfaction. "Let's move the dress frame over here so that when Miss Patterson comes in, she gets the full effect of the cape and the headdress at once."

The morning seemed to drag on, and with every ring of the front doorbell, the knot in Nora's stomach grew larger. But when Greyson Chandler finally escorted his leading lady into the studio, Miss Patterson let out an exclamation of delight. While she primped before the mirror, Chandler spoke with Elise.

"With your permission, Mr. Frost would like to recommend you to the other troupes that come through Lincoln."

Miss Thornhill was delighted, thanking Chandler and asking him to forward a resounding "yes" to Mr. Frost regarding future business.

Miss Patterson finally finished preening before the dressing mirrors. Removing the headdress, she handed it to Miss Thornhill with an imperious, "Have it sent over at once."

As Miss Patterson and Chandler left, the actress pressed two gold coins into Nora's hand. "Thank you so much, dear. You really are an *artiste*." She squeezed Chandler's arm affectionately as they headed out the door.

Nora mumbled her thanks and avoided looking at Chandler, busying herself with packing the headdress in a new bandbox.

The moment the shop door closed, Miss Thornhill crossed the studio to pat Nora on the shoulder. "Congratulations, Miss O'Dell. And thank you. Between your work on the headdress, and my finishing the cape, I think we can call this encounter a resounding success. Mr. Chandler left four tickets to the opening performance so that we can all see our work on stage."

"That will be nice," Nora said noncommittally.

"And," Elise said, "I think you may expect a raise to, shall we say, fifteen dollars a week?"

"Thank you, Miss Thornhill," Nora said sincerely. "It's nice to be appreciated."

"I think you might dispense with the 'Miss Thornhill,' Nora." She smiled. "Please call me Elise."

Nora thanked Elise and bent to her work. She wasn't certain she wanted to go to the theater to watch Greyson Chandler and Mamie Patterson together . . . onstage. She was making a braided straw hat to be worn the next week to a meeting at Epworth Park. She wondered if she would ever be invited to Epworth Park . . . or anywhere, for that matter . . . with a nice young man.

Twisting the end of a straw braid, Nora formed a small rosette that she held firmly between thumb and forefinger while she sewed it in place with hidden stitches. Once the rosette was secure, she continued adding rows of braided straw, stopping after each row to sew the inner edge of braid. The coins that Mamie had pressed into her palm lay on the table beside her. She picked them up and tossed them into a drawer. Miss Thornhill might not mind adopting a servile stance with certain customers, but it was something Nora could not seem to manage. She wondered why receiving a tip should bother her so much. She could certainly use the money.

When she had a straw disk the size of the crown of the wire frame she had selected, she affixed it to the wire frame. As she worked, she continued thinking about Mamie Patterson on Greyson Chandler's arm . . . about Lucy and Mr. Fielding . . . about Shep Roberts . . . and Epworth Park. When she finally admitted it, she realized that she would not have minded being tipped, if it had not been Greyson Chandler looking on as Mamie reminded Nora of her place.

Sighing, Nora pondered whether church might be a place to begin after all. Perhaps there, she could meet someone who would be her friend. Dr. Allbright might not approve of the idea, but Nora was beginning to think that for all her bravado, Dr. Allbright was a bit lonely, herself. Certainly she didn't have all of the answers to the questions Nora was beginning to ask.

Nora was in the workroom sipping tea when Elise appeared at the doorway to the studio, her arms filled with a massive bouquet of yellow roses. "Lucy," Nora teased, "is there something about you and Mr. Fielding you need to be telling us?"

Lucy blushed.

Elise held out the card. "These are for you, Nora."

Nora read the card. *For Miss O'Dell, with sincere thanks. G. Chandler.*

CHAPTER 14

Acting the Part

Who whet their tongue like a sword, and bend their bows to shoot their arrows, even bitter words.
Psalm 64:3

On Sunday afternoon Nora was returning from a cable car ride to Wyuka Cemetery when she encountered Greyson Chandler. He was wearing a pale gray tweed coat with dark gray trousers and a matching felt hat. Nora tried not to stare at the huge diamond pin tucked into the fold of his ascot.

He tipped his hat. "I was just going for a walk. Would you join me for tea?"

Nora said yes and took his arm. They walked several blocks to the Lindell Hotel. Over tea, Chandler asked, "How did things turn out for Lily?"

"The way she hoped," Nora said. "Goldie took her back."

"You don't sound pleased."

"Well, I wonder if it would have been better if she would have had to look for something else."

"But would she have done what you think is best?" Chandler asked quietly.

Nora shook her head. "No. Probably not."

"It's the same with Shep. I see him once or twice a year when we come through Lincoln on tour. This time he's more sober. I guess that's something." He leaned back. "Do you take the cable car out to Wyuka often?"

"Oh, no." Nora laughed. "This was the first time. Shep used to tease me about it. I was terrified of the cable cars when I first came to Lincoln. I guess I just wanted to prove to myself that I wasn't afraid anymore."

"Was your young man busy elsewhere this afternoon?"

Nora look confused. "My—what?" She laughed and shook her head. "I don't have a young man, Mr. Chandler. I'm just me."

He winked at her. "I'm glad to know the roses didn't cause you any trouble."

Nora raised her hand to her mouth. "Oh, how rude of me. I'm so sorry. Thank you. They're beautiful." She put sugar in her tea. "They did cause me a little trouble, though. Lucy and Hannah like to tease me."

Chandler smiled. "Well, if it's any comfort, they caused me a little trouble, too. Mamie found out."

On Tuesday, Chandler ran into Nora when she was on her way to deliver a hat to a patron. He walked with her, waiting at the gate, tipping his hat, and smiling brilliantly while the customer stared and asked Nora if that was really Greyson Chandler waiting for her.

On Wednesday morning, Chandler, came into the shop. He had been just a short distance from Thornhill Dressers when he realized he had a loose vest button. Would Nora mind sewing it on? He accepted a cup of coffee from Hannah and stayed long after the button was reaffixed.

After Chandler left, the hours crawled by. Finally, at five o'clock, Nora rose to lock the door. Just then, a messenger ran up with a package for Miss Nora O'Dell. It contained the lace parasol from Herpolsheimer's. She didn't need to read the card. Who else could have sent it?

Nora told herself it was too expensive, that she couldn't accept it. But when she had donned her green bombazine gown and looked at herself in the mirror with that parasol over her shoulder she couldn't help herself. Besides, she reasoned, any man who could afford a diamond the size of Chandler's tiepin, could afford a parasol.

She might not understand every word of *Hamlet*, but she would be dressed as well as anyone there.

"Who's there?"

"Nay, answer me: Stand, and unfold yourself."

"You come most carefully upon your hour."

"'Tis now struck twelve; get thee to bed, Francisco."

"For this relief much thanks: 'Tis bitter cold, and I am sick at heart."

Nora had not known what to expect at the opera house. Certainly not this. Listening to the opening lines of the play called *Hamlet* by someone named Shakespeare, she frowned. She reached up with a gloved hand to push at an imaginary out-of-place blonde curl, wondering how she would endure the evening. Her eyes wandered over the theater. Gilt pillars soared up both sides of the stage. Atop each pillar was the imposing bust of a man. Miss Thornhill had told Nora he was the one who had written the play they were to see. Between the busts, heavily carved wooden flowers and clusters of grapes and pears arched over the stage. At the back of the stage was a curtain painted to look like a castle. Nora bent over and looked up, wondering what scenes the other curtains she could see high above the stage displayed.

A ghostly figure appeared onstage, catching Nora's attention. Two men blathered on to one another about it. Apparently they thought the ghost was a king. Nora leaned toward Elise and whispered, "Are they really speaking English?"

Elise whispered encouragement. "Don't try to listen to every individual word. Just let yourself follow the flow of it. Get involved with the actors. Watch and listen with your heart as well as your eyes."

When the two men exited, Nora gathered that the action had moved inside the castle. The same curtain remained in place, but two huge chairs were pushed onto the stage. A dozen people filed in from the wings. Nora recognized Mamie Patterson first. She was wearing the crown and cape Nora and Elise had worked so hard to realize.

Greyson Chandler stepped from the background, dressed completely in black. His hair shone more golden than Nora remembered it. She had admired his broad shoulders before, but his stage costume revealed much more . . . all of it very, very pleasing. She had always liked the rich tenor of his voice, but his stage voice was remarkable. Nora would read the next day that critics had described Chandler's voice as having "the ring of the trumpet." People would say that his voice enabled him to "exhibit vast power" and "assume unequaled dignity for a man so young." Nora didn't think in such lofty terms. She only knew that with Chandler's first speech as Hamlet, prince of Denmark, Lincoln, Nebraska, ceased to exist. Gone were the gilt pillars and carvings that soared up the sides of the proscenium arch. Gone were the other theatergoers. Nora was swept up in the drama of the events on stage, oblivious to everything around her.

Clasping her hands in her lap, she listened as Elise had advised—with her eyes and her heart. The next two hours were complete magic. She agonized with Hamlet over the death of his father, wept at the madness of Ophelia, and hated Claudius for his duplicity. When at last Horatio said, "Good night, sweet prince, and flights of angels sing thee to thy rest," Nora was embarrassed to realize that tears were stinging her eyes. She hastily brushed them away, relieved that the gaslights along the theater walls were not yet turned up.

Once the actors had taken their bows and the thunderous applause died down, Elise prepared to lead the way toward the exit, but Nora had barely reached the end of the aisle when a dark-haired young man stepped forward. Bowing low, he introduced himself as Ned Gallagher, handed her a card, and waited.

"It's an invitation to join Mr. Chandler backstage."

Lucy's eyes grew wide.

Hannah covered her mouth with a gloved hand.

Nora felt her stomach lurch. She shoved the card toward Elise. "You go, Elise. I don't want to."

"You cannot refuse, Nora. It would be very rude." Elise bent down and said quietly, "We cannot offend these people, Nora. I want their business. It's not all that unexpected. You are, after all, the one who rescued Miss Patterson's costume."

"But you made the cape," Nora protested.

"But *you* are the one invited," Elise said, with a smile.

Lucy nodded. "Go on."

Hannah agreed. "You have to, Nora."

Nora was not anxious to encounter Mamie Patterson again, especially not with the lace parasol in hand.

"Hey," Ned Gallagher interjected. "I don't know what you've heard about actors, but most of us are perfectly nice." He grinned at Nora, raising one hand to his left eyebrow and saluting. "I won't let them boil you in oil or anything. Honest." He offered Nora his arm. "Come on. It won't hurt a bit. I promise."

Reluctantly, Nora took Ned's arm. Bidding Elise, Lucy, and Hannah good evening, she went with Ned. He led her up a narrow stairway and around the proscenium arch where they ducked behind the stage curtain and headed down a long, narrow hallway crowded with trunks and other assorted baggage.

"You ever been backstage before?" Ned asked.

Nora shook her head. "I've never been to a play before tonight."

"What'd you think?"

"It was magical. Even if I didn't understand everything."

Ned laughed, a friendly, easy sound that helped Nora relax. "Don't worry. I don't always understand everything, either, and I can recite the whole thing—every single part. Even Ophelia's."

He led Nora down a narrow hallway where everything was complete bedlam. Rosencrantz and Guildenstern pushed by them, followed by the two clowns who had been grave diggers. The more portly of the clowns was wondering aloud if dinner at the hotel would be beef or pork that evening. He was hoping for both. Claudius, the king of Denmark, disappeared behind one door. Ned finally stopped at the end of the hallway and knocked on a door. Without waiting for a reply, he pushed it ajar and announced, "Miss O'Dell to see Mr. Chandler."

"Thanks, Ned," Chandler answered. He did not come to the door, but Nora heard him call, "Please come in."

Ned opened the door wide, standing aside for Nora to step across the threshold. A woman's touch was evident everywhere in the room, from the painted dressing screen in the corner to the carpet on the floor. Nora realized that what Hannah had said about Chandler and Miss Patterson sharing a dressing room was true.

Greyson Chandler was standing with his back to the doorway, leaning toward a mirror as he wiped makeup off his face. Nora was amazed at the dark lines around his eyes, across his forehead, down his cheeks. He caught her eye in the mirror. "See what they do to me to make me look mad." He winked at her and continued scrubbing the makeup away. Finally, he ran his fingers through his blond hair and turned around.

"Your fine work helped us be a success this evening, Miss O'Dell. Mamie and I wanted to say thank you."

Mamie stepped out from behind the dressing screen in the corner. She wore a flowing silk robe tied about her waist. Instead of echoing Chandler's gratitude, she reached up and removed a wig. Plunking it onto a stand nearby, she began to take down her own hair, which had been plastered against her head to accommodate the wig.

"The roses said thanks enough," Nora said. She did not miss the effect her comment had on Mamie and hurried to add, "And thank you very much for the tickets."

"Did you like our little play?" Mamie interrupted.

Nora nodded. "It was wonderful."

"I thought perhaps you would join us for dinner this evening," Chandler said. "The cast always dines at the Hathaway House after a performance. Would you be my guest?"

Nora saw Mamie pause, hairbrush in midair, and throw an icy stare at Chandler.

Nora shook her head. "I can't. Miss Thornhill expects me at my workstation no later than five-thirty in the morning."

Mamie spoke up. "You'll have to forgive Grey," she said. "He's so accustomed to the actor's schedule, he forgets that most of the world rises with the sun." She tossed the length of hair she had been brushing over her shoulder and put a hand on Chandler's shoulder. "I'm so glad you enjoyed the performance. When Grey said he had invited you, I was worried. Shakespeare can be so difficult for one who hasn't studied."

Nora looked at Chandler. He had noticed that she was carrying the parasol. She blushed and looked away. "Well, at first, I wasn't certain I would like it, but then you—" She corrected herself. "Then Hamlet began to talk, and everything just—" She stopped. "When Hamlet died, it made me cry."

Mamie had begun to pin her hair up while Nora talked. She moved to recapture center stage in the dressing room. "You'll have to come tomorrow. Grey is hilarious in the lead. It's a farce. And the language isn't nearly as difficult as Shakespeare." She finished pinning up her hair and turned around to look at Nora pointedly as she said, "It's much more like what you would have been used to at Goldie's."

"Oh, Mamie," Chandler scolded. He frowned.

"Oh, Mamie, what?" the actress asked as she disappeared behind the dressing screen. "It's the truth, Grey. She'll understand the farce much more easily."

Goldie's. Total surprise was followed by hurt, which quickly melded into anger. Nora opened her mouth to say something. Then, she thought of Elise. Elise had been treated badly by customers before, and she never ever threw mud back in someone's face. This was different from Mrs. Judge Cranston. If Nora alienated these people, the ramifications for Thornhill Dressers could be terrible. Reaching deep inside, Nora found the will to ignore Mamie's barbs. She said quietly, "Thank you, Miss Patterson. Perhaps I will take your advice and attend again tomorrow night. I have a great deal to learn, and I want to take advantage of every opportunity to do so."

She turned to look at Chandler. Swallowing hard to keep her voice from trembling, she said, "Thank you, Mr. Chandler, for the invitation to dinner. You really don't owe me anything more. You paid Miss Thornhill generously, and hopefully Mr. Frost will continue to recommend Thornhill Dressers to your associates. That's quite enough payment for us." Nora wheeled around, brushed past Ned, and started down the hallway, hoping she was headed for an exit.

Chandler went after her. He caught her arm from behind. "Please, Miss O'Dell—Nora. Wait."

Nora stopped and spun around. "I don't recall giving you permission to call me Nora, Mr. Chandler. I'd appreciate it if you wouldn't—even if I am just one of Goldie's girls."

"Let me apologize. Mamie—" He stopped, seeming to search for words. "Mamie depends on me, and when she feels threatened—"

"I'm just an ignorant milliner, Mr. Chandler," Nora interrupted. "But I don't think I need you to translate what just happened. I understood perfectly. I should have gotten the message the day you two were in the shop and she tipped me. I should have known when she called me 'dear.' And I should never have enjoyed your company at the Lindell, or anywhere else, for that matter."

Angry tears threatened to spill down her cheeks, but Nora blinked rapidly and willed them away. Imitating a flirtatious pose she had learned from Lily, she placed one hand on her hip and the other on Chandler's shoulder. "Listen, honey, you tell Miss Patterson that her feelin' threatened by little ol' me is just silly. Land sakes, I'm just one of Goldie's girls. Nobody takes us seriously." She fluttered her eyelashes. Then, drawing herself up as tall as possible and hoping she seemed dignified, Nora said, "Now, if you don't mind, I've been reminded of my place, and I think it's time I returned to it. And I won't be needing this on my side of the tracks." She handed Chandler the parasol and headed for a door marked "Exit."

Ned followed her. "Hey, that was great. You told *him*. And he'll tell *her*. Can I walk you home?"

"Sure you want to be seen with someone who used to work at Goldie's Garden?" Nora said bitterly.

"What do I care about that?" the boy said.

Nora stopped and stared at him. "Listen up, Mr. Gallagher. I was strictly a housekeeper at Goldie's. A *housekeeper*. Got that? So, if you're thinking—"

"Hey," the boy said, almost angrily, "all I was thinking was you're a nice girl with a lot of spunk and I thought we could have a nice walk. Get the chip off your shoulder, will you? We're not all like Chandler and Patterson."

"All right then," Nora said.

"All right then." Ned held out his arm. They walked along in silence for a block or so, when Ned suddenly asked, "Did Mr. Chandler really send you roses?"

"Yes," Nora said. "Why?"

Ned whistled softly under his breath. "I've known him a long time. He never sent a woman roses before."

CHAPTER 15

Cherubs

Behold, thou art fair, my love.
Song of Solomon 1:15

The Frost Players had been scheduled to remain in Lincoln for a short engagement, but when, at the conclusion of the week, Mr. Funke received a telegram informing him that the next act booked into his opera house would be forced to cancel its engagement, Frost's troupe voted to remain in Lincoln for an extended run. Each of the five women in the troupe flocked to Thornhill Dressers to order new gowns. They didn't seem to mind that the finished work would have to be shipped to their next destination and might need further alterations by another dressmaker.

Ned Gallagher asked Nora for "permission to call." Ned had been in the theater since he was a child, crisscrossing the United States several times and even touring in Europe once. He was a superb storyteller with a generous store of anecdotes. Ned didn't flirt, and he seldom mentioned Chandler or Patterson. Nora spent enough time with Ned that Lucy began to tease her about him instead of Greyson Chandler.

Ned Gallagher's assertion that Chandler had never sent roses to a woman didn't seem to mean anything. Nora had heard nothing from either Chandler or Patterson since the performance of *Hamlet*.

Sewing for the theatrical troupe yielded more than just monetary benefits. Imitating them taught Nora flawless grammar. Knowing them taught Nora not to feel inferior to someone just because they were famous. She knew that the Mamie Patterson the "upper class" invited to dinner was no more real than the innocent ingenue Mamie sometimes played onstage. She knew that Felicia Bonaparte's hourglass figure was created with an ingeniously designed corset, and that beneath her puritanical visage, Rosalind Frey hid a propensity for red and lavender petticoats and outlandishly woven stockings.

Nora would have found a measure of contentment, had it not been for those yellow roses. Lucy reported that Chandler and Patterson dined together every evening and always retired at the same time. But Ned had said that Chandler had never given a woman roses. Hannah saw Chandler and Patterson together in Dover's Dry Goods store. Miss Patterson was examining a pair of striped hose and seemed to be asking Mr. Chandler's opinion. But Ned had said—Nora finally tossed the roses out.

When Chandler and Patterson finally returned to Thornhill Dressers, Nora was out with Ned Gallagher. It had been over a week since the opening of *Hamlet*. The troupe would depart for Denver in two days.

Mamie selected an elegant navy blue watered silk for a new gown, with the stipulation that it must be completed before the train left Lincoln.

In the interest of future business, Elise sacrificed twenty-two of her most treasured French enamel buttons to grace the bodice of the exquisite gown. With Elise and Lucy and Hannah rushing madly to complete it, Nora felt compelled to sacrifice an evening to do her part. "If you can get the thing put together," she said reluctantly, "I'll do the handwork tonight."

On Friday evening, Nora carried the gown upstairs to her tiny apartment, with mixed feelings. She was determined to fulfill her promise to Elise, but she couldn't help resenting the fact that Mamie Patterson, who least deserved it, was once again getting preferential treatment. Set in gilded-copper mountings, the buttons glistened against the navy blue watered silk. Nora was having a great deal of difficulty not envying Mamie Patterson those buttons, each one featuring a cherub painted in white on a blue ground. Nora jerked the sewing thread angrily as it knotted and tangled around a button. Finally, she held the garment up. All twenty-two buttons would march in an unwavering line from Miss Patterson's neckline, across her ample bosom and down to the waist, which, Nora reminded herself, was beginning to thicken.

Nora scolded herself for her unkind thoughts. She had spent a great deal of time trying not to be envious of Mamie Patterson over elegant gowns and delicious buttons . . . and her power over Greyson Chandler. Nora sighed. What *did* he see in that woman?

Downstairs in the studio, Elise closed the shop door and locked it. Although it was a full half hour before her usual closing time, she pulled the cords that lowered the curtains behind each of her four display windows. The drapes operated like individual stage curtains, providing a backdrop to the creations that Elise displayed in her shop windows, while at the same time blocking the view of the shop's interior from passersby. The system of drapes enabled Elise to work late into the night in her shop whenever necessary while protecting her privacy and giving her a sense of security.

Tonight, however, Elise had no plans to work late. A secretive smile played across her face as she produced a gigantic basket from behind a counter and positioned it in the middle of the large table in the center of the studio. She lit the gas lamps, moderating their glow until the studio was bathed in soft golden light. Once everything was arranged to her satisfaction, Elise went to the back door to welcome a latecomer into the shop.

Upstairs in her apartment, Nora stood up and stretched. Picking up the newspaper, she skimmed the headlines. A final review of the production at the opera house caught her eye. She sank into a chair and began to read. The reviewer spoke of Mamie Patterson as "first and last, a natural-born actress." *How right they are*, Nora thought unkindly. She read the next paragraph carefully.

> *It appears that Miss Patterson has invented a new stage kiss. She stands with her back to the audience near the footlights. The husband, played by Greyson Chandler, rushes wildly into her arms. They hold each other at arm's length. Her bosom heaves. He pants. He looks down at her, and she looks up at him. Then he suddenly places his lips to hers. She clasps him about the head and they are, as it were, glued together. Men around town have their watches out timing them. That is the Patterson kiss.*

Nora threw the paper aside, happy that she had planned to be away from the studio when Miss Patterson picked up the garment the next morning.

"Nora," Elise called up the stairs. "I'm leaving. Shall I lock up?"

"No," Nora called back. "I can do it. I'll come down and arrange Miss Patterson's gown on the dress form in the studio before I retire."

"Thank you," Elise said. "I appreciate your extra hours, Nora. Have a good evening. And enjoy your breakfast with Mr. Gallagher."

Regretting that she had read the paper at all, Nora draped Miss Patterson's new gown over her arm and descended the stairs. Halfway down, she thought she heard footsteps in the front studio. She hesitated. Elise was gone and Hannah had flitted out the back door more than an hour ago on some mysterious errand. Lucy was with her Mr. Fielding.

When she reached the bottom step, Nora heard a noise again. Her heart thumping, she called out, "Is someone there?"

No one answered, but Nora knew that someone was, indeed, in the studio. As noiselessly as possible, she tiptoed to the cutting table opposite the back door. Trembling with fear, she grasped a pair of sewing scissors in her right hand. She hid the scissors beneath the folds of Miss Patterson's gown and headed toward the studio.

Nora paused just before launching herself through the door. Someone had lowered the gaslights to cast a warm glow throughout the studio. Someone had pulled the curtains behind the display windows. And someone had covered the worktable with a white linen cloth . . . and then set it with elegant tableware. Greyson Chandler was lighting the last of six candles held by a silver candelabra. What the candlelight did to his already handsome face made Nora take a quick breath.

"What's this?" Nora said.

"I believe it's called dinner," Chandler said. He looked up. "It's also my attempt at an apology. If this doesn't work, I plan to fall on my knees and beg your forgiveness." Nora didn't say anything. He smiled. "If you don't agree to dine with me, I'm going to feel like a first-rate fool. But I wouldn't blame you if you kicked me out."

He walked toward Nora and took the gown into his arms. "Here. Let me help you. This *is* the new gown Mamie ordered?"

Nora nodded, pointing at the waiting empty dress form that stood on the opposite side of the studio. "I was going to put it there. She's to come for it in the morning."

Chandler walked to the dress form. "Well then, let's get the thing on display."

Nora hurried to his side, still clutching the scissors in her hand.

Clumsily, Chandler pulled the gown down over the dress form.

He reached for the scissors. "May I take the fact that you haven't stabbed me with these as a sign that you might consider dinner?"

Nora nodded dumbly. "Of course I'll have dinner. I just—need to—" She fumbled with the gown, wishing her hands would stop trembling. When at last it was arranged to, she stood back to admire it.

From behind her, Chandler asked, "What's this?"

He was standing by her workstation at the opposite end of the studio holding up a string of buttons on a yellow ribbon.

"It's called a charm string." Nora blushed. "It's a silly fad. Hannah and Lucy got me started. Kind of a way to keep memories."

"Tell me about it," Chandler said. He walked toward her. Looking down, he rubbed his thumb across the face of one of the buttons. "What's special about this one?"

"That was my mother's."

He raised his eyes to hers. "I've been 'pumping' Ned for information about you. I didn't think you knew your mother."

Nora stammered a little. "I—I didn't really know her. But there were a few things in a little trunk."

"What do you know about it?"

"Only that it was important to my mother." She felt awkward and groped for a topic that would draw attention from herself. She asked abruptly, "What about you? Do you keep in touch with your mother? She must be very proud of you."

Chandler shook his head. "No, I haven't heard from her in a very long time. She was stunned when I took up acting. It's rather scandalous to be an actor where I grew up." He frowned slightly. "It wasn't at all what they had in mind for me. Lately I've begun to understand why they felt the way they did."

"But surely they would be proud—if they knew. I mean, what could be wrong with *Shakespeare*?"

Chandler leaned against the worktable, fingering the string of buttons. "It's not the Shakespeare they objected to. It's the offstage atmosphere. The temptations." He lowered his voice and said softly, "About which, it seems, they were quite right. I was raised in a very conservative, churchgoing household. They wouldn't be very proud about some of my involvements." He added, "But then, neither am I."

"But they should know how successful you've become. You should write. If you have a family, you shouldn't just give them up." When Chandler looked up, Nora apologized. "I'm sorry. It's really none of my business. I just can't imagine having a family and not wanting them."

"It's not a matter of not wanting them," Chandler said quietly. "It's a matter of if they want *me*." He cleared his throat. "Never mind. Tell me about the other buttons."

Nora pointed to a small white one. "This one is from a dress I mended for Lily at Goldie's."

"And this one?" Chandler pointed to a small black jet button.

Had he meant to touch her hand? Nora took a tiny step backward. Holding both hands behind her back, she recited, "That's the kind I put on my first really good dress. Goldie had it made for me . . . sort of as a farewell. I thought I'd never have a place to wear it, but then you sent the tickets to *Hamlet*."

He looked down at her. "The green dress with the frill at the neck. And a matching bonnet that sits like so—" He gestured with his free hand.

"Yes. That's the one."

He grinned. "You could say, then, that this one commemorates our first evening together."

She nodded.

"Although I suppose you'd just as soon not remember that." He laid aside the charm string. "Let's sit down, shall we?"

They sat down at the table, and Chandler began to take their supper from the basket. While he worked, he asked, "Which story do you believe?"

"What?" Nora asked.

"Which button story is popular here in Lincoln? The one about the old maid or the one about marriage? I believe the thousandth button has something to do with one or the other."

Nora exclaimed, "You tricked me! You already know all about charm strings."

Chandler grinned and shrugged. "A couple of the women in the troupe started strings last year in New York. But you didn't answer my question . . . about the end of the charm string."

"I don't believe either story. I just like buttons." She took a sip of water.

Chandler sat down opposite her and took a deep breath. "You've caused me a great deal of trouble, you know. After Mamie found out about those roses I thought I'd never hear the end of it."

Nora took a deep breath. "You know, Mr. Chandler, you've caused me some trouble, too. Asking me to tea. Walking me to deliver a package. Visiting the shop. You ask me backstage, and Miss Patterson lays into me. What did I ever do to *her*?"

"You attracted my attention," Chandler said quietly. "Mamie knows I've never sent roses to a woman before. Not even her."

"Well, I don't like being in the middle of things," Nora

said quickly. "Especially when I'm not even certain what I'm in the middle *of*."

Chandler reached out to touch her arm. "I had no intention of putting you in the middle of anything." He looked at her. "The real reason for this is—" He paused, seeming to grope for words. Finally, he sat back, raising one hand to stroke his mustache while he looked at Nora. "Would you do something for me?"

"What?"

"Would you consider having dinner with me this evening?"

Nora looked at him, confused. "What?"

"With me." He touched his hand to his chest. "Greyson Chandler, the person. Not the actor, not Mamie Patterson's partner. Just me. Could we do that?"

Nora nodded slowly. She saw Chandler's shoulders relax. His smile became more genuine. He took a sip of water. "I never, ever, expected to be a successful actor. I thought I might get a few minor parts from time to time . . . but what I really expected was to be the music director for a troupe. Then one evening our leading man was taken ill, and I, the understudy, stepped onstage. I wasn't at all prepared for the consequences . . . and I've never been really comfortable with some of them."

"Yes, poor boy," Nora teased. "One *would* get weary of all the fluttering eyelashes and sighs. It must be a terrible trial to have every woman you meet falling all over herself to impress you. And enduring the famous Patterson kiss would be pure torture."

"As a matter of fact," Chandler said quietly, "it gets downright annoying at times. In some cities I can't eat in a restaurant without women giggling and watching my every move." He looked across the table at Nora. "The illusion of Mamie and I as a couple provided a sort of buffer. It all seemed perfectly harmless." He sat back and shook his head. "Unfortunately, somewhere along the way Mamie seems to have forgotten that we're just playacting.

I didn't realize it until I took an interest in a certain blonde-haired milliner."

Nora took a sudden interest in her dinner.

Chandler shrugged. "Sometimes I forget why I'm in the theater at all. Cancelled engagements and destroyed costumes, homesick troupe members and disagreements with theater owners . . . they take their toll. And then there is Mamie." He took a deep breath and let it out very slowly. "Well. Not your problem, obviously. Masculine whining is very unattractive." He changed the subject. "What about you? *Wherefore art thou*, Miss O'Dell?"

Nora smiled. "There's very little to tell about me. I'm from—"

"—Hickory Grove," Chandler said. "Ned told me. What made you leave?"

"Hard biscuits," Nora replied. The expression on Chandler's face made her laugh. "Really. It's the truth." Having begun the story, Nora felt compelled to finish it. Somehow, what Chandler had requested of her happened. She was no longer dining with Greyson Chandler, actor. She told him more than she intended about her childhood, then apologized. "I'm sorry. I didn't mean to sound quite so pathetic. As you said, whining isn't very attractive." She concluded her autobiography. "After the biscuits, I packed a bag and started walking. I stopped when I got to Lincoln."

"Shep told me about Lily bringing you to Goldie's," he said. He pretended to wield a shovel at an imaginary enemy. "Has the Lincoln baseball team heard about you?"

Nora smiled but changed the subject. "I thought your parents were in the theater like Ned's. But from what you said earlier, that's obviously not the case."

Chandler shook his head. "No. I come from plain American farming stock. But even as a child I was much more interested in music than crops. I had other brothers to take on the farm work, so my parents finally let me go. I was studying in Philadelphia when one evening I saw Edwin Booth in *Hamlet*."

Chandler's eyes glowed as he shared the memory. "I can't really explain it, but the moment Booth strode onto the stage, the entire audience seemed to be charged with electricity. I don't know if anyone even took a breath during his soliloquy. It was nearly a religious experience, the communion between that actor and his audience—"

Chandler sat back abruptly. He seemed almost embarrassed and stabbed a piece of fruit with his fork before saying nonchalantly, "What you saw at the opera house here was mere caricature compared to Edwin Booth. At any rate, that was the moment I knew I wanted to be on the stage. I knew I would never have Booth's power over an audience, but I knew I had to try."

"You *do* have power over an audience," Nora said. "I felt it that night when you first opened here in Lincoln. They were all with you. Even the fops in the balcony quieted when you walked onstage. I can't imagine having such a gift. Your family should know about it."

"Oh, I imagine they're very content not knowing about a lot of it," Greyson said.

Nora protested, "They would be very proud of you."

He pulled on his mustache as he considered what she said. "Maybe. About the acting. But there are other things." He looked up at her and shrugged. "I'm not very proud of myself." He sighed. "This Mamie business. I've known it was getting out of hand, but I let it go on, because it was to my advantage. That's despicable." He frowned. "Tell me, Miss O'Dell, what does one do to reclaim one's honor?"

Nora shook her head. "You're asking the wrong person about that. I've been too busy trying to survive to think about anything that philosophical. Just getting the next hat finished has been about all I could manage."

"You don't ever contemplate the future? Plans? Dreams?"

"I want my own shop, if that's what you mean. I'm good at millinery, and it's one of the few professions where a woman can make an honorable living."

"See, you *have* considered metaphysics," he chided. "You've considered the matter of honor in selecting a career." He leaned forward. "Does Miss Thornhill know you're planning a defection?"

Nora smiled. "It won't come as a surprise. She's encouraged me from the very beginning to keep learning and growing."

"Do learning and growing include marrying Ned Gallagher?"

Nora was so taken aback by the question, she stared open-mouthed at Chandler. Finally, she gathered her thoughts. "That would be none of your business, Mr. Chandler."

He smiled. "That would be right. Humor me. Answer it anyway."

"I don't have plans to marry anyone," Nora said quietly.

"Why not?"

She took a sip of water and set the glass down firmly. "I'll depend on me and pay my own way through life."

"It sounds like a lonely life." He looked at Nora. "Don't you think people need each other?"

Nora was sitting with her hand on the edge of the table. Chandler covered it with his. The two sat quietly for a moment. Nora's heart raced. *Memorize this moment* she told herself. She looked down at the tangled pattern of veins on the back of Grey's hand. He squeezed her hand softly. She didn't pull away.

"You haven't eaten your dessert," Grey said quietly. Still, he didn't release her hand.

"I'm not hungry anymore."

He pushed his chair away from the table and leaned toward her, taking her hand in both of his. "If someone named Grey Chandler wrote to you, do you think you'd write back?" His eyes searched hers.

"Yes."

"And if he disengaged himself from a certain actress, would you think that a good thing?"

Nora swallowed. "Yes, but—I wouldn't want to be the cause of trouble for you."

Chandler let her hand go. He rubbed his forehead briskly. "The only one who's causing me trouble is myself. I've made some very poor choices in the past. I think it's time I righted them. And—" He smiled slowly. "I think perhaps it *is* time I wrote home. You're right about family. One shouldn't give them up so easily." He stood up and began to pack their supper back into the basket.

Nora stood up to help him, feeling very self-conscious as they worked side by side. When their shoulders touched, she pulled away.

Grey looked down at her. "I hope—I hope you won't let Ned Gallagher steal you away before—"

"I told you, Ned and I are just friends."

"You'd better tell Ned that," Chandler said softly. Then, before Nora knew what was happening, he gathered her into his arms and kissed her. Her mind told her that she should push him away. She put her hands on his shoulders to do that. But then she didn't push. Instead, she kissed him back.

Chandler finally let go. Taking their picnic basket by both hands, he said quietly, "There are two things you need to know about me. Ned was right. I've never in my life sent a woman roses." He looked at her. "And I've never left after a kiss like that. I'm ashamed of that, but it's the truth. I have some things to straighten out. When I get it done, I'll be back. And I'm going to ask for a good deal more than a stolen dinner and one kiss."

CHAPTER 16

Everything in Writing

Train up a child in the way he should go: and when he is old, he will not depart from it.
Proverbs 22:6

On Saturday morning, Nora awoke before dawn. Leaping out of bed, she washed her face and did her hair before pulling on the green bombazine dress. Her hands were trembling with excitement as she inspected herself in the mirror. *Green with a frill at the neck, and a hat worn like this*. He had even remembered what she wore to the theater!

The morning seemed to drag by. Lucy and Hannah finally arrived.

Nora descended the stairs trembling with excitement. "I've changed my mind," she said. "I'd like to go with you to the train station. Is it still all right?"

Lucy and Hannah exchanged glances. "Of course," Lucy said, nodding. She added, "You sure dressed up for Ned Gallagher. Anything you want to tell us?"

"Ned?" Nora pursed her lips. "Oh, Ned. I'd forgotten—"

Just then, Ned Gallagher knocked on the back door. Once inside, he looked Nora over approvingly. "Say, you look great. I didn't expect you to get all dressed up just for breakfast."

"Well," Nora said, "it's your last day, and I thought I'd look nice for you."

Ned offered her his arm. "I'm taking you to the Hathaway House today."

"We'll meet you at the station later," Lucy called.

Nora nodded vaguely.

As they walked up the street, Ned said, "Say, Nora, we've had some good times, haven't we?"

"Yes we have. Thank you, Ned. I'm going to miss you."

"Do you mean that? I mean, if I write to you or something, would you maybe answer me?"

Nora patted him on the arm affectionately. "Of course I will. I'd love to hear from you. Will you be with the troupe if they come through Lincoln in the fall?"

"If Mr. Frost still wants me, I will be. But it's going to be strange without Chandler in the company. Hard to know what's going to happen."

Nora stopped. "What do you mean?"

"He and Miss Patterson had a huge fight this morning." Ned corrected himself. "Actually, Chandler was calm about the whole thing. It was Miss Patterson who threw the fit. Everyone on the third floor of the Hathaway House must have heard it. Apparently Chandler didn't come home last night. Patterson was furious. He wouldn't say where he was, and that made her even madder. Then Mr. Frost joined the fray, trying to calm them down. Whatever was said, Chandler got canned." Ned shook his head from side to side. "I couldn't believe it, but I saw it with my own eyes. Greyson Chandler walking out of the hotel with a bag in his hand."

"Where do you think he went?" Nora was doing her best to sound only casually interested.

"Darned if I know," Ned said. "All I know is Mr. Frost said we're leaving as scheduled, that he's wired Denver to find a replacement for Chandler."

They walked to the Hathaway House hotel and in to

the dining room. Ned ordered breakfast, and the waiter had just poured coffee when Mr. Frost entered with a red-eyed, puffy-faced Mamie Patterson on his arm.

Miss Patterson had taken up a napkin and spread it on her lap before she saw Ned and Nora. Snatching the napkin up and laying it on the table, she got up and marched to their table. "Miss O'Dell," Mamie said.

Nora stood up, suppressing a smile as she looked down upon the actress. It was difficult to feel inferior to someone so much shorter. "Yes, Miss Patterson."

"If you see Mr. Chandler," she said icily, "or should I say *when* you see him?"

Nora didn't say anything, so Mamie continued. "You may inform him that he can claim his things from Mrs. Hathaway." She drew a lace-edged handkerchief from her sleeve and dabbed at her eyes. "Do you know who Mrs. Hathaway is?"

"Yes. We've met," Nora said.

"Oh, of course. You've made hats for her, I suppose."

Nora began to sit down, but Mamie grabbed her sleeve. "Were you able to finish the watered silk gown?"

"Of course," Nora said. "We always do our best to keep our word, Miss Patterson. I sewed the buttons on myself late last evening."

"Oh," Mamie said, her voice trembling with rage. "You were *sewing* last evening?"

"Yes," Nora replied.

"Well, you can inform Miss Thornhill that I have decided not to take the gown, after all."

Nora narrowed her gaze and stared at Miss Patterson. Mamie had selected some of the most expensive material they carried, and now several yards of it were a complete loss. Could she really be so petty as to cause Elise such a loss because of one dinner? The hatred in the woman's eyes almost frightened her. Nora's anger melted. How unhappy she must be.

"I hope we haven't displeased you in some way, Miss Patterson," Nora said quietly. "The gown is lovely. I'm sure you'd like it."

"I'm afraid that doesn't matter now," Mamie said, lifting her nose in the air and sighing deeply. "I simply cannot bear the thought of wearing that dress. It would be a constant reminder of heartache."

"I'm very sorry, Miss Patterson," Nora said. She almost meant it.

Mamie swept back to where Mr. Frost was seated. Nora and Ned returned to their breakfast, after which Nora accompanied him to the train station. She met up with Lucy and Hannah, and the foursome made their way through the crowd and onto the platform.

As the conductor called, "All aboard," Nora stood on tiptoe and kissed Ned on the cheek. "Good-bye, Ned. I hope I'll see you again."

Ned leaned down to return Nora's kiss, planting a clumsy buss on her lips. He blushed furiously and ran for the train car. Climbing aboard, he took off his hat and waved it in the air. Nora raised her hand to say good-bye. The whistle blew and the train began to move out.

Someone shoved Nora from behind and spun her around. As she raised her hand to steady her hat, Greyson Chandler wrapped one arm around her and kissed her. He shoved the lace parasol in her hands. The train picked up steam, and Chandler ran, bag in hand, to catch it. He barely managed to grab the railing on the last car, pulling himself aboard just at the end of the platform. He turned around and raised his hand. Nora returned the gesture, standing on the platform and watching until the train was out of sight.

Grey kept his word. Nearly every Friday a letter arrived. He was in Denver. He had written home and planned to visit soon. He was living off his savings, trying to find answers to what he called "the deeper questions of life."

Summer's heat brought the dress business to a standstill. In spite of her efforts to the contrary, Nora found herself marking the passage of time by the arrival of Grey's letters.

Dr. Allbright escaped the city and headed for a small town to the northwest called Millersburg. "They've been after me to come out and open a practice there for years," she said.

"But isn't it the worst possible time of year to travel?" Nora asked. "It's so hot. You'll be miserable."

"Exactly," Dr. Allbright replied. "If I see any merit at all to the move, I'll know the worst. If I can bear the heat of summer in Custer County, I can bear anything it has to throw at me."

Dr. Allbright was gone for two weeks. When she returned, she had decided to move. She was more animated than she had been in months. She prepared for the move with gusto, and in less than a month, she had closed her office, and arranged for the railroad to ship her furnishings to Millersburg.

The combination of Dr. Allbright's departure and what seemed to be the death of her millinery business sunk Nora into depression.

"Business always slows down this time of year." Miss Thornhill encouraged her. She had propped the door to the shop open in a vain attempt to capture any passing breeze. "Dressmakers only work a few months out of the year. No one wants to think about layers of cloth when the thermometer is approaching one hundred." She went on, "But we don't have to be idle. Now is the time for us to be perusing all the fashion magazines and making up models for the fall. With the first breath of cool air, we'll be busier than you can imagine."

Grey wrote a strange letter that left Nora feeling more distant from him than ever.

I've had a deep change of heart. A return to my roots. In the Book of Proverbs, it says, "Train up a child in the way he should go: and when he is old he will not depart from it." I don't know if my parents ever claimed that Scripture for their son, but regardless, it has come true in my life.

Have you kept your promise to Miss Thornhill about church? I wish you would. I want you to understand what's happened to me. It's a change at the center of my being. I didn't think that God could forgive all I'd done, but He has.

I can tell you the exact moment it all happened. I was walking alone up in the mountains, and I sat down to read. A grasshopper jumped on the page, and then my eye fell to Isaiah 40. Yes, I was reading the Bible. No one will ever be able to convince me that that grasshopper was coincidence. You must read the entire passage, Nora, to understand the impact it had on me . . . the reminder that I am but a grasshopper, and yet God has His eye on me.

Lessons from my childhood came roaring back into my head. I was overcome with a sense of my own sinfulness and I wept. But then followed a sense of God's great love. I looked at the mountains before me and knew, as surely as I know I am writing this, that I was forgiven. I understood that Christ had to die . . . not for the entire world in general, but specifically and personally for me.

I'm going home a new man, and I'm going to get on my knees and ask my dear mother to forgive her erring son. And then, when the time is right, I'll be back in Lincoln, calling on a certain blonde beauty, and as I promised when I left, I'll be expecting much more than dinner and a kiss.

Each time Nora reread the letter, she had new questions. She knew that Miss Thornhill could probably answer them, but then Miss Thornhill would know more about her and Grey. Nora wanted to keep their growing friendship to herself. She had begun to hope it was a romance, but she didn't want to risk it by telling anyone. Grey's letter made her feel uneasy.

She bought a Bible and found the passage that Grey had referred to, but the only impact it had on her was impressing her mind with the less-than-comforting picture of God blowing on things and making them wither.

As for going to church, she remembered Goldie's opinions about preachers. What if Miss Thornhill's pastor was *that* kind? She remembered what Lucy and Hannah had said about Madame Hart, too. She was a "high-muck-a-muck" in her church, and yet Lucy and Hannah knew her for her cruelty as an employer. Nora didn't know what had happened to Grey, but she hoped he hadn't found the kind of religion that would make him a self-righteous hypocrite.

Just when Nora had determined to write to Dr. Allbright and ask her opinion about some of the things Grey mentioned in his letters, she received an invitation.

Dear Nora,

I am writing to encourage you to take a vacation to Custer County. I enclose a copy of the Millersburg Republican *so that you may see for yourself the spirit of our bustling little city. I also extend an invitation from Mrs. Cay Miller, wife of the proprietor of the largest dry goods store in town (indeed, wife of the gentleman who owns* most *of the town), to meet with her to discuss opening a millinery shop in connection with Miller's Emporium. She is no Elise Thornhill, but she is fair and honest, and your business would be an instant success.*

If the opportunity appeals to you, please let me know at once. I can provide lodging and would be happy to meet your train, if you only forward your travel particulars. You can buy a ticket straight through to Millersburg, only be certain you don't change trains at Grand Island and you can't go wrong.

Yours—Maude

Nora read the letter with mixed emotions. She smiled at Dr. Allbright's having signed her name "Maude." It felt good to be on a first-name basis with a physician.

She opened the newspaper that Dr. Allbright had enclosed. The ladies of the First Church were hosting a strawberry and ice cream social. A first-rate cobbler was needed in town. "Italian Chris" would provide music for a dance at the Delhommes' on Friday night. Professor E. A. Garlich offered piano and violin lessons in his home every weekday except Monday, when he traveled to Merna to instruct the young people there.

Nora chuckled reading a humorous article purporting to be the membership roster of the "Millersburg Bachelors' Club." Lonesome Pratt, Askme Thompson, Gotleft Smith, Allgone Andrews, and Willing Williams begged the ladies of Millersburg to "hear their cry" and attend the dance at Delhommes' on Friday night.

Nora liked the friendly tone of the newspaper. She could write Grey and let him know her new address. He had only hinted of the future, and if he had gone off on some religious tangent, she dare not plan her future around his half-promise to return to Lincoln "for more than dinner."

Nora slept fitfully that night. When Elise came in the back door of the shop the next morning, Nora was waiting. "I'd like your opinion of something," she said, wishing her hand would stop shaking as she held out the letter.

Elise read it.

"It probably wouldn't work out," Nora said. "I haven't

saved nearly enough to open my own shop. The timing is a little off, but—"

"You should definitely go and see what it's like," Elise said firmly. She smiled. "If this Mrs. Miller wants you badly enough, she'll be able to help you with setup expenses. It's a dry goods store, and that means they already have a stock of supplies. It might not cost all that much to get started."

Nora shifted her weight from one foot to the other. "I wouldn't want to leave you shorthanded."

"Business is slow right now. It's an excellent time for you to go exploring this new opportunity. And, if you decide to move, I'll have time to find and train your replacement before we get busy." She patted Nora on the shoulder. "I didn't expect to keep you forever, Nora. I knew you'd be wanting your own shop. And I won't hold you back."

She reached for a pad of paper and a pencil. "Sit down. Let's talk about some of the things you'll need to check into." Elise was already making notes. She spent the next hour educating Nora on opening her own business. "Before you leave, I'll write out a list of questions. Dr. Allbright can refine it to fit Millersburg before you ever talk to Mrs. Miller."

She disappeared into the studio and returned with a huge box. Taking off the lid, she pulled out Mamie Patterson's blue silk gown. "What would you say to our cutting this down to fit you for the trip? You can't be seen in green bombazine for the rest of your life, you know. This will make you look like the prosperous businesswoman I know you'll be. Although," she said, grinning, "I would recommend more conservative buttons."

Nora blinked back tears. She stood up and hugged Elise. "Thank you. I was nervous about asking."

"Well, there's no need to be nervous. I'm happy for you.

And I don't envy you Millersburg one bit. Custer County can be an oven this time of year."

Nora wired Dr. Allbright that she would be coming for a visit. Early on Monday morning, Lucy, Hannah, and Elise all accompanied Nora to the train station. As Miss Thornhill had predicted, Nora looked like a very prosperous businesswoman in Mamie Patterson's remade blue watered-silk gown. They had replaced the cherub buttons with pewter.

"I only wish I felt as confident as I look," Nora said on the platform. "My stomach is tied in knots." Elise hugged her and she climbed aboard, finding her seat and opening the window.

Elise reached up from the platform to squeeze her hand. As the train began to move, she said, "Don't forget to get the answers to all the questions we discussed. And don't let Mrs. Miller push too hard." She walked alongside the train, still talking. "Remember that you have something the entire city needs. Don't sign anything until you have a lawyer look it over." The train chugged off. Elise called out, "Get everything in writing!"

CHAPTER 17

Explanations

Execute true judgment, and shew mercy and compassions every man to his brother.
Zechariah 7:9

Nora had considered many of the "what-ifs" surrounding her move to Millersburg. But one thing she had not contemplated was *What if I get sick on the train?* What she had dismissed as nervousness the morning of her departure soon proved to be a full-blown case of the ague. Nora knew what it was, for her own symptoms were almost an exact copy of those Pap had once suffered. First, she began to feel weak and feverish. She barely made it onto the platform at the front of the train car before her stomach revolted against breakfast. Weak and shaky, she clung to the railing around the platform as the train moved west. When the wind blew the smoke from the engine around her, she moved back inside, choking and gasping for breath.

Once in her seat, Nora felt chilly. Grabbing her shawl, she burrowed into it. She had barely stopped shivering when a sudden flash of heat made her throw it aside and head outside for fresh air. No one on the train seemed inclined to help her. She finally realized they must be afraid of contagion. She longed for a drink of water and rejoiced when the train pulled in at Grand Island for a scheduled stop.

Nora stumbled into the station, splashing her face with water, then dampening her handkerchief, and pressing it against the back of her neck. She knew she had a raging fever. Shivering, she stumbled back toward the train. That was when she saw him.

Greyson Chandler was walking away from her. Nora leaned against the station wall, staring after him in disbelief. She squeezed her eyes shut, thinking to clear the mirage away. But when she opened them again, Grey was still there. She opened her mouth to call to him, but he had removed his hat and was waving to someone—a woman—coming toward him, smiling. It was Iris! She ran to him and they hugged. Grey picked up her bag . . . and together they boarded another train.

Nora stumbled on board her train. Leaning back against her seat, she closed her eyes. *I will not cry. I will not.* Hurt and disappointment washed over her. Everything he said about a new start . . . about religion . . . about his family. Nora wondered if any of it had been true.

Iris was beautiful and educated. Nora certainly couldn't blame Grey for being attracted to Iris. She wondered when they had spent time together. Why hadn't he told her in one of his letters? As the rails of the train clicked by, Nora's mind swirled with scenarios and explanations . . . but always, she came back to one reality: Perhaps he had meant the kiss at the station, but he couldn't have meant the letters. Nora wanted to be angry, but she didn't have the energy for anger. It seemed, however, that hurt did not require any effort at all, for it washed over her in waves until she finally fell asleep, slumped over against the window.

At some point in the night, a stabbing pain in her back awoke her. How could it be even hotter when it was dark? Nora threw her shawl off and dozed again, until a voice called through the haze of deep sleep, "Ticket. Ticket, please."

Frowning, Nora croaked, "But you saw my ticket when I boarded. I'm to get off at Millersburg, remember? You told me you'd wake me if I was asleep."

"Millersburg?" the voice grated. "You want to go to Millersburg, you're on the wrong train, lady. This train arrives in Loup City at midnight. And that's a good ways east of Millersburg. You shouldn't have changed trains in Grand Island if you wanted to go to Millersburg."

Through a fog of sickness, Nora realized that she must have stumbled back onto the wrong train. She squinted at the rack overhead. It was empty. Overtaken by near-panic, she half stood. "Wait, a moment, please. Let me just look—" Grasping the backs of each seat as she made her way up and down the aisle, she searched in vain for the carpetbag that held her ticket and a small amount of cash.

Slouching back into the seat she had thought was hers, Nora looked up at the conductor. "My bag is on the other train. The one that goes to Millersburg."

The conductor peered at her suspiciously. "You sure you had a ticket to Millersburg?"

"Please," Nora begged. "I'm ill. I can send a message to a friend in Lincoln. Or Millersburg. Will they telegraph for me?"

"I don't know what they'll do if you've no money," the conductor said. "Guess you'll have to see when we get into Loup City."

Nora sighed and closed her eyes. The conductor wasn't being much help, but she was too sick to care. If she could just close her eyes and sleep . . .

Some time in the night the train lurched to a halt, throwing a half-conscious Nora onto the floor. Landing with a thud, she was immediately awake and aware that the sleep had done nothing to improve her condition. She curled up in a ball, trying to forget the acute pain in her head and back. She was aware of shapes moving in the darkness, intense whispering, but she could not tell if the sounds were real or simply part of the remarkable dreams she had been having. Pulling her shawl closer to her, she hunkered on the floor and fell back into a sleep so deep it was close to unconsciousness.

Sometime near dawn, Nora awoke again, this time because of an urgent need to find a relief station. Barely remembering where she was, she half walked, half crawled up the aisle of the empty train and out onto the platform. When she crept down from the train, her feet slipped out from under her and she went down, floundering in the dirt for a moment. She pushed herself to a sitting position. She needed to find water . . . and a place to rest. She could not make herself move. Nora lay down for what she intended to be only a moment.

Mikal Ritter started awake. Cocking his head to one side, he listened. Yes, there it was again. Far off in the distance he could hear the shrill whistle of a train. Turning over, Mikal looked at the face of his sleeping wife. When he reached up to gently touch a lock of her thick brown hair, she opened her eyes, smiling.

"I've always loved that," she said sleepily.

"What is that, *mein shatz*?"

"When *you* are the first thing I see in the morning." She reached for him, snuggling close.

Far off in the distance, a train whistle sounded. Karyn Ritter sighed. "The end of the dream." Kissing her husband on the chin, she said, "You had better get going."

Mikal sat up reluctantly. Flinging his long legs over the side of the bed, he quickly pulled on his overalls, fastening only one strap while he poured water from the pitcher on the washstand into a bowl. He plunged his hands into the water, splashing his face and running his hands over his long mane of black hair. As he pulled on his red plaid shirt, he padded across the hotel room to the window and looked out. "Perhaps it will be cooler today."

Karyn sat up in bed, leaning her forehead on her knees. She reminded him. "If you don't like the weather, stay another day—it will probably change." She slid out of bed and pulled her simple cotton dress over her head.

Standing before the small mirror over the washstand, she wrapped her long dark hair about her head.

Mikal reached from behind to lay one giant hand across his wife's abdomen.

Karyn put both of her hands over her husband's. "I think we have a boy this time, Mikal." She arched one eyebrow at him and said playfully, "Perhaps even two, if God answers my prayers."

Mikal nuzzled her ear. "I will get the team."

When Mikal entered the livery next to the hotel, the first thing he saw was the great black head of his Percheron stallion thrust over the edge of the stall. It was as if the horse were looking for him. At the sight of Mikal, he whickered softly, nodding his head up and down.

"Yes, Midnight, yes. I heard it, too. The train arrives. Time to get to the station."

Mikal reached out to pat the velvet-soft nose of the gigantic horse. He fed the team their morning ration of grain before leading them out of their stalls.

As Mikal worked at harnessing the team to his farm wagon, the grizzled owner of the livery stable clomped in.

Patting Midnight on the rump, he asked Mikal, "You going to be hauling from here often? I'll let the word out if you want to offer thisun' at stud from time to time. He's a fine one. Fellers would come a far piece to breed him."

Mikal shook his head. "Thank you, but I am only here to do a favor for an old friend. The railroad sent an important shipment here instead of leaving it on the train for Millersburg. They finally located it, but it had been unloaded and delivered somewhere farther north. My friend's wife thought they could not wait for the railroad to right the problem. I offered to come this far and haul it to help keep the peace in his house."

Jake nodded knowingly. "When the missus ain't happy, a man's got no peace." He spit out a stream of tobacco juice. "That's the reason I'm still single. No woman's gonna keep me from enjoyin' my cigar when the sun goes down."

Jake walked to the front of the stable and slid the two gigantic doors open, creating a wide berth for Mikal to lead his young team through. Mikal climbed up on the wagon seat and headed for the hotel to find Karyn waiting by the front door.

The bright morning sun promised a warm day. Helping his wife up beside him, Mikal turned the team west and headed for the train station to wait for the new arrival. It had been promised that the misplaced load of goods for Cay Miller's store would be on board. The train was pulling in when Mikal rounded the corner from the hotel. Helping Karyn down from the wagon, Mikal encouraged her to wait inside the station while he drove the wagon down the tracks to the train car. "I should not be long," he said.

Karyn found a seat inside the station, glancing over at the half-dozen passengers who were waiting to board the train. As she watched, a young woman came in from the side of the station near the train tracks. She seemed to be headed for the ticket window, but suddenly she stumbled and crashed to the floor.

Some time after Nora had fallen asleep in the dirt the night before, something had awakened her. Through the waves of nausea that flowed over her she had realized that she must not stay where she was. Half crawling, she had managed to get up onto the station platform where she collapsed on a bench that sat just outside the locked doorway to the station. She spent the night there. In the morning, she felt more miserable and sick than ever.

Finally, someone unlocked the door from the inside. After a few moments, Nora willed herself to get up and go inside. She would go to the ticket window and beg them to let her wire Elise or maybe Dr. Allbright. Perhaps she could find out if her bag had been found on the train she had left. She tried to think clearly, but she was so very ill—she felt herself waver and fall.

A woman's voice pierced the fog about her. There was a hand on her shoulder. More hands pulled her upright and then half carried her back to a bench.

Blinking and squinting against the sunlight coming in the station window, Nora stared up into dark brown eyes. She realized that the sweet voice she was hearing must belong to those eyes. The voice was asking her something—something about where she was going.

Nora forced herself to concentrate. Where was she going? "Millersburg," she mumbled.

"Millersburg!" Karyn said.

"She got on the wrong train in Grand Island," someone was saying. "At least that was what she claimed. She didn't have a ticket. Said it must be in her bag on the other train."

Nora's head was clearing. She recognized the same conductor from the night before.

The conductor said defensively, "I figured if she showed up this morning we could wire Millersburg. You know, to see if anyone found her bag—or asked about her."

Karyn's voice had a hard edge to it as she asked, "And where did she spend the night?"

"I don't know. In the hotel, I guess."

Karyn asked, "You left a sick woman alone? Knowing that she had no bag and no money, you left her *alone*?" She was angry. Her dark eyes blazing, she glared at the uncaring young man. "How could she have stayed at the hotel?

Do they give rooms without cost? And what if she had been seriously ill. She could have died, all alone, here in the train station!"

"Now see here, lady." The conductor raised his voice angrily. "I'm not paid to be nursemaid to every passenger on the train. I'm just the conductor, and—"

"—and if you wish to continue being the conductor, you will lower your voice and speak with respect when you are talking to my wife."

The conductor wheeled about. The retort in his mind died, as he came face-to-face with the buttons of a red flannel shirt. Looking up into the man's icy blue eyes, the conductor swallowed hard. "I only meant—"

"Yes," Mikal said quietly. "I know what you meant." He tipped his hat to the man. "We will take care of the young lady. Good-bye."

The conductor hurried toward his departing train.

Mikal knelt on one knee next to where Karyn sat. She explained, "She was to go to Millersburg."

Mikal said to Nora, "You must come with us. We are from Millersburg. I am Mikal Ritter." He turned to look at Karyn. "And this is my wife, Karyn. We came to Loup City on an errand for our friends, the Millers. We would be happy if you would come with us."

Nora nodded, blinking back grateful tears. She half whispered to Karyn, "Thank you. I didn't know what I was going to do."

"Sometimes God answers our prayers even before we say them," Karyn said, patting Nora on the shoulder. "Do you have friends in Millersburg?"

"Dr. Allbright. I was to stay with her and then talk to a Mrs. Miller about—"

Karyn interrupted her. "You are the new milliner! *Ach*, such a way to meet. Mrs. Miller is my sister."

Mikal stood up. "I will ask the ticketmaster to wire Cay so that he knows what has happened. He can tell Dr.

Allbright so that she will not be concerned." He strode away.

"You have not had any breakfast," Karyn said. "Can we get you something before we leave? We have plenty of food in the grub box in the wagon, but you should have something now."

"Oh, no. That's all right," Nora said, shaking her head.

Karyn asked, "You said that you have been ill?"

Nora described her symptoms, finishing with, "I'm afraid it's the ague. I feel better now, but if it's like my pap's was when I was little, it could come back."

"I know," Karyn said and nodded. "Mikal suffered terribly last year." She smiled, "And I know just what to do, so you don't have to worry. Wait here."

Karyn followed her husband to the ticket window. Nora watched her go, marveling as Mikal bent low to speak to her. The man was fully eight inches taller than his wife. Nora had never seen such a giant of a man. He bent his ear to his wife, and then, reaching into his pocket, pulled out a leather coin purse. He counted some change out to Karyn, kissing her on the cheek as she turned to go. She left the station while Mikal turned back to the ticket window.

A sharp whistle sounded, announcing the departure of the train. Mikal came back to where Nora sat. "I have sent word that you are with us. They wired back that your bag was found on the train in Millersburg last evening. Dr. Allbright has it. All is well."

Karyn came hurrying back into the train station, bearing a mug of hot tea and a warm biscuit.

"I'll go and make certain the load is packed properly," Mikal said.

When Nora and Karyn exited the train station, Nora saw that Mikal had rearranged the load in the wagon, to make room for a narrow bed of comforters just behind the wagon seat. He had even created a pillow by tying a quilt into a roll with a length of twine.

Nora sat in the wagon box, leaning against the side where Karyn only had to look down and back over her right shoulder to talk to her. As they rumbled out of Loup City, Karyn said, "We travel until noon. Then we will give the team a brief rest. We will sleep one night on the way, and tomorrow you will be in Millersburg."

CHAPTER 18

Love Never Fails

I have loved thee with an everlasting love:
therefore with lovingkindness have I drawn thee.
Jeremiah 31:3

"Don't be in such a hurry," Dr. Allbright scolded. "You've only been here for a little over a week. The ague can be tricky. Folks think they are well and then have a relapse of more chills and fever."

Karyn was sitting at the foot of Nora's bed. "You listen to the doctor," she said, patting Nora's legs. She pushed herself awkwardly up off the bed with a little "oof." Laying her arm across her belly, she said, "I like having company. Mikal doesn't worry so to take building jobs in town because you are here." Karyn went to the door of Nora's room. "Better to stay a little longer than to just begin and get sick again."

"But what if Mrs. Miller gives up on me? I don't want her renting my shop space to someone else."

Karyn shook her head. "I know Sophie barks and growls, but she only means to show that you are needed. She has waited this long for a milliner. She will wait a little longer."

Dr. Allbright agreed. "Mrs. Miller doesn't care when you open as long as she has enough notice to advertise in the paper."

"But I'll need time to make some samples before she does that."

"If you can tell me what you need, I'll bring it out when I come at the end of the week," Maude said. She looked at Karyn. "I'll need to be checking on you then, Mrs. Ritter."

"Maybe by then you'll be checking on a new baby, as well," Karyn said hopefully. She nodded at Nora. "Mollie and May are making you a surprise. Shall we share it while Dr. Allbright is here?"

Nora sat up. "I'd love it. Tell them we'll be right out."

"No, no," Karyn said, motioning for Nora to stay put. "You wait. They will come for you."

When Karyn disappeared from the doorway, Dr. Allbright said, "Having you here keeps Mrs. Ritter's mind off her own troubles. I see improvement in her mood since you arrived."

At Nora's questioning look, Dr. Allbright nodded. "She's a very strong woman, but she has been unusually concerned for this baby. Sons are important out here."

Nora nodded. "I know. But Mr. Ritter doesn't seem the kind to—"

"No," Dr. Allbright said. "He's a rare thing—a man who truly adores his wife. I don't think Mr. Ritter would care if Karyn gave birth to kittens, as long as she was well. She puts the pressure on herself. She wants to give her husband the one thing only she can give—a way for his name to continue."

Dr. Allbright sighed. "The older I get, the less I understand. So often it seems that it's the people who trust in God the most who receive the least from him." She shook her head. "And yet even when they are denied what they want, they are more determined than ever to serve the God they believe in."

Two pairs of incredibly blue eyes peeked around the doorframe. Two girlish voices called out, "Please join the Misses Ritter for tea, served in the parlor."

May and Mollie had created a parlor in one corner of the room that served as kitchen, dining room, and living area by setting up a serving table and five chairs. A lace tablecloth had been spread, and a fine china tea set awaited the twins' guests for tea.

"Please be seated," May said, holding Nora's chair for her. Mollie did the same for Dr. Allbright, while Karyn set a basket of steaming muffins on the table.

Mikal appeared at the doorway. "I believe I was commanded by the Princesses May and Mollie to be present at tea," he said. He bent down and held both arms out. "May I escort the ladies to their places?"

"Oh, Papa," the girls said in unison, skipping to the doorway.

May and Mollie served tea as only four-year-olds could. A pat of butter flipped onto the floor when May attempted to butter a muffin. Tea was spilled, and muffins crumbled. Laughter and love reigned, and all in all, the event was a great success.

Thinking of it later, Nora shed bittersweet tears. She was learning something from the Ritters. She was learning that she was lonely.

After Dr. Allbright left, Karyn asked Nora to help her unpack the contents of one of the trunks that served as a night table in May and Mollie's room.

"Mikal has already taken the trunk outside. I don't want things smelling musty. It's time they were aired out."

While May and Mollie swept the floor in the house, Karyn and Nora went out back where Mikal had strung a clothesline from the back corner of the house to the windmill and back again.

Karyn opened the trunk and removed a sheet of tissue paper to reveal a layer of infant's clothes, each item beautifully made, each item unused. There were two identical blue knit caps and two pairs of booties lying atop two sacques trimmed with several rows of wide, handmade lace. Karyn picked them up and handed them to Nora, explaining, "We have two sons. Over there." She nodded toward the ridge. "You can't see it from here, but walking up the ridge you find it. Beneath that tree. A little white fence. That's where my boys are." Karyn's voice trembled with emotion.

She pulled two indigo blue-and-white crib quilts from the trunk. Hugging the quilts to her, she wiped away tears, as she said, "Of course I know the boys are not really there. They are with our blessed Savior." She sighed, handing Nora one small quilt while she put its twin on the line. "I am so thankful their little bodies are nearby, where I can visit them."

Karyn added softly, "I have much to be thankful for. Mikal loves his daughters." She sighed. "But a farmer needs sons. Every day I ask God for sons for Mikal."

Nora marveled at Karyn's sweet acceptance of her circumstances. Pap had allowed the loss of his wife to destroy his life. As far as Nora knew, Pap had never visited his wife's grave. And instead of taking comfort in his children, he had treated them cruelly. Not one day had passed when Nora was not aware that her very existence caused Pap pain. Seeing Karyn's sadness, yet knowing that she had not allowed her grief to block out the light in her life gave Nora an odd feeling. She began to think that perhaps she was not responsible for all of Pap's misery after all. Maybe Pap could have acted differently. If only—if only what? Nora wondered. What was it that enabled Karyn to bury two children and still smile and laugh and sing?

After the trunk's contents were hung out to air, Karyn called to her daughters, who had been playing nearby. "It's time for you to do your stint at sewing, girls."

May pouted, "I don't want to today, Mama. Can't I have just this one day to play? The wind isn't blowing and"—she smiled prettily—"I'll pick you a bouquet of goldenrod. And take some up the hill." She nodded toward where Karyn had said her babies were buried.

Karyn chuckled knowingly. "That's a very clever attempt at getting out of your work, May. You can collect flowers later. Now, we sew."

May sighed deeply, but she headed for the house.

Karyn called after her, "You and Mollie get your little baskets and meet Nora and I at the front. We can sit there in the shade."

Karyn had cut squares of fabric for the girls to stitch together into nine-patch blocks. "I have them sew a little every day," she explained. "Next year they will begin knitting."

"Did your mama make you sew?" Mollie asked Nora, stabbing angrily at the fabric in her lap. Her little-girl fingers struggled clumsily to hold the needle.

"No," Nora answered. "I didn't have a mama. There was only Pap and my brother, Will."

Both girls looked up, their eyes wide. "You didn't have a mama?"

Karyn interrupted. "Girls, it is not polite to ask so many questions of our guest."

"Here, Mollie, let me show you something that might help." Nora reached down and demonstrated how to make a knot at the end of the thread. "It doesn't have to be so big as you think. Try it." Nora snipped the knot she had just made from the end of the thread. Mollie tried Nora's method, succeeded, and smiled triumphantly.

Karyn hauled her mending basket outside and lifted out a girl's pinafore. "I need to take one of the tucks out along the hem of this, but first—" She disappeared back inside the house. Presently she reappeared, with a blue wool dress thrown over her arm. Her right hand held an outdated hat. "I thought perhaps you could make a few suggestions," she began. "Something I could do to update these."

Mattie looked up sharply. "But Papa said you were to have a new dress for winter, Mama," she protested.

"I know what Papa said," Karyn replied. "But I don't need a new dress. This one suits me."

"We're getting a new house, and you're getting a new dress. That's what Papa said." The little voice was stubborn.

"We must be thankful, Mollie, for all the blessings God has already given us. And we must not be greedy for more. The new house will come in time, but not this year." Karyn smiled at Nora and shook her head. She sat down, still holding her dress and hat. "Mikal dreams of a new house instead of the soddy." She sighed. "But the last two years have not been so good. God gives us perfect weather and abundant harvest, but the railroad takes the profits in shipping fees."

While Nora inspected the worn dress, Karyn repeated, as if reminding herself, "Already we have so much more than when I first came." Hat in hand, she turned to look at the soddy. "When Mikal brought me here, there was just the one little window and the parlor. It was our kitchen, our bedroom—everything. I was nineteen, and I had left Germany with visions of a white cottage in a meadow. Mikal's tiny house made of dirt was quite a shock."

Nora said, "I don't think I would have stayed."

"Almost I did not," was the answer. "But then—" Karyn shrugged, blushing. "I learned to be content. One year Mikal built the first bedroom. When the girls came, we built the trundle." Nora had helped put the girls to bed one night and seen that Mikal had built a special little bed for his girls that rolled out from beneath the high spool bed where their parents slept. She had thought how nice it was for them to be so near their parents where they knew they were safe and loved.

Karyn continued, "When the boys were coming, Mikal added a second bedroom." She said softly, "But then we didn't need it." She smiled at Nora. "So that is how we have a guest room for visitors." Karyn went on, "When Mikal built the little lean-to on the back, it made things so much easier for me. Now I have a place to store my garden tools and the washtub, and I don't have to walk so far to the well."

She absentmindedly ran her finger down the row of buttons on her well-worn dress. "Mikal is always speaking of a new house. But we manage fine just as things are. He needs a new team, a bigger barn. And another corncrib." Karyn sighed. "Life is hard, but God is good."

Nora was inspecting the dress. "The fabric on these buttons is wearing very thin. If we could replace them, and perhaps add a lace inset here—" She indicated the sleeve of the dress. She took up the hat. "Feathers are popular this year."

Karyn was enthusiastic. "Mikal can go hunting. I'll tell him we need something for stew that has beautiful, long tail feathers." She laughed. "It's a blessing to have God send me such a talented friend."

By the time May and Mollie had finished their sewing stint, their mother and Nora were hard at work ripping seams and removing buttons. When Karyn left to prepare their dinner, Nora remained outside, humming as she worked on her friend's dress. *Friend.* She paused with needle in hand while she tasted the word. With a sudden rush of happiness she realized that yes, Karyn Ritter was becoming her friend.

After dinner that evening, May and Mollie showed their father their sewing. Mikal dutifully praised their progress, pulling the girls into his lap for a hug.

Mollie spoke up. "Mama says we're not going to have a new house this year. Does that mean the new baby can sleep with us when he comes?"

Mikal looked at his wife, who busied herself clearing the table as she spoke cheerfully, "A new team and a bigger barn. And the second corncrib. We need those things more than a new house."

Mikal raked his hand through his hair in a gesture that expressed at once frustration and resignation. "You are right, of course. The house will have to wait. Again." His shoulders slumped wearily. "Perhaps some of the railroad barons should descend from their gilded mansions just long enough to visit our little soddy . . . maybe then it would make a difference in their shipping fees."

Karyn looked at her husband. "Not one of those gilded mansions holds more love than our home, Mikal."

The girls scrambled off their father's lap, and Mikal began to help his wife clear the dishes from the table.

Nora spoke up. "Please, Herr Ritter. Let me do this. The fresh air is good for me. Dr. Allbright said so. You two sit and enjoy the sunset together."

"Thank you, Nora." Karyn turned to Mollie and May. "All right, girls. Time for bed."

Mikal hauled the washtub filled with dirty dishes outside and set it on a bench near the well. He pumped cold water into a cooking pot and said, "I will bring this out as soon as it is hot." He ducked beneath the porch overhang and disappeared inside.

While Nora waited for Mikal to bring heated washwater outside, she made her way up the ridge at the back of the house to where a cottonwood tree marked two little graves. A short black-iron fence surrounded the little plot. Set inside were two small stones, atop which rested a stone lamb, curled up as if asleep. Beneath each lamb, the inscription read, *Onser Liebling*. There were no names, only the dates *December 27* and *31, 1885. She lost two babies within a few days of each other. Right after Christmas*. Nora shivered and headed back for the house.

The sun was setting as Nora finished the dishes. She felt tired, but happy. Her strength was returning. In the remaking of Karyn's best dress and hat, she had found a way to repay her new friend for her care. Soon she would be in Millersburg, with her own shop, and a tiny room that was all her own. How wonderful it would be.

When Nora carried her stack of clean dishes back inside the soddy, Mikal had settled his huge frame into a creaking rocker by the window. He had lit the lamp that sat on the broad windowsill and was reading a news-paper, his profile outlined against the backdrop of golden light and the red geraniums blooming in the window.

Nora sat nearby, removing old trim from Karyn's hat, and contemplating how she would redesign it.

From the bedroom, Mollie's voice could be heard begging, "*Please*, Mama. Just one story. One very little story."

"It's too late, girls."

"But, Mama, we always sleep so very, very, much better when we have heard a story."

There was a pause, and then Karyn began, "Once, a long, long time ago, there was a giant."

"Was he a very big giant, Mama?"

"Yes, Mollie. He was very big indeed."

"And did he have dark, flashing eyes, and white hair, and—"

"Mollie, be quiet," May snapped. "It's Mama's story. You always interrupt."

"As it happens," Karyn said quietly, "this giant had black hair. And flashing blue eyes."

"Black hair like Papa?"

"Just like Papa," Karyn answered.

Nora saw Mikal look up from his paper.

Karyn continued the story. "He was very tall, and his black hair was long and scraggly. His eyes flashed in such a way that he frightened anyone who saw him. They did not know that the giant only growled and acted fierce because he was sad, for he was very, very lonely. One day, the giant went on a journey to the mountains. On his journey he captured a young girl and carried her home to be his wife. He brought her to his hut made of dirt.

"The girl was very strong-willed and very high-spirited. She refused to let the giant know that she feared him. But every night, when the giant slept, the girl went to the doorway of the little house where he kept her, and looked at the stars, and away toward the mountains where she had once lived. She longed for her home, because although the giant treated her well and gave her gifts, he never told her that he loved her.

"At last, the girl became so lonely that she ran away. But as she ran, a terrible thing happened. A prairie fire came rushing from where the sun rose each morning. It encircled the girl and rushed off toward the giant's home. Miraculously, the fire passed her by and did not harm her.

"Far, far away, the giant awakened and saw the fire. Immediately, he ran to the house where he kept his girl. But she was gone. He looked toward the east, toward the mountains, and he knew that the girl had run away. Terrified that she had been caught in the fire, he jumped on his best horse and charged swiftly across the blackened earth, in search of his girl.

"When at last he found her, he jumped from his horse, his eyes blazing with light. Thinking that the giant was angry with her, the girl cringed with fear. But then, a great tear slid down the giant's cheek. He clasped her to his breast, hugging her so tightly, she could hardly breathe.

"And then, the girl knew that the giant loved her. She went back to the hut of mud, and together the giant and the girl lived happily.

"When the girl grew older and had children of her own, she would often tell them the story of the giant and his girl, and she always ended the story this way: 'I grew up where there were mountains, and God took me to a country where there were no mountains, but He gave me mountains of blessings and mountains of love, which are better than any mountain made only of earth and grass. I am content.

"'I grew up where there were clear, sparkling rivers, and cool, clean lakes. God took me to a country where there are only small springs, and narrow ribbons of muddy water crisscrossing the parched earth. But He gave me the knowledge of Jesus, who is the living water and quenches the thirst of men's hearts. I am content.

"'I grew up where there were many, many, people. God took me to a country where there were few people. For weeks at a time, I saw no one, except a fearsome giant. But the giant has become my best friend, and my dearest love, and I am content.'"

Karyn stopped talking abruptly. There was a brief pause before she spoke again. "And now, my darlings, you must go to sleep, or I will have *our* giant come in here and—"

"And what, Mama," Mollie teased, "*hug* us to death?"

"Just so," Karyn retorted.

Nora bent her head to hide the tears in her eyes.

The girls murmured their good nights, and Karyn came back into the room. Mikal laid his paper aside. He got up and went to her. Placing a hand on each of her shoulders, he stared down at her for a moment. Then, he dropped his hands to his sides and went outside into the moonlight. Karyn followed him.

Nora bent to her needlework, feeling strangely embarrassed. When she finally laid it aside and retired to her room, she lay awake for a long time, trying to reconcile what she thought she knew of men, and what she had seen of Mikal Ritter.

Pap's behavior had convinced Nora that most farmers valued their children only insofar as they provided free labor. But then she met Mikal Ritter, concerned that his wife was working too hard, gentle with his daughters, never failing to give them their nightly "horsey-ride" by crouching on the floor so they could clamor up onto his back.

While Goldie's clientele had varied widely, Nora had come to regard them all as tragic players in a poorly scripted play. By day, many of the "regulars" were admired citizens. One or two enjoyed the power to mold city affairs after their image. But by night, these men succumbed to fluttering eyelashes and rouged lips like any other weakling. Nora had seen them behave so ridiculously she had to bite her lips to keep from laughing at them. She had finally concluded that true manhood was a clever myth created by someone with a tremendous sense of humor. Power and self-assurance, Nora decided, were only a veneer pulled over the truth that all men were equally weak and vulnerable. But then she met Mikal Ritter.

Karyn and Mikal came back from their walk. Through the doorway, Nora saw Karyn turn toward her husband. He put his arms around her, and she leaned against him, nestling her head against his shoulder as they tiptoed into the bedroom.

Nora lay awake for a long time, trying to push the image of Greyson Chandler from her mind. She relived the last day she had seen him. The day Iris was running to meet him in Grand Island . . . throwing her arms about him . . . their boarding a train . . . together. Nora sighed.

Unlike Greyson Chandler, Mikal Ritter didn't make pretty speeches about finding God and living for others. He just did it. The realization that lasting goodness and happy marriages existed left Nora feeling depressed. If true goodness existed, and if it gave the kind of happiness the Ritters had, Nora wanted it. But she had no idea where to get it.

Interlude—1998

Reagan and Irene were baking Christmas cookies at Irene's one frigid Saturday in December when a red Dodge Ram drove up the drive.

Reagan looked out the kitchen window in time to see Noah climb out of the cab and stretch. He leaned back in the truck to retrieve his coffee cup.

"You didn't tell me you were expecting Noah." Reagan hastened to put down a cookie sheet and brush her hair back out of her face.

Irene was sitting at the table giving frosting smiles to row upon row of gingerbread people. "Oh, didn't I?"

"Irene Peale." Reagan's tone was accusing.

"What?" Irene said with mock innocence.

"What are you up to?"

"Me? I don't know what you mean. Goodness, girl, can't a woman's nephew come to visit without causing a stir?" Irene gave the cone of frosting in her hands an expert twist. Her soft blue eyes twinkled as she said, "You might want to freshen your lipstick, dear."

"Right," Reagan said. She pulled her apron off and disappeared up the back stairway just as Noah reached the back door.

"Is that Reagan's 'bug' out front?" she heard him ask. Then, she forced herself to go on up the stairs and into the bathroom. She inspected her "American-girl-no-makeup-today" face in the mirror. *I'm going to kill Irene. She could have at least warned me. I don't even have my makeup bag with me.*

Reagan lingered as long as she could upstairs. Finally, she descended to the kitchen, where Noah was sprawled in a corner chair, his long legs stretched out before him, a pile of cookies on the table. He greeted Reagan while he chewed.

Reagan said hello and then looked at Irene. "Should I make some fresh coffee?"

Irene moved to get up. "No. Come and sit. I'll make the coffee." She pushed herself to a standing position and headed for the stove, dragging one foot a little.

"Aunt Rini," Noah said firmly, "sit back down. In fact, both of the 'cookie queens' should sit and relax. *I'll* make the coffee."

"Listen, sonny-boy," Irene retorted. "I'm showing off, so don't ruin the moment. It wasn't all that long ago I couldn't make coffee—at least not while standing on my own two feet. So just sit there and watch."

Irene moved slowly across the kitchen to the sink, filling the glass coffee carafe with water, pouring the water into the top of her drip-o-lator. She reached to a shelf above her head for a box of filters. "Watch this, Noah," she said. "Do you have any idea how many weeks I spent in therapy learning to reach above my head again?" Inserting a filter in the coffeemaker, she added grounds and then flipped the "on" switch with a flourish and a bow. She made her way back across the kitchen and sat down. "You can pour when it's ready. I know I am truly amazing," she teased, "but I can't be trusted with a tray of cups filled with hot coffee."

While the coffee was brewing, Noah described his latest project at the farm. He had plans to restore an ancient windmill dragged out of a nearby field. "Judd Hayes up at Ansley said he'd come down and help me get it all hooked up in the spring. Right now, it's just lying out back in the weeds." He went on. "With the cold, I haven't been able to accomplish much else outside. But I'm almost finished getting all the old laths out of the rest of the rooms. Wiring and drywall next. New windows next spring," Noah said. "You wouldn't believe how much cold air blows in around those windows."

"Oh, wouldn't I?" Irene said. "I remember as a little girl, lying in bed at night when I visited Oma and Opa. I swear I saw snow come in around the windows more than once. There were times when ice formed nearly a half-inch thick on the windowpanes."

"Aunt Rini said you're trying to do some research connected to Custer County," Noah said to Reagan. He looked over at the coffeepot, got up and poured coffee for them. Before sitting down, he picked a half-dozen more cookies from the cooling rack.

"That's the absolute end, young man. Those are promised to the church for the children's program tomorrow evening," Irene scolded.

"Tell me about your research," Noah asked, settling back in his chair.

Reagan answered, "There was a tin of buttons in one of the rooms we cleaned out last month." Reagan explained the charm string, without the added folklore. "Irene said it came to Karyn Ritter from a milliner in Millersburg. Apparently they were good friends. There isn't much to go on."

Irene added, "When Reagan sorted the buttons, she found a business card. I'm certain Oma told me Nora had a shop in Millersburg. But the business card said she was working here in Lincoln."

"Have you checked the city directory?" Noah asked.

"Yes," Reagan answered. "Thornhill Dressers was in business from 1880 to after the turn of the century. But I never found the name Nora O'Dell. I found an advertisement in the newspaper for the dressers, but again no reference to Nora."

"What about the Sittler's Index? It would tell you if her name ever appeared in the newspaper."

Reagan looked surprised. "You sound like you've done historical research before."

Noah shrugged. "I'm just learning. But I've been to the archives here in Lincoln a few times. They have some terrific pioneer records from Custer County." He took the head off a gingerbread person, chewing while he talked. "I could help you do some research if you want." He swallowed. "I was going down there tomorrow anyway."

"Sure," Reagan said.

Irene nudged her. Imitating Reagan's voice she said, "'Oh, right, Irene, that's just how all hunks dream of spending their Saturdays, poking around the historical society archives looking for information about dead people.'"

Reagan blushed furiously and jumped up to rinse out her coffee cup. From the sink, she said, "Thanks, Irene. I was really hoping you'd embarrass me at least once today."

Noah got up and crossed to where she was standing. He leaned against the counter while she filled the sink with water and began to scrub cookie sheets. He leaned over and nudged her with his shoulder. "I said the same thing a couple of weeks ago on the phone. 'Oh, right, Aunt Rini, that's just how all babes want to spend their Saturdays, poking around the library looking for information on dead people. What a great idea for a first date.'" He walked to the back door. "I've got to get my backpack out of the truck. Do we have a date or not?"

Reagan didn't turn around. "The archive opens at ten o'clock. I'll meet you there."

She turned toward Irene. "And you're coming, too, right?"

"Wouldn't miss it," Irene said.

"Runza® sandwiches for supper, Aunt Rini?" Noah called from the back porch.

"Only if you earn it by packing all these cookies up and delivering them over to the church for me."

"Deal." The screen door slammed.

Reagan whirled around. "I-am-going-to-kill-you!" she hissed at Irene. "I've never been more embarrassed in my life!"

"Oh, settle down, Ray-ray," Irene said. "I'd have to be deaf and blind not to see the attraction between you two. I'm not getting any younger. I don't have time to wait for young love to blossom freely. If I can give it a jump-start, I'm going to do it."

Reagan finished the last cookie sheet and removed her apron. "I'm going home and try to resurrect my self-respect."

"No you're not," Irene said firmly. "We had a date tonight and you're going to help me make Runza® sandwiches and then we're watching *North By Northwest*. Just because you have a hot date with my nephew tomorrow does not give you permission to stand me up tonight, young lady!"

Noah came back in and lumbered up the back stairs to the bedroom that had been his since he was a child spending his summers with Aunt Rini and Uncle Henry. He returned and began to help Irene pack cookies into wax-paper-lined shoeboxes, then loaded them into the truck and headed out to deliver them to the church.

While he was gone, Reagan browned hamburger in a skillet, adding onion and then leaving Irene to add her "secret spices" while she kneaded bread dough. She rolled out the dough on the kitchen island, cutting it into rectangles. Irene spooned the ground beef filling in a long line down the center of each rectangle of dough. Then, the women rolled the dough into what resembled long hoagie-style buns. After a few minutes in the oven, the buns began to rise, filling the kitchen with the aroma of fresh bread and spices.

Noah returned with a grocery sack in one arm. He pulled six pints of Ben and Jerry's ice cream from the sack, explaining, "I couldn't decide on a flavor."

The three spent the rest of the evening in Irene's "informal parlor." They ate hot Runza® sandwiches off of TV trays while they watched Cary Grant escape from an airplane intent on dive-bombing him. By the time he was climbing the face of Mt. Rushmore, they were sitting side by side on the couch, eating Ben and Jerry's straight from the carton with a spoon.

Noah stole a bite of Reagan's "New York Super Chunk Fudge."

"Watch it, mister," she warned. "I get very hostile when it comes to sharing chocolate."

"I'll remember that," he whispered back.

By the end of the movie, he was sitting so that his shoulder touched hers.

"Got it!" Noah leaned on one elbow so that he could see around the side of his microfilm reader to where Reagan and Irene sat. They got up and came to look over Noah's shoulder. "There," Noah said, pointing at a few tiny lines of type. "Read that."

Miss Nora O'Dell invites the ladies of Millersburg to inspect her new line of millinery goods, just arrived from the East. Fair prices and the latest styles. At Miller's Emporium, corner of Main and First.

Reagan patted him on the shoulder. "Good work, Sherlock. At least we know she was in Millersburg."

"You know," Noah said, "maybe she wasn't in Lincoln long enough to appear in the city directory."

Irene added, "Maybe she trained at Thornhill Dressers. Then she moved to Millersburg to have her own business."

"But why Millersburg?" Reagan asked.

Noah shrugged. "The railroad arrived in 1887. That would have made it a 'boomtown,' at least for a while. Maybe she was a real 'go-getter.' The 'entrepreneurial spirit' and all that."

"I wish they had a city directory for Millersburg! I can't imagine reading every issue of every *Millersburg Republican*, just hoping for some mention of one business!"

One of the research librarians walked by. "Excuse me for butting in, but since you know the address, you could check *Sanborn's* and at least know how long the dry goods store stayed at that location. And if a millinery shop pops up right next door, it would be a good guess that it was Miss O'Dell expanding."

"*Sanborn's*?" Reagan asked.

The librarian explained, "*Sanborn's Fire Maps* have been made since the 1800s. They provided a schematic of cities for the fire departments. They show the location of businesses and details like type of construction, location of windows—all kinds of things." She said, "I have to help someone check a census record, but if you'll meet me at that big table across the room, I'll be over in just a minute."

"Census records," Noah said. "I know how to check those. You go ahead and look at *Sanborn's*. I'll check for Miss O'Dell in the census."

Noah found Miss O'Dell in the census, and Reagan and Irene found Miller's Emporium on the *Sanborn* maps. They wondered aloud what might be available in the Custer County museum.

"You don't dare travel to Custer County in December," Noah warned, "unless you're willing to get snowed in."

He teased, "Although that would make for an interesting second date."

That evening Irene called Reagan. "What about it? You want to brave Custer County in winter?"

"I don't think so, Irene. There's still a lot I can do here. I have five books on the history of buttons piled on my desk right now." She started to say something more, but decided against it.

"What aren't you telling me?" Irene said quietly.

Reagan took a deep breath. She shifted the phone from one hand to the other. "Things are going too fast. At least from my end."

"But I thought you wanted to learn all you could," Irene answered.

"I'm not talking about the research."

"I know that."

Reagan heard Irene sigh before she said, "What *is* it about young people these days? So much caution. Henry proposed to me after our second date, and we were married for over fifty years."

"That's what scares me," Reagan said. "If Noah asked me, I might say yes. That's stupid. I don't know him at all."

"You know he likes ice cream, he's crazy about history, he's kind to old women. What's to know?"

Reagan blurted out, "Look, your nephew is the hottest thing to come my way in a long, long time. But he has a history, and so do I. And mine says that I have to know that a man's relationship with God is personal. I know he said something to you about getting things straight with God, but I need to know exactly what that means."

"Ask him."

"I will. But I have to get my head on straight first. It's too much, too soon. I've never had anything like this happen to me before. Frankly, it's scary. I feel like there's this giant magnet pulling me toward him . . . I just want to make certain God is the source of the magnetic field. But before I do that, I have to make certain that if his answers aren't the right ones, I can walk away. Right now, tonight, the way I'm feeling, I'm not certain I could do that."

"All right. I give up. For now. But I reserve the right to meddle in the very near future." Irene wished Reagan good night and hung up.

Fifteen minutes after she had hung up the phone, Noah Ritter arrived at Reagan's door. The moment she opened the door, he said, "Aunt Rini said to tell you that she didn't define 'very near future' when she said she'd be meddling. May I come in?"

Reagan shook her head. "I don't think that's a good idea."

"Then come for a ride with me. We'll drive around and look at Christmas lights or something."

Reagan shook her head again. "Sorry. My Sunday school kids are all in the children's program at church tonight. I need to be there."

He smiled. "Care if I come along?"

"You don't know when to give up, do you? I assume Irene told you every word I said."

"You assume correctly. And, no, I don't give up easily." He pulled on the bill of his ball cap as if it were a cowboy hat. "Haven't met any foxes like you up in Custer County, ma'am."

"What about the one in California?" Reagan blurted out. "I think her name was Angela."

Noah tilted his head and looked away for a moment. He pressed his lips tightly together and shook his head. "Let me take you to the children's program. Have coffee with me afterward. I'll tell you everything you want to know."

He put one hand on the doorframe and leaned against the door. "Look, Reagan. This is all moving pretty fast for me, too. The magnet isn't just pulling in one direction. I feel it, too. But does it have to be so difficult? Can't it be fun?" He raised one eyebrow and looked at her. "I mean, it's not often two such good-looking people strike up a relationship over microfilm and maps. I'd say it was meant to be, if you look at the evidence." He grinned. "And you did, after all, share your New York Super Chunk Fudge with me. That has to count for something."

"Stop being so blasted charming and get in here," Reagan ordered. She opened the door and headed off to the back of the house. "I'll get my coat. The program starts in fifteen minutes."

CHAPTER 19

A Child Is Born

Lo, children are an heritage of the LORD:
and the fruit of the womb is his reward.
Psalm 127:3

"*Push*, Mrs. Ritter, *push*!" Dr. Allbright sat at the foot of Karyn's bed, holding out her hands, urging her patient on. Nora stood beside Karyn, mopping her brow, feeling generally incompetent. She had offered to leave several times, but each time Karyn would gasp, "No, please, it is so much easier with you here."

Karyn had been in labor since early morning, and already it was near dark. She was exhausted. With each increasingly difficult contraction, she reached up to grab the headboard for leverage to push. Finally, with Dr. Allbright's urging, she yelled at the top of her lungs and forced her reluctant infant into the world. The baby cried, and Karyn's entire being lit up with joy.

"You have a son, Mrs. Ritter," Dr. Allbright said, swaddling the infant in a soft white towel before handing him to Nora and returning to stitching and disinfecting.

Karyn's German exclamations needed no translation. She held out both hands to take her newborn son, cuddling him close while tears streamed down her face.

Nora mumbled something about making a supper for them all. She headed for the doorway to call Mikal and the girls, but they were already running up the hill from the pond, where Mikal had taken the girls to look for baby ducklings.

Dr. Allbright came to the bedroom door just as Mikal arrived. "Congratulations, Mr. Ritter. You have a son."

"And my wife?" Mikal asked.

"Fine," Dr. Allbright assured him. She looked at Mollie and May with a smile. "In fact, you can all take one quick peek at him before I check him over. I'll leave you all alone to get acquainted without my intrusion. Bring him with you out to the kitchen later for a bath."

Mikal ducked his head and entered the bedroom, followed by his girls. He knelt by the bed, reaching out to stroke his wife's cheek and admire his son.

"What's his name?" Mollie wanted to know.

"Friedrich Mikal," Karyn said. "But you may call him Freddie."

"Mama," May said, stroking the back of the baby's hand. "Now we can use all the baby boy things from the trunk."

Karyn smiled, her eyes shining with happy tears. "Yes, *liebling*, now we can."

"No, we need *another* boy to use 'em all," Mollie said.

"Girls," Mikal interrupted. "One baby at a time, please. Let us enjoy this one before we ask God for another." He reached for the baby as he said to Karyn, "Go to sleep, little mother. He will want to eat soon enough." He bent to kiss Karyn and left the room with his son held against his chest, one giant hand supporting more than half the baby's body.

Dr. Allbright had prepared a tub of warm water in the kitchen. "Come here, girls," she beckoned. "You watch and then you can help Nora give Freddie his bath tomorrow." She slipped the baby out of his blanket and into the warm water. "See how he kicks and squeals," Dr. Allbright said. "That's good for him. It gives him strong lungs and muscles."

"Look how big his feet are!" Mikal exclaimed. "He will be a big boy."

"This is a child, Mr. Ritter, not a puppy," Dr. Allbright retorted, with mock sternness. "But you're right." She put the palm of her hand against one of Freddie's feet. The baby pushed back against her hand. "He does have good-sized feet. And strong legs."

Freddie quieted abruptly. "He likes it," Mollie said.

"I believe he does," Dr. Allbright said. "Sensible boy." But by the time Freddie had been bathed, diapered and dressed, he was squalling again.

May clamped her hands over her ears. "Does he have to yell so *loud*?" she wanted to know.

Mikal chucked her under the chin. "Little Freddie is not half so loud as you girls were—and think of it, your mama and I had to listen to two of you!"

Dr. Allbright took Freddie to his mother. Mikal emptied the dishpan that had served as a baby bathtub, and Nora set the table. She had cooked fried sausages and potatoes for supper. Watching the family sit down at the table with Dr. Allbright, she could hardly suppress a smile. Goldie would have been amazed at how quickly the family was devouring her cooking.

While Mikal hitched up Dr. Allbright's horse and buggy, Nora and she sat beneath the crude covering that jutted out over the front door of the soddy.

"I want to stay and help Mrs. Ritter with the new baby," Nora said, "but I think that as soon as she has recovered, I need to be on my way. Elise has been very understanding, but I don't want to take advantage of her patience. She needs to know if I'm going to be there for her busy season this fall or not."

"I think you're safely through with the ague," Dr. Allbright said. "I'll tell Mrs. Miller to expect you next week. You'll stay with me, of course."

After Dr. Allbright left for Millersburg, Mikal went to do his evening chores. Mollie and May were clearing the table when Nora went in to check on Karyn. She was asleep, her arm curved around Freddie, who slept with his tiny infant bottom up in the air. For some reason, Nora found herself blinking away tears. She turned away and hurried outside.

Mollie was standing on an overturned barrel by the well, pumping water into the washtub full of dirty dishes. May waited patiently, a dishrag in one hand and a bar of lye soap in the other. Down the hill, Nora could see Mikal forking hay over the corral fence. Everywhere she looked, Nora saw happiness and contentment. She thought ahead to Millersburg and her fledgling business in the corner of Miller's Emporium. She doubted that success as a milliner would ever give her the happiness that existed among the inhabitants of the soddy on Mikal Ritter's homestead.

"What are you saying!" Karyn said hotly. "You will insult me if you do such a thing. I thought we were friends."

"But I only want to repay you for your kindness," Nora was saying. "Heaven knows what would have happened to me if you had not found me that day in Loup City."

"Exactly," Karyn said. "Heaven knows and Heaven knew, and that is why God sent us to you. You cannot pay someone for doing God's will. That is sacrilege! Would you have me pay you for caring for Freddie and me?"

"Of course not," Nora said. "That was—oh, all right. But how can I thank you?"

"Take my sister's offer to open a little shop in her store. Every woman I know needs a new hat! And that is only among my friends out here on homesteads. Millersburg grows every day."

Nora smiled. "If everyone in Millersburg is as kind as you, I will not be able to say anything but yes."

"Remember what I told you about Sophie," Karyn said. "She can be difficult, but she has a good heart. And be certain you call on Celest Delhomme. She will introduce you to everyone. If there is anything you want to know, ask Celest."

"And if there is anything you *don't* want to know, count on Sophie," Mikal said, laughing.

"Mikal!" Karyn said sternly. "Shame on you. Sophie has made great improvements."

"I know," Mikal said. "But seeing you jump to her defense lets me know that you are completely recovered from having our Freddie." He hugged her briefly. Tipping his hat to Nora, he said, "God's best to you, Miss O'Dell, and thank you for all you have done for us. Please greet Celest, and tell her we will be bringing her new godchild to visit her soon."

Nora bent down and held her arms out to Mollie and May. They hugged her until she was breathless and laughing. Finally, she climbed up beside Dr. Allbright. As Dr. Allbright's carriage pulled away from the Ritter homestead, Nora looked back. She waved one last time and then turned around. She sighed. "I'm going to miss those two."

"Maybe you'll have some of your own someday."

"I never thought I wanted children," Nora admitted. "But if married life could be like that—"

Dr. Allbright tapped her horse's rear with the buggy whip. "Get along, Grady. It's near dark and you still have to pull us a good four miles." The carriage made its way slowly along two well-worn wagon tracks. As far as they could see around them, there was only a vast, waving sea of grass and wildflowers.

They had ridden along in silence for a while when Dr. Allbright said, "If I could bottle the Ritter's secret for happiness, I could be a very rich woman." She chuckled. "Can't you see it right next to the Lydia Pinkham's Remedy on drugstore shelves—Dr. Allbright's Bitters—Marital Bliss Guaranteed."

"I hardly think you'd want to call it 'bitters,'" Nora said.

"Anti-bitters, then," Maude offered.

"Much better." Nora hesitated before saying, "Karyn told me what it was like when she first came. I doubt things turn out so well for most of the mail-order brides. She credits God with everything."

"Yes,"Maude nodded "I've noticed that about her. What seemed different to me was that Mikal seemed to share her beliefs. I've met plenty of women out here who seem to cling to religion almost as a refuge from the insanity of loneliness. It isn't often, though, that I come in contact with a man who is so open about his own faith in God."

"It seems genuine."

Maude shrugged. "I think it is. In fact, quite a few of the folk in Millersburg seem to credit God with things." She said thoughtfully, "I called on an elderly woman in town only last week. Poor thing, she's suffering terribly from arthritis. Can barely get out of bed anymore. Unfortunately, there isn't much I can do. But she didn't complain—and she had her Bible handy and spoke about God like He was a personal acquaintance."

Dr. Allbright shook her head. "It's curious. Even with the pain she's in, she had baked biscuits for me. Said she knew I lived alone and thought since I usually eat at the hotel I should have some home cooking." Dr. Allbright smiled. "I'm sure you'll hear about Amalia Kruger's biscuits from someone. Personally, I hope she pays me in biscuits for every fee. She lives with Celest Delhomme. You're certain to meet her."

Maude began to tell Nora about Millersburg. "The town is laid out around a public square. Right now the square is just an expanse of grass, but they have plans for a courthouse as soon as they win the county seat. Mrs. Delhomme is heading a drive to plant trees along one section of the square to create a park. There are two hotels. Stay away from the Commercial. The Grand isn't too bad. Lots of open lots as yet. You'd be the first milliner. There's a two-story building next to Miller's for sale. I checked and it rents for $150 a month. I know you're not ready to think about that kind of money, but I might be interested in the building as an investment. If I can get out of my current lease and move my office there, I could give you a better rate."

Maude flicked the buggy whip toward her horse. "Get up there, you!" She muttered, "Oh, how I miss Casey . . . ," then she returned to the subject of Millersburg. "You'll like Mrs. Delhomme. She lost her husband a few years ago. They owned one of the largest farms in the county. When he died, Mrs. Delhomme turned the place over to her children and moved into Millersburg. She's a pillar of the church and at the forefront of civic improvements. Last winter, she organized a series of quilting bees to send quilts to the Indian reservation up near Wounded Knee." Maude paused. "I think she may be the nicest woman I've ever met."

"What about Mrs. Miller?"

"Hmm." Maude hesitated. "I think I should let you decide about Mrs. Miller without my commentary."

"Now you're making me nervous," Nora said. "Even her own sister says she 'can be difficult.'"

Maude nodded. "Yes. That would be accurate."

"I'm not suggesting you violate doctor-patient privacy," Nora said.

"Let me think how to say this," Maude said. She handed Nora the reins while she reached up to adjust her hat. Taking the reins back, she said, "Mrs. Miller is, next to Celest Delhomme, the most prosperous woman in Millersburg. Her husband dotes on her. She has absolutely everything a woman could want—except children."

"And so she isn't happy," Nora said.

Dr. Allbright nodded. "Right. She is very astute in business, as is her husband. They have a good marriage insofar as they seem to be good friends, and their talents make them very compatible. However, I would caution you that Mrs. Miller is not very—ah—flexible. She has definite ideas about how things should be done."

"Well, it is, after all, her business," Nora offered.

"I really don't think you have anything to worry about. Neither she nor her husband would have made the decision to expand their millinery department if they weren't certain it would succeed. And while there are several other general merchandise stores in Millersburg, theirs is definitely the most well-run with the widest selection."

"You sound like an advertisement for the store. For the entire town, for that matter," Nora said.

"I love it," Maude agreed. "Coming here was the best thing I could have done. The city board has bent over backward to make certain I'm happy and well-received. Everyone is interested in growth. It's a lot like Lincoln was when I first arrived. A little backward, but moving steadily forward. I think you'll like it, too."

She looked out of the corner of her eye at Nora. "You'll definitely like the female-to-male ratio. Prepare to be swamped by male suitors. That article you mentioned about the Bachelors' Club was meant as a joke, but it wasn't far from the truth." She chuckled. "Believe it or not, even *I* get asked to dances."

Nora said firmly, "Well, I'm going to be a hard catch. I'm not going to be swept off my feet by some handsome pretender wanting to play 'Mr. Right' to my 'Mrs. Right.'"

"Had your fill of the theater, eh?" Maude said.

Nora sighed. "Yes. Quite."

"Well, beware, Miss O'Dell, because Millersburg just opened an opera house and I've heard rumors that the Millers are doing all they can to attract a first-rate theatrical troupe for the opening. There will be actors about."

"I'm not worried," Nora said stoutly. "Besides, I don't even know that I'll *like* Millersburg."

CHAPTER 20

Millers and Men

With all lowliness and meekness, with longsuffering, forbearing one another in love.
Ephesians 4:2

"It won't be so late when we get there," Nora remarked, nodding towards the cluster of lights flickering just ahead.

"Don't let the sight of those lights fool you," Dr. Allbright warned. "Distance is very deceptive out here. We're still at least three miles from town."

Nora settled back against the carriage seat. The night breeze was cool. Once, she was lulled almost to sleep. But then a carriage wheel fell into a wagon rut so deep the carriage pitched sideways. Nora nearly fell out.

Dr. Allbright laughed. "Hold on there, girl. I don't want to lose you before you've even seen Millersburg!"

Nora laughed nervously and held on tighter. To keep herself awake, she ran down a mental checklist of the things Elise had said were important for her to remember. Elise had said to "get everything in writing." She should offer to pay rent for a certain square footage of the Miller's store, making certain it was clear that Nora was not an employee of the store, but rather an independent entity. "Show her you are confident in your abilities, that you don't need an overseer, because you don't. Dr. Allbright will be able to guide you to a good business mentor, but it shouldn't be Mrs. Miller. You want to keep your interests and your financial affairs to yourself."

Nora was anxious to see Millersburg. The idea of a town smaller than Lincoln appealed to her. If the Ritters were any indication of the kind of people she would meet, she knew she would be happy. She wondered who the "Mrs. Judge Cranston" of Millersburg was and hoped that Celest Delhomme would prove to be as kind and helpful as both Karyn and Dr. Allbright had said she would be. Nora determined to get involved right away with one of the charity projects Mrs. Delhomme was heading. She longed to become part of a community, and she knew that giving of herself to those less fortunate was a good way to do it. She had seen that even Goldie Meyer received grudging acceptance because of her philanthropy. Nora was glad she wouldn't have to overcome the stigma of Goldie's.

Her mind wandered to Dr. Allbright's comment about the number of eligible bachelors in Millersburg and the surrounding area. She hoped they were more reliable than Greyson Chandler had proved to be. Starting a new business would keep her very busy, but she no longer thought strictly in terms of business.

Thinking back over the past year, she realized that she had been learning bits and pieces of something that had finally fallen into place for her. Respectability and wealth were sometimes just a thin veneer hiding deep-seated faults. People who seemed to be religious were sometimes the worst of all. Nora thought back to the circuit-riding preachers who stopped at Goldie's after their services. She still didn't understand how that could be.

For a while she had thought Greyson Chandler was different. Beneath all the glamour of fame and good looks, there had seemed to be a genuine person she could really like. But he had proved himself to be no better than the rest of Goldie's customers. All the while he was writing to her about his "return to God," he was planning to run off with Iris. Nora's hurt had subsided. When she thought of Chandler now, it made her angry.

By the time Grady plodded into Millersburg, Nora had decided she was going to like the small town. If it grew marriages like the Ritters', she wanted to be part of it. She hoped that Dr. Allbright was right about the number of eligible bachelors, and she hoped that among them there was another Mikal Ritter—although she had to admit she preferred blond hair and a little less height . . . something more like Greyson Chandler, without the hypocrisy. She might even bear with a little religion, if it was the genuine kind. She wondered how one knew if religion was genuine.

"There's Miller's," Dr. Allbright said, nodding as they drove by a two-story general store. "Cay Miller began everything you see around you with a soddy built right next to that site. Mikal Ritter and one of Celest Delhomme's sons built this store."

She pulled Grady up and they sat, looking across an open field toward the opposite side of the square. Light from a full moon bathed the little town in a soft glow. "Over there, just behind that block, is where you should have gotten off the train." She gestured with the buggy whip as she talked. "As you can see, there are still a few vacant lots, but in the morning what is now a deserted square will be bustling with activity. There are piles of lumber everywhere, and there are always a dozen or more wagons coming and going from the train station hauling in new building supplies."

Dr. Allbright urged Grady forward. They passed another two-story building. "This is the one that's for sale. I'll show it to you tomorrow. But you can see it's well placed. Someday there will be a courthouse in the middle of that open field—unless Broken Bow captures the county seat—and these folks are determined to put up a respectable fight about that. Celest Delhomme has a drive started to plant trees along the east end to begin a public park. It's going to be a great little town someday."

They made their way around the square, and then Dr. Allbright turned east on what she called Cedar Street. Pointing to a two-story house, she said, "That's where Mrs. Delhomme lives. It's the nicest house in town." She chuckled. "Something that grates terribly on Sophie Miller."

They pulled into an alley. "This is it. We're home." Nora helped unhitch and tend to Grady while Dr. Allbright pulled the carriage under an overhang next to the small barn. They walked through a patchy yard and onto a small back porch. Inside, Dr. Allbright lit a kerosene lamp. Its glow revealed an immaculate white-washed kitchen. She led Nora through the kitchen and toward the front of the house, then up a narrow staircase. "You get the bedroom at the front of the house. I'm being selfish," Dr. Allbright said. "When I'm out half the night I want to be able to sleep, and I wanted the room as far from the street as possible. It's quieter, and there's more of a chance I can actually sleep during the day." She went to the door, "I'll let you get settled. Breakfast at dawn." She added, "I hope you decide to move here, Nora. The older I get the less I like rattling around in an empty house."

Seven years of living in Custer County, Nebraska, looked more like fifteen when applied to Sophie Miller. Karyn had told Nora that Sophie had come to Millersburg not long after her sister, and that she had enjoyed a long reign as the "belle" of every "ball" in the area. Nora could tell that the petite woman had once been a beauty, but the years had taken their toll.

"Sophie had so many suitors, it was hard to keep track,"

Karyn had said. "But persistence won out. Our dear friend Cay would not give up, and finally Sophie had the sense to marry him." Karyn had sighed. "Sophie always wanted a glamorous life, but she finally realized the worth of financial security and the devotion of a dear man."

Nora was not as certain as Karyn that Sophie appreciated her husband's devotion. Cay Miller was slightly built, with a perfectly trimmed mustache and a black eye patch earned over twenty years earlier while he was serving the Grand Army of the Republic. He had given over the running of his store to his wife, and now served on various civic committees and the board of the First Bank of Millersburg. He had a genuine smile and a twinkle in his one good eye. Nora liked him the moment they met.

Mrs. Miller treated her husband with practiced deference. While Nora and Mrs. Miller talked over their agreement, Cay was present. His wife appeared to consult him, but it quickly became clear that Mr. Miller's presence was for effect only. Miller's Emporium could have been renamed "Sophie's."

Talking things over with Dr. Allbright that evening, Nora said doubtfully, "I don't know. As a business, it's a good opportunity. But you were right when you said that Sophie Miller is no Elise Thornhill. She's almost overbearing."

"Don't let her scare you off," Dr. Allbright urged. "She has a hard shell, but underneath it there's a fairly decent woman."

The next day, Nora was back at Miller's. She had agreed to make a few sample hats for display. She settled in to "her" corner of the store, grateful to be near one of the large front windows.

The worktable was huge. Three mirrors, positioned down the middle of the table, divided it into halves, one for work, one for display. Several hat racks of different heights stood around each mirror. Sophie had ordered elegant cane-seated chairs and upholstered wooden footstools to encourage patrons to relax and shop. The entire wall behind the table was a mass of shelves and drawers, replete with a surprisingly good selection of trims and hat frames. Bandboxes and tissue paper were stored beneath the worktable. Nora's work chair was fitted with casters enabling her to move between each of the five hat stands permanently mounted to her side of the worktable and open the drawers behind her without ever getting up.

Removing her hat, Nora asked, "What would be the best style to start with?"

"I'd like two matching girl's bonnets," Mrs. Miller said. "Make them quite frilly. Something for Sundays." She opened a drawer and pulled out a pile of plain infant's bonnets. "And these need to be trimmed," she said. "I bought them sight unseen from my wholesaler. He can usually be trusted, but these are just—"

"—boring," Nora said.

Sophie smiled. "Exactly."

Nora reached into her bag and drew out some fashion magazines. Opening *The Delineator*, she pointed to a drawing of a child's dressy bonnet. "Is something like this what you had in mind?"

"I don't think I have a frame for anything like that," Sophie said doubtfully.

"I can use those plain straw bonnets on the top shelf."

"You can turn straw into that?"

"All it takes is cutting away half the brim at the back of the hat. The straw will be completely covered. No one will ever suspect I didn't use a wire frame."

Sophie nodded. "Wonderful. You've probably already guessed that these are for Mollie and May."

Nora smiled. "And a baby bonnet for Freddie." She was already pulling the ladder over and climbing up on her chair to reach the two straw bonnets. Nora worked for the rest of the day on Mollie's and May's new hats. By late afternoon, the straw forms were completely covered with a layer of fine white linen. Over the linen, Nora gathered white net with an edging of lace that dipped down in the front over the forehead. A huge bow nestled between the brim and the crown at the front of the hat, tied in place with long streamers that twisted along the edge of the crown to the back of the hat where there was another, smaller bow. White linen and lace streamers flowed off the hat and down the back. Two panels of lace ran across the flat top of the crown of each hat.

The minute Nora had finished the bonnets, she met the "Mrs. Judge Cranston" of Millersburg in the person of a woman who was intent on buying one of the bonnets.

"I'm sorry," Nora said. "these are already sold."

"But my daughter's party is this evening. You can't possibly make another in time."

"No, ma'am. I can't," Nora said. "But I'll be happy to take an order."

"I can't see why you can't just sell me this one and make another for—whoever."

Sophie interrupted. "Hello, Mrs. Smith. I'm sorry, but these are for my nieces. Miss O'Dell is correct. They aren't for sale."

"Are the Ritters coming into town tomorrow?" Mrs. Smith asked.

"I can't be certain," Sophie replied. "It all depends on the new baby and his mother."

"Then there's no reason you can't sell me one of these hats."

"Yes, there is," Sophie said calmly. "These are for Mollie and May."

Mrs. Smith ignored Sophie. "I'll pay you twice the price," she said to Nora.

Nora stood up. "Actually, Mrs. Smith, it's not an issue of price. Mollie and May's mother took care of me when I was ill not long ago, and I made these hats as a way to say thank you. So you see, their sentimental value is what's important. There's a lot of affection stitched into them. I really can't sell them."

Mrs. Smith departed. Sophie shook her head. "It does take all kinds." She turned to Nora. "Most of the people you will meet in Millersburg are easier to please."

Nora shrugged. "Don't worry. We had our Mrs. Smiths in Lincoln. Only there we called them all 'Mrs. Judge Cranston'—although I wouldn't want you to let that be known."

Sophie smiled. "Your work is very good, Miss O'Dell. I hope you decide to become a citizen of Millersburg."

Nora worked until closing time fashioning a spray of blue ribbon forget-me-nots for Freddie's bonnet. From her workstation she had a view of the entire interior of Miller's Emporium. Sophie Miller knew all of her customers by name. Nora also noticed that not a single child left the store without at least one piece of penny candy. Sophie Miller might be an astute businesswoman, but Nora suspected that at the heart of the free candy was just that—a heart.

The next day, Mikal and Karyn Ritter came to town. Mollie and May clambered across the boardwalk and into the store calling for "Aunt Sophie," who grabbed the two girls around their waists and swung them about laughing. She gave them candy and insisted they sit and tell her all about their new brother.

When Karyn came into the store with Freddie, Sophie kissed her sister's cheek. She took the baby in her arms. When Nora saw her struggling to control tears, she suddenly understood. Running the store might keep her busy and provide a sense of accomplishment, but in a world where motherhood was the epitome of success, Sophie Miller felt like a failure. Beneath her terse, businesslike exterior, she was a hurting woman desperate for children of her own. Nora wondered if Cay Miller had realized his wife's need for the store. She suspected that should Sophie Miller become pregnant, Cay Miller might suddenly become interested in running his store again.

That evening, Nora asked Dr. Allbright, "I don't mean to ask you to betray any doctor-patient confidence, but is Mrs. Miller unable to have children?"

Maude set her cup of tea down. "I see you broke through the facade."

"I was there when Karyn and Mikal arrived to show off Freddie. An entirely different woman appeared."

"To answer your question, I don't know why they have no children. As far as I can tell, Mrs. Miller is completely healthy in that respect."

Nora got up and went to the window. Across the street someone was building a new home. In what would be the front yard, a carpenter was constructing a picket fence. "I think I'll walk up to the train station in the morning and get a ticket for the next day. There's no need to put it off. I'm coming to Millersburg."

Packing for the move to Millersburg was no great challenge. Between Nora, Lucy, Hannah, and Elise, they had things ready in half a day. Nora sighed, "I don't have much to show for the last year of my life, do I?"

"Nonsense," Elise said. "Don't look at it in terms of *things*. When I think back to the girl I hired away from my sister, I'd say you have a lot to show for the last year of your life. You're self-assured, you know what you want . . . and you're going to get it." Elise hugged her. "I'm going to miss you, but I wouldn't keep you here for anything."

Early in the afternoon, Nora paid a last visit to Goldie's, where she urged Lily to consider joining her in Millersburg and promised to help her friend find a good job.

Lily shook her head. "That's real nice of you, Nora, but I'm better off here with Goldie. I got a regular string of clients now, and I've settled down a lot." She smiled. "I quit the bottle, and I figure in another year or two, I'll have money saved to do whatever I want."

Nora opened her mouth, then closed it.

Lily said, "I know what you are thinking. You're wishing I'd follow Iris's example. Well I'm not smart like Iris, and I don't have a Greyson Chandler ready to help me out."

At the mention of Grey's name, Nora almost flinched. Not wanting to hear any more, she hugged Lily and said, "Well, just remember, you'll always have a friend in Custer County." She gave each of the girls a hair comb adorned with handmade silk flowers. For Goldie, she had a monogrammed silk scarf. After another round of hugs, Nora left.

The next morning, Nora boarded the train for Millersburg. "I'll be sure to stay on the train at Grand Island," she joked as she stepped up onto the train car. Hidden in her bag were several unopened letters from Greyson Chandler.

Nora opened the first letter as the train went from Lincoln to Woodlawn. Grey was in Denver. He sent her greetings from Iris, who was at last settled in a little house near the heart of the city. She had taken in three children. Grey had put her in touch with an influential benefactor he knew from his "days in the theater," and she would be able to grow her charity without worries for the future.

> *Do you remember that I told you I had some things I had to do. Helping Iris was one of them. I know I have not written as I should, but I did not want to boast about what I was going to do . . . until I had done it. And even now, I do not boast, only in that it has been a blessing to be used in this way. I don't know what He has for me next. Please write and tell me your impressions. I wonder if you have tried any of the Lincoln churches yet.*

Nora read and reread the letter, finally laying it open in her lap while she looked out the window. Her inherent mistrust of men may have destroyed her relationship with Greyson. Why was it so easy for her to categorize him among the "good-for-nothing so-and-so's only interested in one thing"?

Feeling guilty, Nora ripped open the second letter. There was another letter to read while she passed through Marengo . . . Round Grove . . . Janesville. The final letter said that Grey had received Miss Thornhill's note about Nora being away and being ill.

> *I wish I knew where you were so that I could come to you. What are you thinking, Nora? I need to hear from you. I keep praying, but no answers seem to come.*

Nora finished Chandler's last letter just as the train pulled into Millersburg. It was little more than a terse note. He was coming to Lincoln to find out why she hadn't answered his letters.

Nora climbed down from the train in Millersburg, clutching the bundle of Greyson Chandler's letters. As Dr. Allbright hurried toward her, she stuffed them into her carpetbag.

"Well," she said. "Here I am."

"You look as white as a ghost. I hope it's not another attack of the ague," Maude said.

Nora shook her head. "No. Just an attack of terror. I've been asking myself all the way here who I think I am and what I have done."

Maude took her arm and guided her inside the small station. She nodded toward the door. "Go over there and take a look at your new town. See if it feels like home yet. I'll see to having your trunk sent to the house."

Nora stepped outside the small train station. Across the street the new opera house gleamed white in the morning sun, wearing a new coat of whitewash. A few wagons were parked in what would one day be the town square, but for now was simply a wide-open field of prairie. Nora tried to envision a park and a courthouse. The streets around the square were unusually wide. Two children ran by chasing iron hoops they had set to rolling with sticks. Somewhere a dog barked. Remembering her introduction to Lincoln, Nebraska, Nora realized how much better this was. It didn't feel like home yet, but Nora thought it could. Except for the bundle of letters in her carpetbag, she would not have given Lincoln a second thought.

At Dr. Allbright's house, Nora settled into her room. Later in the day, Dr. Allbright joined her for tea. "There was an entire packet of letters from Greyson Chandler waiting for me in Lincoln. The last one said that he was on his way there to find out why I wasn't answering his letters." Nora set her tea cup down and asked, "What do you think I should do?"

"What do you *want* to do?" Maude asked.

Nora took a deep breath. "I don't know."

"You can be downright irritating at times, young lady. Constantly asking questions I have no answer for. First it was questions about God, when you know I'm agnostic. Now questions about love and marriage. I'm divorced." At Nora's look of surprise, the doctor said tersely, "Scandalous, but true."

Dr. Allbright stood up. "You're searching for answers I can't give you, dear. Not because I don't want to. Because I don't *have* the answers. If I did, I'd be happily married and singing in the choir at First Church." She headed for the back door. "I have to get back to my office. I leave you with this: It has been my experience that when we don't know what to do, it's best to do nothing. The same train that takes Mr. Chandler to Lincoln can bring him to Millersburg. Why don't you just let time take care of that. In the meantime, perhaps you should take a drive out to the Ritters and interview Karyn about marriage and metaphysics. Or talk to Mrs. Delhomme."

Nora lay on her bed that evening staring at the ceiling. She thought back over the day. She had reread all of Greyson Chandler's letters and come to one conclusion. She did, at last, know what she wanted. She wanted to be loved the way Mikal Ritter loved his wife. Nora turned over and pounded her pillow. I wonder if Mikal Ritter has a brother. *Maybe it runs in the family.*

CHAPTER 21

Will

A friend loveth at all times,
and a brother is born for adversity.
Proverbs 17:17

Dear Will,

I am sending this to Mrs. Johnson for her to give you. I don't know but what Pap would throw away a letter from me without ever giving it to you. If you've left home, I'm hoping the Johnsons can find you.

It took nearly four days to walk to Lincoln. Did you know that was where I was headed? It's been a long road since the day I left. I spent last year in Lincoln, but I'm settled in Millersburg now, on the Burlington line west of Grand Island.

I'm a milliner, with my own little corner in Miller's Emporium. I have a room at a Dr. Allbright's, a woman doctor I met in Lincoln. She's the one who suggested I look Millersburg over, and I'm glad I came. Folks make you feel welcome and the town is growing fast. I hope it never gets as big as Lincoln. Don't imagine it will.

I hope you don't hold it against me for not telling you I was leaving, but I figured if you really didn't know anything, Pap couldn't hold it against you. I've wanted to write for a long time, but made myself wait until I felt I had something to offer. What I'm writing for now, Will, is to say that if you ever want a place to go, and if Millersburg sounds good to you, come on out.

There is a big spread just northeast of here owned by a family named Delhomme, and they always need hired hands. I already talked to Mrs. Delhomme, and if you decide to come, she is sure her sons, who run the farm, would have a job for you. It won't pay much, but it would be a way to start. The Delhommes have a decent bunkhouse for their hired hands, and as hard as you work, you'd be a foreman in no time. They raise sheep and cattle, and grain enough to feed their own herds. Mrs. Delhomme told me their foremen all have their own houses—one on each section the family owns.

Will, I'll never forget all the times you stood between me and Pap. You were more of a father than a brother to me, but you were pretty good at both, and I'm grateful. Don't let Pap ruin your life. He made his own choices and he didn't have to end up so bitter and unhappy. Since I left home I've met people who've been through much worse than Pap, and they are happy and have good lives.

The difference seems to be that a lot of the happy ones have a strong faith in God. I'm not talking about going to church. I mean these people seem to know God like you and I know each other—maybe better. I've been too busy to learn much about that, but as time goes by and I get more settled, I'm thinking I will check into it for myself. Things that have happened make me think maybe Someone has been watching out for me. It's like maybe God took over when you weren't there anymore. Come to think of it, maybe God was the one who put you there in the first place.

Hope it doesn't embarrass you for me to say I love you, Will.

Your sister, Elnora
(Forgot to tell you I call myself Nora O'Dell now)

A few days after Nora posted her letter to Will, a messenger came into the emporium and called out, "Telegram for Miss O'Dell."

"Telegram?" Nora was terrified. Had something happened to Elise?

Arriving Friday. Have money for second-rate hotel and big hug for little sis.

Will

Nora clutched the telegram to her chest and cried.

"What is it, Nora—what's wrong?" Sophie hurried to Nora's side and put a hand on her shoulder.

Nora shook her head. She held the telegram out. Sophie read it. "A brother! Coming to visit! How wonderful!"

Nora swallowed hard and tried to regain her composure. How would she ever wait until Friday?

"Well, he's certainly not staying in a 'second-rate hotel,'"Sophie said. "If Dr. Allbright doesn't have room, he's welcome to stay with us."

Dr. Allbright stated firmly that Will would most certainly stay with her, and Nora did not get a complete night's rest for the remainder of the week.

He had already climbed down from the train and was headed for the station to claim his bags when there was a flash of blonde hair in the crowd. Something familiar about the way she moved caught his eye. He raised his hand and started to call her name, but just as he did, she threw herself into the arms of a lanky young man in dire need of a haircut and a new suit of clothes.

The stranger bent down to hug her fiercely, brushing her cheek with his mustache as he kissed her. She was crying, almost clinging to him. When the couple turned to head into the station, Greyson ducked in ahead of them. He grabbed an abandoned newspaper and sat down, watching them over the top of the front page.

Well, at least I know what she's been doing . . . and why she hasn't answered my letters.

Nora and the other man left the train station arm in arm. Grey stood up wearily. He grabbed his bag and headed up the street. It would be suppertime soon. He doubted he would be hungry.

Nora hung on her brother's arm as they crossed the street. After her initial joy at his appearing, she felt awkward. She couldn't think what to say next, and from his silence, she thought Will must feel the same way.

They passed the new opera house, and Nora pointed to a posted announcement on the door. "There's a performance tomorrow night. The whole community's been working hard at it. Millersburg is growing so fast they need a new school. This is the beginning of a long list of fund-raisers."

She went on, "Mrs. Delhomme is at the heart of it. I helped with some of the costumes. Mrs. Delhomme wrote away and got scripts for that comedy." The playbill said that *Love's Lottery* would be performed on *Saturday evening, September 22, 1887, one performance only, at eight o'clock*. "It's supposed to be very funny. Even with amateur actors, it should be fun. Mrs. Delhomme won't tell anyone, but there's some kind of big surprise planned. Nearly the entire town should be there. You could meet a lot of people." She looked up at Will. "Want to come?"

Will shrugged. "I guess."

Nora finally asked, "How's Pap?"

"The same."

"Did you tell him?" Nora hesitated. "About me, I mean."

Will nodded. "Sure."

"What'd he have to say?"

Will shook his head. "Nothing you want to hear."

"Oh." Nora took a deep breath. "Well, I guess I shouldn't be surprised."

They had arrived at Dr. Allbright's. A note tacked to the front door read, *Called to set a broken leg north of town. Welcome, Will! Probably back late. Sorry.*

"We could have used her horse and buggy to get your trunk."

Just then, Celest Delhomme came up the street. "Nora!" she called, smiling. "And this must be Will."

Nora introduced them before Celest said, "Maude stopped by my place on her way out of town. You two are welcome to use my horse and buggy if there's anything to be brought over from the station."

"Thank you, ma'am," Will said, pulling on the frayed brim of his straw hat. "I travel light."

Celest excused herself. "You two have so much catching up to do," she said. "I'm going to head back home. If there's anything you need, just let me know." She turned toward Will. "We've already talked about the fact that you're a good farmhand, Mr. Calhoun. You must have dinner with me after church on Sunday so we can talk about that. The boys will all be here. You can meet the entire family."

Will and Nora accepted Celest's invitation, and she headed for home, leaving them still feeling awkward with one another.

Nora opened the front door and gave Will a tour of Dr. Allbright's house before leaving him to observe his new surroundings on his own. He plopped his small bag on the bed in his room before heading downstairs to where Nora was rattling pans in the kitchen.

He sniffed the air. "That supper?"

"You bet," Nora said. She gestured with a wooden spoon. "Smells good, doesn't it? Tastes good, too. I've learned a lot since I left home." She smiled wryly. "And you can't skip my biscuits across the water like rocks anymore, either. I finally got a lesson from the champion biscuit-maker in all of Custer County."

"Now, Elnor—Nora," Will said, "I never used your biscuits like that. 'Cept maybe once or twice."

Nora laughed. "It's so good to have you here. Now I know what I've been missing. It's family. Tell me you're going to stay."

"Guess I will," came the answer. "Pap made it real clear I better not plan on coming back once I walked down that road with my bag in hand." He pulled a chair out and sat down. "I got a little surprise waiting for you over at the train station. We can walk over and get it after we eat, if that's okay."

Nora had dished up two bowls of stew and was pulling biscuits from the oven. She exclaimed, "You brought Mama's trunk!"

Will nodded.

After supper they retrieved their mother's little trunk from the station. Opening it finally bridged two years of silence. By the time Nora and Will retired, it was as if they had never been apart.

CHAPTER 22

The Prodigal Son

To every thing there is a season, and a time to every purpose under the heaven: . . . a time to embrace, and a time to refrain from embracing.
Ecclesiastes 3:1, 5

Compared to Funke's Opera House in Lincoln, Millersburg Opera House was little more than a large room with a stage at one end. Instead of theater seats, patrons occupied folding wooden seats. Set up in rows for performances, the seats could be moved against the walls for dances, or arranged around tables for meetings. Lighting was provided by reflector kerosene lamps instead of gas. There was no carved proscenium arch. Instead of being decorated with scenic views, the walls around the stage were painted a soft sage green. There was no crystal chandelier, but urns and cupids formed an elaborate design in the pressed tin ceiling.

Nora and Will found seats near the front of the room where Will could sit on the aisle and have more room for his long legs. After they were settled, Nora looked around. Mr. and Mrs. Miller were just coming in. Sophie hurried to the front of the room to reserve seats for Mrs. Delhomme and her sons, who would be late getting to their seats.

Nora introduced Will, pleased that he remembered his manners and stood up to shake Mrs. Miller's hand. She wondered if Dr. Allbright would be at the performance. It seemed that more and more she was working long into the evening.

Looking up at the stage curtain, Nora remembered her first theater experience in Lincoln when she asked Elise how many yards of velvet she thought had been used to create the stage curtain, which was painted with a scene Elise called "The Rajah's Triumphal Entry into Singapore." Remembering the title, Nora smiled as she looked at the white canvas curtain before her. There was a simplistic landscape painted in the center, but all around it an array of painted portrait frames created ad space. Most were lettered with the names of businesses owned by Cay Miller. *The Millers' Triumphal Entry into Custer County,* Nora thought with a smile.

The capacity of the opera house had been said to be "over one hundred." Nora guessed at least double that had crowded into the room. She leaned toward Will. "Mrs. Delhomme said there was a surprise, but I didn't think this many people would turn out!" Will tugged at his collar. "I sure hope they open the windows before too long."

Finally, at eight o'clock, Mrs. Delhomme peeked through the opening in the center of the curtain. A trickle of applause greeted her, and after ducking back out of sight for a moment, she finally parted the curtain and stepped in front of it. A second round of applause died down. Everyone waited. She opened her mouth to speak, then closed it. Finally, she clasped her hands before her and began. "This is the beginning, friends. The beginning of our efforts to build a better school for our children and a better future for all of Custer County."

When the whoops and cheers died down, Celest said, "I didn't expect so many to come, and I hope my surprise is big enough to merit this evening's attendance. As many of you know, my sons now farm the land their father and I homesteaded when we first came to America. Many of you also know, that one of our sons has been away from home for many, many years."

Celest bowed her head for a moment. Her clasped hands were shaking. Not a person in the large room stirred. "This son left to become a musician, but the stage became his vocation. His father and I were not pleased. We were raised in a home where the theater was believed to be a playground for evil." She tried to make a joke. "But then, the same thing was said about America when we told our parents we wanted to emigrate." There was a trickle of laughter.

Celest smiled nervously before continuing. "This evening, I want to share something with all of you. My prodigal son has come home." There was a murmur in the room. "He is with us, this evening, as my gift to Millersburg. I want to thank the good Lord for answering this mother's prayers and for bringing my boy home to me. And I also want to thank Luc for having the grace to forgive his parents their foolishness."

Celest dropped her hands to her sides and smiled. "He is known by another name in theatrical circles. But here, he is Luc Delhomme. He has come home, and his family rejoices. And now, without any more comments from this foolish old woman, I once again thank you all for coming. We hope that you enjoy our performance of *Love's Lottery*.

Celest disappeared behind the curtain. There was a stir in the room. The kerosene lights along the walls of the hall were turned low. The curtain parted, and the play began. When Luc Delhomme stepped on stage, there was rousing applause, hooting and screeching such that Nora could see him fighting back tears. He finally stepped out of his role long enough to bow to the audience. He saw Nora. He looked at Will. And then he stepped away from the edge of the stage and into *Love's Lottery*.

The play was hilarious. The crowd laughed and applauded, and the paper the next day would report that "a good time was had by all." Nora was to remember nothing of the play itself. Her head was swimming from the revelation that apparently Greyson Chandler's real name was Luc Delhomme.

There was a brief intermission added to *Love's Lottery*, to give the citizens of Millersburg time to bid on a mountain of decorated boxes on a table at the back of the room. Each box was supposed to contain dessert for two, and proceeds from the sale provided another way for the citizens of Millersburg to contribute to their new school.

"Do you want to go?" Nora asked Will, when the lights were turned up and the parade of boxes began. A relay line of eligible bachelors had formed along one wall, and they passed boxes to the stage where Cay Miller was acting as auctioneer.

"No, we should stay," Will said.

"It's so hot in here," Nora said. "And it's only going to get hotter. I didn't make a box, and I don't really care about the play. We can go if you'd like."

"Well," Will said doubtfully, "maybe a walk around the square while the auction is going on. We can come back up later. We don't want people to think we're rude."

"We can give our seats to someone else," Nora urged. "No one is going to notice we're gone."

"All right. If you want to." Will looked at his sister quizzically.

Nora stood up and pulled him after her. Someone slid into their seats immediately.

Outside, Will clamped his limp hat on his head and hurried to catch up with Nora. "You gonna tell me what's wrong? You look like you just saw a three-legged hog jump a fence."

"I'm just so mad I could—*ooo*!" Nora clenched her fists and marched away.

"Hey, I thought it was funny. That one scene was a little risqué . . . but, Nora, it wasn't all that bad. Even Mrs. Delhomme laughed." He stepped in front of her, bent over, and looked at her until she made eye contact. "You mad 'cause that Luc fella was ogling you from the stage?"

Nora closed her eyes and shook her head. "No. I'm not mad about that."

"Well, what is it, then?"

Nora shook her head and closed her eyes. She held her hands up and stepped around her brother. "Just let me walk a little while, okay? I need to think."

"Well, okay, Nora. Walk all you want. I'm gonna head back to Dr. Allbright's and get some of that lemonade you made earlier. When you want me, that's where I'll be."

Nora was already striding away from him. She turned around and walked backward three steps as she said, "Fine. Good. I'll be there directly. I just"—she turned around again—"need to think."

"And that's why I was so mad. I feel like an idiot. He never *once* told me Greyson Chandler wasn't his real name. He never once told me he grew up in Nebraska. Every time we talked about it, he was—vague. I've been corresponding with a man I barely know . . . and now I find out I know even less than I thought I did."

Will pulled on his mustache while he considered what his sister was saying. "Uh, Nora—" he began.

"Don't do that!" Nora said, slapping his hand. "Grey does that and I hate it."

Will put his hand down. "I was just wondering, did you ever tell him your real name is Elnora Calhoun?"

Nora blinked. "Why would I do that? It doesn't matter." She glowered at Will. "Don't look at me like that! It's not the same thing."

"Were you ever—uh—vague when you told him about where you grew up?"

"Of course I was vague. I didn't want to sound like a poor oppressed child."

"Gee, Nora," Will said. "Maybe Mr. Chandler didn't want you to think of him as a poor, disinherited child."

"You're just sticking up for him because you're a man." She slammed her teacup down and stood up. "Wait until Dr. Allbright gets here. She'll understand how I feel."

"And how is that, Miss Elnora-Nora-Calhoun-O'Dell?" Greyson Chandler/Luc Delhomme was standing at the back screen door. "Exactly how do you feel?" He nodded toward Will, who got up and opened the door.

He held out his hand. "I'm Luc Delhomme. And I understand you are Nora's"—he nodded toward Nora—"or is it *El*nora's—brother? Glad to meet you." He looked at Nora. "Aren't you going to invite me to sit down?"

Realizing that Grey had apparently been eavesdropping from the back porch made Nora blush. She folded her arms across her chest. "It's not my house, but it is a free country as far as I know. I guess you can sit down if you want to, Mr. Chandler/Delhomme."

"Actually, now that I'm home, Delhomme sounds much better to me. And I always liked the name Luc. My brothers have stupid names like Serge and Remi. Thank God Mama and Papa used up Thierry before I came along. Luc's much more sensible, don't you think?" He smiled benignly. "Care to tell me why you changed *your* name? Oh, and while you're at it, I wouldn't mind hearing why you didn't answer my letters." He stroked his mustache. "Let's see, it would be about ten letters by now, I suppose?"

Nora glowered at him. "You are having fun at my expense, Mr. Delhomme. And I don't appreciate it. I cared for you. At least I cared for Greyson Chandler and—"

Luc leaned forward and put both elbows on the table. "Now we're finally getting somewhere."

Nora blushed. "I can't talk to you. This is too confusing."

Luc sat back. Turning toward Will, he said, "I was at the train station the day you arrived. I don't mind telling you how relieved I was when my mother told me you're Nora's brother. Mother says you're thinking of working on the place?"

While Nora simmered, Will and Luc talked. Nora looked from her brother to Grey, practicing the name Luc in her mind. She poured a cup of tea for the two men and finally got up to make coffee.

While she moved about Dr. Allbright's kitchen, she watched Luc. She had forgotten how much he gestured with his hands when he talked. The memory of her two hands being held in his made her blush. When she finally sat back at the table, Will had been given a good idea of the size and layout of the Delhomme farm. He had also been invited to ride out with Luc when he visited on Monday.

"You should come along, Nora," Luc was saying. "My father built probably the most unique sod house in the state. Have you ever seen one?"

Nora nodded. "I stayed with a family for a while when I first came. Do you know the Ritters?"

"*Know* them!" Luc boomed. "Mikal and I could tell you stories . . . but how did you come to stay with them?"

"It's a long story," Nora said.

"Tell him," Will urged. He could see that his sister was calming down. And he had not missed the way she looked at Luc Delhomme.

Nora shrugged. "I got sick on the train coming out. In Grand Island, I got off to get a cool drink of water . . . but I mistakenly got back on the wrong train and ended up in Loup City. Fortunately, Mr. and Mrs. Ritter had gone there to retrieve a lost shipment for the Millers. They rescued me. I stayed with them for about three weeks." She smiled. "I was there when little Freddie was born."

Luc smiled and nodded. "So, Mikal finally got his boy."

"They have two others," Nora said quietly. "Up on the hill behind the house."

Luc ran a hand through his blonde hair. "I didn't know about that."

"And they have twin girls, about four. Mollie and May."

"Has Mikal added on to the house?" Luc wanted to know.

Nora nodded. "There's a kitchen on the back and two bedrooms."

"Still the soddy?"

"Yes. But all plastered and painted white on the inside, with a wood floor. It's very cozy."

"I know all about that plaster," Luc said. "I'm the one who hauled the clay for the main room. We did that right after Karyn came." He laughed and shook his head. "I had my doubts about Mikal's German bride. I didn't think she'd stay. You could tell she was pretty horrified by the conditions she was expected to live in. But she surprised us all. Did she ever tell you about getting caught out in the prairie fire?"

Nora shook her head. "No."

Dr. Allbright's grandfather clock struck midnight. Luc hesitated. "It's getting late. I shouldn't be keeping you."

Impulsively, Nora reached out and touched the back of his hand. "Please stay." She blushed and looked at her brother. "We'd like to hear about it. Wouldn't we, Will?"

Will leaned back in his chair. "Well, I would, Nora, but I think I'll be turning in." He looked at Luc. "If you won't take offense."

An unspoken message passed between the two men. Luc grinned and nodded. He stood up and offered his hand. "Good night, Will. I'll see you at my mother's in a few hours."

Will left. Nora moved into his chair opposite Luc. Suddenly the air in the kitchen seemed close. Nora reached up to wipe sweat off her forehead.

"It's cooler outside. There's sure to be a breeze. Why don't we sit on the porch?" Luc suggested. They made their way in the dark through Dr. Allbright's parlor and outside. Maude had dug some wild vines in the country and stuck them in the ground on either side of the path that led up to the porch. They had taken hold in spite of her neglect, climbing up the posts and trailing across the overhang.

"Unfortunately," Nora said as she sank into the cushions that covered one of the cozy chairs on the porch, "Maude hardly ever has leisure time to relax out here." She paused. "It looks like she's to be gone the night again. I don't think I'd like being a doctor much."

Luc perched on the railing opposite her and leaned against a post.

"You were going to tell me about Karyn Ritter and the prairie fire," Nora said.

"When Karyn married Mikal, they were complete strangers. Did you know that?"

"She told me," Nora said. "It was a surprise. I assumed they were sweethearts from childhood. They seem so—perfect for one another."

Luc laughed softly. "They are. But it took about six months for them to figure that out." He looked at Nora. "I guess sometimes it can take even longer."

Nora fidgeted in her chair. "Tell me about the fire."

"Karyn came to America with a group of about forty German women. They arrived one day, filed off a train, lined up in a church and picked mates. Then, Mikal took her to his little one-room soddy."

"She said she almost didn't stay."

"Right. Apparently Karyn's family in Germany was fairly well off." He shook his head. "Whatever she expected, it certainly wasn't Custer County. But she liked Mikal."

"And she had her sister with her," Nora said. "That had to help."

"Oh, no. Karyn came alone. Sophie's arrival was a complete surprise."

Nora took note that Luc called Mrs. Miller by her Christian name. She wondered what the significance of that might be.

Luc quickly told the story of Sophie's arrival. "She stayed with Mikal and Karyn, of course. And somehow Karyn got it in her head that Mikal cared for Sophie. After a few months, she decided things would be better if she left. So she rode out one day to check on another homestead. I guess she was thinking she might try to make a go of it alone. While she was gone, a prairie fire came up."

"And Mikal went after her . . . and when he found her they finally knew they loved each other."

"Yes. She did tell you."

Nora said, "I heard her tell it to Mollie and May one night as a bedtime story. I never guessed it was true." She paused and then said thoughtfully, "I thought they had a fairy-tale romance. But they've worked hard to have a good marriage."

"I don't think there are many fairy tales coming true these days," Luc said thoughtfully. "My mother and father were crazy for one another, but there were times when she wanted to throw him all the way back to Belgium."

"My pap was so crazy about my mother he *went* crazy when she died." Nora shivered. "That's an awful way to live."

"Different people respond differently when bad things come their way. Some can handle it, some can't." Luc peered at Nora through the moonlight. "And some just run away and try to ignore it."

"I didn't run away from home because I wanted to ignore my problems."

"I wasn't talking about that. But I have wondered if you ran away from Lincoln because of me." He reached up to stroke his mustache. "Although I suppose that's giving myself too much importance in your life." When Nora said nothing, he asked, "Are you ever going to tell me why you stopped writing? I know you were sick for a while, but—"

Nora interrupted him. "I saw you and Iris in Grand Island."

"What?!"

She nodded. "I got off the train to get a drink of water. I came out of the station to get back on board the train, and there was Iris running toward you. You took your hat off to hug her. You picked her up and twirled her around."

Luc was quiet for a moment. Without saying anything, he knelt before her on the porch, took one of her hands in his, and kissed the back of it. He held her hand next to his cheek for a moment before speaking. "No wonder you didn't write."

Nora pulled her hand away. "I guess I have to admit that Grey had more than 'turned my head.' Being squired through the streets of Lincoln by the heartthrob of the theater was pretty heady stuff for a little country girl. And that dinner the night before you left." She took a deep breath. "Well." She paused again. "When I saw you and Iris, I thought I had just been a pleasant interlude for you. I told myself that was all right, that that was probably the way actors did things. And I had had fun, so I didn't have any right to whine and feel sorry for myself. And I figured it was time to move on." She paused again to keep her voice from trembling. "I didn't even open your last few letters until I was on my way back to settle here. I almost threw them away."

"Did you believe what I wrote about Iris?"

Nora nodded. "Of course. She told me herself about her plans to settle in Denver." She paused. "But then she stayed in Lincoln so long, I thought it was just talk. That she was just like the other girls, after all." She added softly, "It was wonderful of you to make her dream possible."

"But you still didn't write."

Nora shook her head. "I didn't know what to say. Dr. Allbright reminded me that the same train that took you to Lincoln could bring you to Millersburg, if you really cared."

Luc sat back on the porch floor and leaned against the railing. He raised one knee and balanced his arm on his knee. He could just reach Nora's skirt, and he stroked the fabric where her hand had been. "And here I am."

"To do a benefit performance as a favor to your mother," Nora reminded him.

"—and to find you."

Nora took a deep breath. "Grey—Luc. I'm too confused. I didn't really know Greyson Chandler all that well, and I don't know Luc Delhomme at all."

"Karyn and Mikal Ritter married complete strangers. They're happy."

Nora fidgeted in her chair.

"Do you even *like* me?"

"I can't believe Greyson Chandler is asking that question. He never seemed to have any doubts about his power over women."

"Well, Greyson Chandler isn't asking that question. This is me. Luc Delhomme. Are you going to answer me? Because if I'm not mistaken there is still something pulling us toward each other." He knelt before her once again, putting one hand on each arm of the chair she was sitting in. "I'm not moving until you answer me, Nora. Do you even like me?"

In a very small voice, Nora said, "So much it frightens me." He leaned toward her, and she immediately held a hand up, pushing against him. "I built my weeks around those letters you sent. I can't tell you how hurt I was when I saw you with Iris . . . and then how relieved when I finally read your letters. But, Luc—"

She heard a carriage coming up the street. "That's probably Dr. Allbright—"

Suddenly, Luc leaned forward and covered her mouth with his. He kissed her fiercely before pulling away and standing up. He stood and walked to the stairs that led down into the yard. "I'm going to walk around back and help Dr. Allbright unhitch her horse. She must be exhausted. Will you come to church with me this morning?"

"Yes."

"And you're coming to dinner at Mother's, right?"

"Yes."

"And on Monday, I'd like it very much if you'd ride with Will and me to see my home. We could stop at the Ritters' on our way back if it doesn't get too late."

"That would be nice."

Luc stepped down off the porch. He started around the edge of the house, then stopped. "Nora."

"Yes?"

"You *were* kissing me back just now. I didn't just imagine that, did I?"

Nora got up and crossed the porch. She leaned out over the railing and softly kissed him again. "I just need a little time."

He touched her cheek. "Take all the time you need. I'm not going anywhere." He walked down the side of the house, whistling softly.

CHAPTER 23

The Promise

I am he: before me there was no God formed,
neither shall there be after me.
I, even I, am the LORD; and
beside me there is no savior.
Isaiah 43:10–11

"I have a promise to make to you this morning. What I am going to say is guaranteed to help you overcome any past. What I am going to say this morning will fit you for the future. What I am going to say this morning will make today richer and fuller than you thought possible."

The pastor stood back from his pulpit. "How is that possible, you wonder? How can this short, ugly little man make such an outlandish promise?" He paused and looked about the congregation slowly.

Reverend Martin Underwood was balding, and the fringe about the hairless crown of his knobby little head had a propensity to stick out in all directions. He wore spectacles so thick they made his eyes appear much larger than their actual size. His voice was too high, his face too long, his teeth too large. Nothing about him even approached the confidence and authority with which Greyson Chandler had commanded the attention of an audience. And yet, when Reverend Underwood took the pulpit, Nora could not take her eyes from him. She was certain he was looking directly at her.

The service had begun benignly enough. The Delhomme family was recognized. Luc was welcomed home. The choir sang. Someone announced an ice cream social Thursday evening. Someone else got up and invited the women of the church to a quilting bee at Lottie Hanson's house on Tuesday morning. The offering was taken. But then Reverend Underwood got up and made his outlandish promise.

"It is possible, my friends, for me to make this promise, because the promise is based on this book. The only book God ever wrote. The only book that fits us for life." He picked up his Bible and read, "'Acquaint now thyself with him, and be at peace: thereby good shall come unto thee.' Do you want peace, my friend? Acquaint now thyself with Him."

Reverend Underwood laid his Bible back on the pulpit and, once again, stared at Nora.

He smiled "Let us begin with love. God is love. He is the very essence of the very thing that humankind longs for. He is the source of eternal, infinite, unchanging, gracious love. I propose, dear brethren, that it is not incompatible with God's love that He permits us to suffer. God's promises are not to remove all affliction. His promise is that when the world hates us, He loves us. He causes all things to work for good. Hate cannot triumph, for God is love.

"Our loving God is patient. How long has He been waiting for you, dearly beloved, to acknowledge His rightful place in your life? How long does He wait while you blame Him for your troubles and refuse to accept His loving comfort for the evils of men? How long does He wait while men deny His Son and refuse the forgiveness freely offered?

"Our loving, patient God is holy. He cannot admit sin into His holy presence. And so, His love is demonstrated in that He provides His own Son to cover our sin. He loves His poor creation enough to give His only Son that we might be saved. He waits for us to come to Him. He allows us to rail against Him, to shake our fist in His holy face . . . and all the while He is loving us. But one day His Holiness will say, 'Enough'! Those who refuse His love must feel His wrath."

Reverend Underwood leaned toward his congregation. "Do not tempt His wrath, dearly beloved. Know His love through His Son, Jesus Christ. Contemplate His wonderful, magnificent person. For in God alone will you find the ability to overcome the past, to ready yourself for the future, to live today fully. He is all, and all in all. I invite you to Him." Reverend Underwood stood back from the pulpit and opened his arms, as if inviting people to come.

The congregation sang a hymn, and then everyone began to file out of the church. Luc was surrounded by old friends welcoming him home. Nora took Will's arm and followed him out of the church. As they left, Reverend Underwood took Nora's hand. His larger-than-normal eyes seemed to look right through her as he said, "I'll be praying for you, my dear." When Nora looked up at him quizzically, he smiled. "I am available at any hour to meet the needs of my flock. And I pray you become one of the flock very, very soon."

Nora shook his hand and said something noncommittal. Will complemented the reverend's "talk" and led Nora down the stairs of the small, white-framed church and out onto the scrubby lawn. They waited in the shade of a tree until the Delhomme family joined them. Mrs. Delhomme introduced her sons Remi, Serge, and Thierry, and their families.

"Mother said that Mrs. Miller had allowed for some time away from the emporium while your brother gets settled," Remy's wife said. "I hope you can come to the quilting on Tuesday morning." She motioned to the other wives. "We're all coming in together. Five of us could command our own quilting frame. It would be fun!"

Celest said, "Luc is taking Nora to visit the Ritters tomorrow. I'll have him ask Karyn to come in that morning, too."

Serge's wife nodded. "Even better. I haven't seen the baby yet."

"Let's get together tomorrow at home and see if we can't whip up a layette," Thierry's wife chimed in. They began discussing who had which fabric and what they would make.

While the wives were planning Karyn Ritter's impromptu baby shower, Nora looked around for Will and Luc. Luc was standing on the steps of the church, surrounded by young people—mostly female. Just as Nora felt a little pang of jealousy, he looked over at her and smiled. He dismissed himself from the group and came across the church lawn to where she stood, boldly taking her hand and tucking it under his arm.

"Mother, I'm starved," he said.

"Well, some things never change, do they?" Celest laughed. The families headed for their carriages.

Thierry called to Will, "Why don't you ride with us, Will? I can describe the place to you."

"Already did that," Luc said.

Thierry frowned at his brother. "And a lot you know, Mr. I-want-to-be-an-actor-don't-bother-me-with-farming."

Luc dodged the imaginary rock. "All right, all right. I see your point."

Thierry laughed. "Good. And don't interfere the next time big brother tries to provide time alone with your best girl." He looked pointedly at Nora.

Will walked off with Thierry.

Luc turned to Celest. "We'll walk, Mother. If that's all right."

Celest nodded and followed Serge and his family to their carriage. The family drove away, creating something of a parade as they made their way around the future town square and up Cedar Street.

"I like your family," Nora said. "The wives invited me to a quilting here at the church on Tuesday morning. We're supposed to invite Karyn to come."

"I don't know if I like that idea," Luc said as they walked along. "Those women can tell far too many stories about my wayward youth . . . you might get the wrong impression."

Nora was not yet ready to let go of Luc's arm when they reached Mrs. Delhomme's. But she disengaged herself anyway and helped carry heaping bowls of food from the kitchen, out the back door, and to the yard. A huge grape arbor ran the entire length of the west side of Celest's house, and beneath it the men had erected makeshift tables with sawhorses and planks. Every kind of chair imaginable had been hauled from the house, and the Delhomme children had brought chairs with them in the backs of their wagons.

Sophie and Cay Miller, Dr. Allbright and Reverend Underwood had also been invited.

From where she sat, Nora looked about her. The table was at least twenty feet long, lined on both sides with members of one family who loved one another. What it must be like to be part of such a family. She ducked her head, trying to hide the tears that welled up in her eyes.

"What is it?" Luc said softly, reaching over to squeeze her hand.

Nora shook her head. "Nothing," she murmured. She swallowed hard, finally leaning toward him to whisper, "I just never saw a family like this before, that's all. It's—" She stopped herself just in time, blushing with embarrassment, grateful that Reverend Underwood had stood up to say grace.

Nora had heard recited blessings before, but she had never heard anyone talk to God the way Reverend Underwood did. He said what was on his heart and mind, sounding absolutely certain that the Almighty Himself was paying attention.

"Heavenly Father, thank You for every one around this table. Thank You for the love You have given them for one another. Thank You for the gift of healing represented in Dr. Allbright, for the talents and skills you have given the Delhomme family in raising crops and children, for their willingness to help those less fortunate. Thank You for providing for our material needs through the Millers. Thank You for bringing Luc home, and for his talents in making us laugh—something we all need to do more of. Thank You for Miss O'Dell and her brother, Will. We pray that You would guide them in the decisions that await them in the coming week. May they be decisions that will bring them closer to You. I pray that for us all, dear Lord. That whatever happens in the week ahead may be perfectly designed to make us more like Your dear Son, our Savior, Jesus Christ. And now, heavenly Father, we thank You for this food so lovingly prepared. And that the Delhommes have been so unselfish as to include me in their precious family time. In the name of our Lord Jesus. Amen."

Reverend Underwood sat down and chaos erupted. Remy, Serge, Thierry, and Luc seemed to have regressed several years in age. Bowls of food were passed around the table several times. Nora had never seen so much food consumed. The boys were still at it long after their children had begged and received permission to run to the town square to play. Dr. Allbright and the Millers left after the second pot of coffee. Still, the Delhomme boys ate. Finally sated, Remy tossed a biscuit at Luc. The threat of a food fight was abated only by Celest Delhomme's stern admonition.

The women cleared the table and did the dishes in shifts while the men sat beneath the grape arbor talking of crops and cattle, houses and dreams. In the late afternoon, an impromptu baseball game was organized. The women spread blankets and quilts where it was hoped a courthouse would one day stand. Children played and skinned knees, were comforted and sent on their way.

As the sun set, the Delhomme men collected their families into their carriages and rolled out of town. Will sat on the steps of Miller's Emporium, deep in conversation with Cay Miller. Luc walked Nora home to Dr. Allbright's, hoping for a glass of lemonade and a kiss. Both were willingly offered.

CHAPTER 24

Faith and Peace

If any of you lack wisdom, let him ask of God,
that giveth to all men liberally,
and upbraideth not; and it shall be given him.
James 1:5

Nora, Will, and Luc rode out of Millersburg at dawn on Monday morning. Luc's mother had loaned Nora a split skirt and boots. The three headed north and east across open prairie toward what Luc called "French Table." They rode for about two hours along a barely discernible ridge, then down into a valley, across a creek, and up a steep incline.

Once her horse had climbed the hill, Nora could see a house in the distance. As they approached it, Luc said, "Everyone thought Papa was crazy when he said he was going to build a castle made of sod, but he did it." The house was two stories high, with curved turrets at the corners and a peaked wood shingle roof. They rode into the yard and were greeted by Thierry's wife, Jennie.

"Come in. Are you hungry? The girls are helping our cook make bread."

Luc and Will departed with Thierry to look at outbuildings and discuss Will's future.

"Is that where Will would stay?" Nora pointed to a long, low building a few yards from the barn.

Jennie nodded. "Yes. Thierry and Serge built the bunkhouse not long after Mother Delhomme moved into Millersburg." Jennie shook her head. "I thought she would just curl up and die when Papa Emile died. They were so devoted to one another. But she surprised us all. She's made a whole new life for herself in Millersburg." A black puppy frolicked up, jumping on Nora's skirt, wriggling and demanding attention.

"If Mother Delhomme could see the way I let her misbehave, she would be horrified. This is one of a long line of Newfoundlands. Mother's dog was named Frona. She was the best-behaved dog you've ever seen." She laughed easily. "This one, on the other hand is incorrigible!" She bent down to rumple the puppy's fur. The puppy rolled on the earth, all four paws dangling in the air, begging for a belly rub. Jennie obliged her and then led Nora inside where a slightly built older man was overseeing the making of bread. "This is Lee, our cook," Jennie said. "He works miracles out of this kitchen. Feeds us and the bunkhouse roustabouts." Jennie introduced Nora and directed her two daughters to take lemonade outside for the men.

"We'll take some coffee into the parlor, Lee. And do you have anything sweet?"

Lee whisked a basket down off a shelf. "Cornbread muffins left from breakfast," he said. "I can put some jelly on the tray. Sound good?"

Nora followed Jennie into the sumptuous parlor. It was carpeted and furnished with elaborately carved pieces that brought Goldie's to mind. In place of a piano, the Delhommes had an organ.

Seeing Nora eye the organ, Jennie asked, "Do you play?"

Nora shook her head. "No. I like music, though."

"That's Luc's. If he ever stays in one place long enough

to have it moved." Jennie laughed easily. "Tell me about yourself. You learned millinery in Lincoln?"

Nora nodded.

"So your family is in Lincoln?"

"No. Our mama died when I was born, and Pap doesn't want much to do with us. There's only Will and me."

"I'm sorry," Jennie said, quickly changing the subject. "Do you like Millersburg?"

Nora nodded. "I like being in a smaller town than Lincoln but not so little as where I grew up. Thanks to people like you, Will and I feel very welcome."

Luc stuck his head in the door. "We're riding to take a look at the place. Want to come?"

Nora looked doubtfully at Jennie, but she encouraged her. "Please, go ahead. In fact, I'll join you. Just let me run upstairs and change."

Nora went outside where Thierry and Will were waiting with the horses. When Jennie came down, the party headed out. They looked over a vast herd of cattle grazing one section of Delhomme land. They stopped at Serge and Remi's, and met the foreman for each of the sections. Finally, Luc said, "Well, if you've seen enough, Will, I promised Mother and Nora we'd ride to the Ritters' before the day was out."

Will nodded. "You go on. I'm going to ride back into Millersburg and collect my things. No reason not to get moved right in and get to work." He looked at Thierry. "That is, if it's all right with you, Mr. Delhomme."

Thierry nodded. "Glad you've decided to stay on. When you get back, check in with Jack at the house just south of the bunkhouse. He'll get you introduced around and get you a horse out of the herd."

Thierry added, "If he suggests a long-legged bay with a white blaze, turn him down flat out. That horse's name is 'Killer,' and the boys use him as sort of an initiation to the place. Save yourself the aching posterior and take the buckskin mare or the piebald gelding. They're ugly, but they're reliable."

"Thanks." Will rode up next to Nora and laid a hand over hers. "Well, baby sis. See you at church on Sunday."

Nora looked at him, surprised.

Will laughed. "Don't act so surprised. I want a whole new life." He grinned. "I've got Ida Johnson waiting for me to make good. Figure she'll be real impressed if I tell her I go to church regular. And it never hurts to try to impress the parents, either." He turned and rode off toward Millersburg.

Halfway to the Ritters', Luc suggested they walk for a while.

"Thank you," Nora said, climbing down off her horse. "It's been a long time. I'm going to feel this tomorrow."

"I suppose you'll be back at Miller's before long."

Nora nodded. "Mrs. Miller has been very kind about letting me take this time away so soon. I don't want to take advantage of her."

"Are you glad you moved here?"

"Absolutely," Nora said. "The best thing I could have done."

"I don't mean to pressure you or anything," Luc began.

"Something tells me you're about to pressure me."

"I've had a letter from Daniel Froman. It got mixed up in someone else's mail. They brought it over to Mother's last night. It was waiting when I got back from talking to you." He took a deep breath. "I know that name doesn't mean anything to you, but it's quite something that he's after me. At any rate, he's brought over a married couple from England named Kendal. They're long-established favorites in domestic melodrama. Mr. Froman wants to know if I'd join the touring company."

He waited for Nora to react. When she didn't, he said, "They need me in Denver three weeks from today." Still, Nora said nothing. "They could also use a costume mistress.

Daniel heard about Thornhill Dressers from Mamie Patterson. He asked if I knew anyone who might be lured away from Lincoln. I don't. But then I thought perhaps there might be someone who could be lured away from Custer County."

Nora said, "I signed a contract with Mrs. Miller that promised I would never give less than six weeks' notice if I decided to leave. And I'm just getting settled—"

"There, Mikal—just a little farther. I think they were there by that big rock."

Luc and Nora had just topped a rise that overlooked the Ritters' homestead. Down below them, Mikal was creeping along the banks of the pond while Karyn directed him. "There were at least six eggs."

Mikal bent over the water, brushing aside some long reeds growing at the edge of the pond. The moment he bent over, Karyn rushed up behind him and pushed him into the pond. He stood up, sputtering and laughing, slinging water everywhere as he shook his head. "Karyn Ritter, you're going to pay for this!" he roared.

Karyn screeched and started to run up the hill, but Mikal caught her and dragged her, kicking and screaming, back to the pond. He swept her up in his arms, stomped into the pond, and dumped her. They laughed and splashed about like two children for a few moments, and then it grew very quiet as suddenly, Mikal reached for Karyn, pulled her into his arms, and kissed her passionately.

Nora put her hand on Luc's shoulder. "*Say* something so they know we're here. This is already embarrassing enough."

Luc shouted, "Hey, you! Mister! Stop trying to drown that woman or you'll have to answer to the Delhommes!"

Nora saw Karyn's hand go up to her mouth. She hastily reached up to brush her hair back out of her face and began to climb out of the water, but Mikal pulled her back. He kissed her again, then put his arm around her, and together they dragged themselves out of the pond and up the hill. By the time they reached Nora and Luc, they were laughing again.

Mikal clapped Luc on the back and then hugged him. "What a welcome we give you, eh?" He smiled down at Nora. "I ask your forgiveness for such behavior, but even yet I sometimes forget I should be acting more like an old married man." He chucked Karyn under the chin. "She had me out looking for duck's eggs." He turned toward Karyn. "Now tell me, *schatz*, are there really duck eggs?"

"Of course," Karyn said. "Mollie and May have them safely nestled beneath one of our hens."

Mikal grinned and shrugged. Then he said, "You must excuse me to get some dry clothes." He nodded at Luc. "Please put your horses in the corral. Make yourselves as if you were at home." He looked once again at Karyn. "I think you deserve to shiver in the cold after the trick you played on me." He made for the house. Karyn excused herself and followed him.

Luc and Nora walked down the ridge toward the corral, where Luc opened the corral gate and led their horses in. He looked around approvingly. "This corral used to have a sod wall." He nodded at all the trees around the homestead. "Karyn dug every single one of those out of the creek bed and planted them." He shook his head. "And that was before there was a windmill up at the house to pump the water for her to water them with. She had to pump it one bucket at a time, one bucket per tree, every day, for weeks and weeks and weeks."

He unsaddled the horses, and perching the saddles and blankets on the corral fence, then took the bridles off and hung one on each saddle horn. The horses trotted around the corral, snorting and tossing their heads.

Luc put one hand on the top board and jumped the fence. Leaning against it, he looked up toward the house.

"Those trees by the porch were just this tall—" He held his hands about a foot apart. "None of the outbuildings were here, except for this dugout behind us." He nodded over his shoulder. "Mikal lived there for two years before he married Karyn."

Nora looked over her shoulder and back around her. "He must be a very determined man."

Luc nodded. "It takes a special breed to succeed here. But, it won't be long before the soddy will be gone. They'll have a new house, and by the time the girls are grown, the hard times will be behind them."

Karyn and Mikal came back down the hill. Karyn was holding the baby in her arms, but Mollie and May ran ahead, calling to Nora. She crouched down, and the girls threw their arms around her neck and hugged her.

Luc admired Freddie, and they all walked up the hill to the little house where a table had been set outside the front door. Karyn put Freddie back to bed and promised supper soon. She put her hand on Nora's shoulder and shoved her into a chair. "You sit. The girls can help me. We want it to be special."

Mollie and May followed their mother into the house. While Mikal and Luc reminisced, Nora watched them, thinking she had never seen two such different men enjoy such a close bond. Mikal was a lumbering giant compared to Luc's trim, athletic physique. Mikal's mane of black hair was slightly unkempt. He reminded Nora of a barely tamed bear she had seen once at a circus in Lincoln. Luc was blond and fair although he had begun to tan since he was home. Watching the two, Nora decided she much preferred Luc to Mikal. She stood up and went to the door of the house. "Are you certain I can't help?"

"I'm certain," Karyn said firmly.

Nora sat back down at the table just as Mollie and May brought dishes out. Both kept a wary eye on Luc as they set the table. Supper was served and the table cleared before Mollie finally said, "Are you the one that got knocked out by the hail?"

Luc nodded. "That's me."

"Can I see the scar? Mama says she helped sew your head back together."

Luc laughed. He leaned down and made a part in the back of his head. "Can you see it?"

Mollie pointed to Luc's head. "Look, May. It's a big scar. Mama had to sew a lot."

"Girls, what are you doing?" Karyn had gone inside to make a fresh pot of coffee and came back outside just in time to see her daughters examining the back of Luc's head. "Where are your manners?"

"We wanted to see where the hail split his head open," Mollie said.

Karyn shook her head. She looked apologetically at Luc. "I'm sorry. Our little adventures make good bedtime stories. But sometimes I exaggerate a little."

Luc laughed. "Don't apologize. It's nice to know I have the leading role in one of their favorite bedtime stories."

Karyn asked, "Do you stay home now, Luc?"

He shook his head. "No. I have to be in Denver three weeks from today."

Karyn looked from Mikal to Luc, to Nora and back to Luc again. She set the coffeepot down. "Well, gentlemen," she said abruptly. "I want to ask Nora some advice about a new hat. So, if you will excuse us."

Nora got up and followed Karyn into the house.

The women were barely through the doorway when Karyn said, "I see what is between the two of you. What is he saying about Denver?"

She turned to Mollie and May. "Girls, I want you to get ready for bed now and to listen for your brother. If he wakes, bring him to me out back. Otherwise, you may play quietly. If you want to do tomorrow's sewing stint now, you will have tomorrow free." The girls scrambled for their sewing boxes. Karyn led Nora through the lean-to and out back, where two crudely made benches provided seating in the shade.

"Someone famous wants Luc to join his company."

"And he is going?" Karyn asked.

Nora looked down at the log bench and pulled at a piece of loose bark. "He said they need a costume mistress. He said—" She blushed and looked up the ridge. "Well, he started to say something, but then we came over the top of the ridge and you were getting dunked in the pond."

Karyn blushed. "The girls were napping. All three were napping at once. Truly a miracle. Time alone with my Mikal." She sighed.

"Did you know right away that you loved Mikal?" Nora asked abruptly.

Karyn laughed quietly. "I knew right away . . . but then it took me a few weeks to admit it to myself . . . and a few more before I admitted it to Mikal." She told Nora what Luc had already said about being selected from the group of women at the church, about the shock of living in a house made of dirt . . . and then she began to talk about Mikal. Her face shone with love.

"How is it that after seven years and three children, you still have this—this—feeling between you?"

Karyn shrugged. "Oh, the feeling comes and goes," she said.

"But you're so happy."

"Yes," Karyn said. "Mostly, we are happy. Except for the times when we are not."

Nora asked earnestly. "What is it that gets you through the times when you are not? What makes the feeling come back? Do you ever fear that you'll lose the love? Lose the will to keep trying?"

"Come with me," Karyn said quietly. She held out her hand, leading Nora up the ridge to the two little graves. The two sat down in the tall grass, and Karyn said, "When this happened, I feared losing the love. For a while, I didn't have the will to keep trying." Her voice trembled with emotion. "But Mikal tried for me. He wouldn't let me give up. Every night, I would cry, and every night, he would cover my cheeks with his kisses, and then he would hold me and tell me that if we never had another child, he would be content. He reminded me of all that God had done for us, of the love of the Lord Jesus, of all the blessing that we had together. He read the Psalms to me while I cried. He did these things over, and over, and over again. Until one night I didn't cry anymore."

Karyn was quiet for a while, looking at the two little graves. "Now I can look back and see that God used those little boys to grow my love for Mikal. Our marriage is stronger because of them. And my love for God is deeper. After we have walked with God through the valley, we learn truly that He is the Good Shepherd."

"Where did you get your faith in God?"

"Where?" Karyn looked at Nora in such a way that she knew that no one had ever asked such a question of her. She thought for a moment. "Somewhere in the Scriptures it says that God gives us the faith that we need."

Nora said, "I wish He'd give me some faith."

Karyn put her hand on Nora's shoulder. "Dear Nora, has no one ever told you that you only ask and He gives? If you are longing so to know God, then He is calling you just as the shepherd calls to his sheep."

"I don't know if it's God I want or not," Nora said honestly. She thought for a moment before saying to Karyn, "But I do know I want to be loved the way Mikal loves you."

Karyn looked soberly at Nora. "I think already you are loved very much by a good man. But better than that, even, is God's love for you. Remember your Sunday school lessons?"

Nora shook her head. "My pap didn't let us go to

church. Most of what I know about God comes from talking to people like you. I've read the Bible a little, but I never got past that book where they were numbering the children of Israel."

"Well then, let me tell you the best story of all." Karyn told the story of Jesus Christ's birth, His death, and His resurrection, as if she were talking to Mollie and May. By the time Karyn explained that Christ would be coming again, Nora interrupted her. "I want to believe that's all true. I really do. But I can't." She shook her head.

"Of course you can't," Karyn said. "'For by grace are ye saved through faith; and that not of yourselves: it is the gift of God.' Do you see, Nora? Even the faith is a gift of our loving God."

"Elise Thornhill once said I could talk to God, just like He was a real person."

"Anyone can," Karyn said softly.

"Okay. I will. I'll ask Him to give me the faith I need." Nora was quiet for a moment. "I hope He answers real fast," she said. "Luc has to be in Denver in three weeks."

Karyn laughed and stood up. "Come along, my friend. The men are probably wanting a second piece of pie, and already you will be riding back to Millersburg in the dark."

CHAPTER 25

The Last Letter

Make haste, O God, to deliver me; make haste to help me, O Lord.
Psalm 70:1

Nora and Luc rode away from the Ritters at sunset. It was Nora's favorite time of day, those few moments when the sun casts an eerie light over the entire landscape. Nora had not yet become accustomed to the vast sky, the seemingly endless prairie that was Custer County. Even as the sky darkened, and dots of light shown around them marking the location of at least a dozen homesteads, the feeling of aloneness did not diminish.

The evening star appeared low on the horizon, twinkling brightly against a sky that was orange-gold, changing to several shades of violet, then dark blue. A full moon glowed warm orange on the horizon before rising to cast a bluish light over the landscape.

Karyn had promised to drive into Millersburg for the quilting. Nora felt strangely content. What Karyn had said about asking God made sense. In fact, she had done it, right there by the little graves. She had asked God to help her. Looking up at the stars as she rode along, she felt a presence . . . almost as if, this time, there would be answers. With Luc riding along beside her, she felt that perhaps she was on the brink of true happiness, after all. If only she could dissuade Luc from leaving.

Luc was strangely quiet as they rode along. Nora had hoped that he would resume the talk of Denver, but he did not. Nora cleared her throat. "In your letters—the ones I didn't read right away—you talked a lot about God. I remember you saying something about returning to things you knew when you were a child. What did you mean by that?"

"My mother and father were devout Christians. By that I mean they really did try to live as Jesus would want. Believe it or not, around here, 'Christians' like you met at Goldies are usually outnumbered by the real ones like my parents. We read the Bible together at home, and we were expected to abide by what it taught—at least on the outside. My parents knew they couldn't change my heart. Only God can do that. They taught us what we needed to know and left the rest in God's hands.

"When I left home, I got away from their teaching. You already know about all of that. As I said in one of my letters, when I met you I was ashamed of what I had to offer. I knew I had to break things off with Mamie, but even when I did that, I still felt terrible. I didn't want to look back on my life and have it be year after year after year of the same kind of thing. I knew all the right answers about how to find God, but I had to make a personal decision—for me. That day I walked up into the mountains, it all came together." He chuckled. "Who would have thought a little thing like a grasshopper could make such a difference in a man's life?"

"Don't you worry about what could happen if you go back to the theater?"

"Of course. I know my weaknesses. But I'm serious about my relationship with God. I know He's forgiven all the things I've done, and I'm going to do my best to live my life in a way that pleases Him."

He went on, "There are many different kinds of theatrical troupes, Nora. Mr. and Mrs. Kendal from England are well-known for their strong family. They travel with their children. They don't participate in anything questionable. Regular hours, no gambling, no drinking, no shared dressing rooms. It's very nearly puritanical from what I've heard. We'll be doing entirely different material. There won't be any 'Patterson kissing' going on, and I'm going to steer clear of single women—present company excluded, of course."

He thought for a moment. "I think my talent is a gift from God, and I can do a lot of good with the money I make. Which, by the way, is quite a lot. I want to continue supporting Iris's school in Denver. And Mother has given me some other ideas about good causes I could get involved in."

"How often does a traveling troupe get to go home?" Nora saw Luc look up at the night sky, thinking.

"That depends. Probably twice a year."

"Twice a year for how long?"

"A month, a week. It depends on how completely the troupe is booked." He added, "Families that travel together create a kind of home wherever they are. The Kendals have a cottage in the mountains somewhere. They always try to spend a month there in the summer. I think they even get back to London once in a while. But there's no denying that it's a different life from what most expect."

"How can you be certain God wants you to do it? I mean, how does a person know when God is talking to them?"

Luc shook his head. "It's not always easy. Asking advice of people who are more mature in the faith than you, reading the Bible, that sort of thing. I've talked hours and hours with Mother. She's very wise in so many ways."

"Does the Bible talk about being in the theater?"

Luc chuckled. "No. I don't think so. I think I'm into a decision where it could be right for me to go and right for me to stay."

"How can both be right?"

"I think it's right for me to go now. But if I were married, once I started a family, I would want to come back home. Teach music. Help with home talent productions at the opera house. Live happily ever after."

They rode into Millersburg, dismounting in front of Dr. Allbright's house, and tying the horses to a fence post. Luc opened the gate, and they walked up the path to the porch.

"Thank you for including me today," Nora said. "My head is so filled with things to think about, I probably won't sleep for days."

Luc pulled her close. "Tell me something, Nora. Could you see yourself in 'happily ever after' with me?" He was looking down at her with such intensity that Nora felt her face growing hot despite the cool night air.

She looked away from him. "It's so different from what I've planned for my life."

Luc released her. "Not the man of your dreams, is that what you're trying to say?" He stepped away from her, walking back down the pathway and to the gate before saying "good night" over his shoulder.

"Luc, wait," she called softly. "You're not—I didn't mean." She shook her head. "Luc, come back. I love you." He didn't turn around right away. "Did you hear what I said? I love you. But it's such a long way from being a milliner in Nebraska to all those stages in all those big cities. I don't like big cities, Luc. I don't like crowds . . ." Luc was still standing at the gate. She moved toward him, reaching out to touch his sleeve. Then, she put her hand on his arm.

Luc turned around. "Oh, Nora," he whispered intensely, "can't you see—don't you know—" There was a kiss, and then he pushed her away. "I have to get out of here," he said. He was breathing heavily. Quickly, he mounted his horse and gathered up the reins to the horse Nora had ridden. "I've made promises to God, Nora. I hope you can understand, but I have to get out of here." He moved the horse into a trot.

Nora stood trembling at the gate until his form was lost in the darkness, her hand lifted to her lips.

Dearest Nora,

Another letter. Perhaps the last. I will not be back to see you today. I hope you understand. I told you there would be no more flirting, no more candlelit dinners . . . I'm done with those things, Nora, because I've found you. I don't want flirting and stolen kisses in the dark. I want you—all of you. I don't want to escort you to church, and to friends' homes, and to church picnics, and then say good night. I want to live, breathe, eat, love, and die with you. But I want it honorably and before God so that He can bless it. That means marriage.

There is a one-way train ticket in this letter. It will take you to Denver. There is also money to pay for a cab to the Larrimer Square Theatre, where our company will be for the next three weeks. I know that you said that you promised Mrs. Miller that you wouldn't leave without giving her six weeks advance notice. Perhaps she would change that if she knew it would make an old friend very happy.

Marry me, Nora. I know I don't offer the life you planned, but I offer you my entire heart and soul. Mikal told me that you told Karyn that you want to be loved the way Mikal loves her. Well, I'm not Mikal, but I dare to say that the love I feel for you right now is far more than Mikal Ritter felt the day he married

Karyn. Greyson Chandler is dead . . . but Luc Delhomme adores you.

I will pray every day for the next three weeks that God gives me the chance to make you happy. After that, I'll begin to pray for the grace to get over you . . . and that, my precious Nora, will take a good deal longer than three weeks. Please come. Let me love you.

Luc

Nora could not face the Delhomme women at quilting on Tuesday. She went to work instead, grateful that Mrs. Miller didn't ask questions. She kept Luc's letter in her reticule, withdrawing it to read every couple of hours. Even after she had memorized it, she still took it out, running her finger along the lines of ink.

Nora worked until it was nearly dark before finally allowing Mrs. Miller to shoo her out the front door. She walked with her head down, distracted, thinking. *Why can't I just throw it all to the winds and follow him*?

When a familiar voice called her name, Nora looked up, startled to see that she was right in front of Mrs. Delhomme's house. Celest stood on the porch. "You look tired, dear. Why don't you come up on the porch and join us for a glass of lemonade?"

Nora dreaded a confrontation, but something drew her to Luc's mother. "Thank you," she said, opening the gate and dragging herself up the path to Mrs. Delhomme's inviting porch. In the corner, sitting in a rocker, was the wizened old woman who stayed with Mrs. Delhomme.

Mrs. Kruger's face was deeply lined with wrinkles. She wore a cap over her nearly bald head and sat with her hands clasped before her. Nora had never seen such hands. Not one finger was straight. The tip of one index finger was twisted so badly it stood at nearly a right angle to the rest of the finger. Where knuckles should have been, Mrs.

Kruger had bumps, some so large it looked like marbles had been inserted beneath her skin. She was sitting with a ball of yarn cupped in one hand, making minuscule movements with the hand.

Although she was crippled with arthritis, Amalia's mind and hearing were keen. When she heard Celest call to Nora, she rose up in her chair with a grunt and watched as Nora walked up the pathway to the porch. Nora's foot had just reached the top step when Amalia Kruger said in a thick German accent, "Come close. Let me see the girl who broke Luc's heart."

Nora obeyed, blushing as she moved across the porch to where Amalia sat.

"Why don't you sit there by Amalia, Nora. I'll be right back with some lemonade."

Nora looked after Celest with dismay. Finally, she said politely, "You're the woman who is so famous for her wonderful biscuits. Mrs. Delhomme showed me how to make your recipe."

"*Humph*," Amalia grunted. She held up both hands. "Not much biscuit making anymore." She eyed Nora closely.

Nora stirred nervously. Did everyone in Millersburg know about her and Luc? She thought back to earlier in the day, when two women had come into Miller's. They had stood across the store from Nora's workstation, whispering. Nora had thought that once they both turned and looked at her, but she scolded herself for being so paranoid. *The entire population of Millersburg does not care about what happens between you and Luc Delhomme.* Sitting beneath Amalia Kruger's critical gaze, Nora began to wonder.

Celest came back out on the porch with three tall glasses of lemonade. She held Amalia's glass for her while the old woman drank, smacking her lips with satisfaction as she tasted the sweet liquid. Celest seemed to know when Amalia had had enough. She set the glass down and sat down across from Nora.

She took a sip of lemonade before saying, "We missed you at quilting today." She sighed. "I wish there were some way I could help you to feel better. Being young is so difficult sometimes."

"I thought," Nora began, then hesitated. "I thought you would hate me."

"Hate you? Why on earth would you think that?"

Barely holding back her tears, Nora said, "I don't mean to hurt Luc. I love him. I just," she spoke so quietly that Celest had to turn her head sideways and strain to hear. "I'm just so frightened by the thought of leaving this—to go there—when I—I—" She shook her head and was silent. She finally let the tears go and sat, holding the lemonade in her lap, crying quietly.

Celest reached over and took the lemonade from Nora's hands. She set the glass on the tray, sat down next to Nora, and pulled the girl into her arms. "Everything will work out. I told Luc the same thing. You just need time. And, he needs to be patient. You can't live the way Luc has lived and then expect a girl to follow you to the ends of the earth just because you say you've changed."

"I don't doubt he's changed," Nora said. She sat back up in the porch swing and dabbed at her nose with a handkerchief. "It's me." She looked at Mrs. Delhomme. "I think I used up all my courage just leaving home and getting things started here in Millersburg." She took a deep breath. "I wish I knew what to do."

Celest smiled and shook her head. "If you truly love my son as you say you do, you can't be happy here. Security is no substitute for love."

Nora sighed. She looked up at the roof of the porch, then bent her head, and reached back to rub her neck. "He could have stayed here. He could teach music. We could have a normal life."

Celest reached out to take one of Nora's hands. "The kind of love that builds walls around people eventually stifles everything . . . even itself. You have to be willing to help Luc do what his heart tells him. The more you push him toward that, the more love will flow back to you."

The only sounds for a few moments were the creaking of Amalia's rocker and the soft swish of Nora's and Celest's skirts brushing the floor of the porch as they moved back and forth in the porch swing. Finally, Nora leaned forward to put her elbows on her knees and her chin on her clasped hands. "He just left, and already I miss him. It's like—" She laughed sadly. "This sounds stupid, but it's like the sun isn't shining quite so brightly anymore. I must have thought of him a thousand times today." She nodded toward the fence where Luc had planted a row of rosebushes for his mother. She shook her head. "He sent me yellow roses once."

Amalia stopped rocking. She grunted with the effort of reaching forward to pat Nora with one of her crippled hands. "I followed a man once to where I did not want to be," she said, "and into years of unhappiness. I decided that love was not enough to make a couple happy." She paused. "I was wrong. My unhappiness was because I did not know God's love. I knew only passion. But love from God never fails. It is always enough. Once you know God's love, you can do anything. Go anywhere. His love goes before you, follows you, surrounds you." Amalia reached up to stroke Nora's cheek with a crooked finger. "Such a lovely young girl and so sad. Don't let it be this way, little one. You must have courage. You must fight for what you want."

Amalia grunted and began to get up. Celest helped pull her to her feet. The old woman grimaced in pain as she put one foot in front of the other. She bade Nora good night by saying, "Remember what I have said. You must fight for what you want. And in your case, I think that means you get on a train."

When the door closed behind Amalia, Nora stood up to go. "Thank you. For everything."

"Come back any time, Nora."

"If you hear from Luc would you tell him—" She shook her head. "Never mind." She made her way down the path and through the front gate. Closing it carefully, she waved good night to Mrs. Delhomme.

CHAPTER 26

L.A.C.D.

Bless the Lord, O my soul:
and all that is within me,
bless His holy name . . .
who forgiveth all thine iniquities . . .
who redeemeth thy life from destruction;
who crowneth thee with lovingkindness and
tender mercies . . . so that thy youth
is renewed like the eagle's.
Psalm 103:1, 3–5

When Will sent word that he could not come to town on Sunday, Nora went to church alone. Somehow it seemed right to go. It was something Luc would want her to do. She came in late and sat in the back. Perhaps, she thought, Reverend Underwood would say something profound that would answer all her questions at once and give her the courage to follow Luc.

In the end, God used a hymn. There was a new song leader, a young man who moved energetically and had the congregation stand to sing. He directed them to page 195 in the hymnal. Nora didn't know any hymns. Perhaps that was why she followed along so closely.

How firm a foundation, ye saints of the Lord,
Is laid for your faith in His excellent Word!

What more can He say than to you He hath said,
To you who for refuge to Jesus have fled?

Nora mouthed the words, afraid she would get the notes wrong. She liked the strong tempo, the straightforward kind of marching through each line. The woman next to her sang loudly and off-key. It didn't matter. As they progressed through each verse, it seemed that every word they sang applied personally to her.

Nora barely heard what Reverend Underwood said that morning. Instead of listening to his sermon, she sat with the hymnal in her lap, reading the verses over and over again. What more can He say . . . Her answers were waiting . . . if she fled to Jesus.

Fear not, I am with thee; O be not dismayed,
For I am thy God, and will still give thee aid;
I'll strengthen thee, help thee, and cause thee to stand,
Upheld by My righteous, omnipotent hand.

She did not have to be afraid of taking the train to Denver . . . of the big city . . . of traveling with a theatrical troupe. God said He would be with her. He would be her God and give her aid. He would strengthen and uphold her. Nora remembered Karyn Ritter sharing how God had upheld her in the early days of her marriage, in the times when the feelings dimmed.

When through the deep waters I call thee to go,
The rivers of woe shall not thee overflow;
For I will be with thee thy troubles to bless,
And sanctify to thee thy deepest distress.

Sorrow had overflowed Pap's life, because Pap didn't have God. He tried to go it alone. Karyn Ritter had almost drowned in sorrow, but she looked to God, and He helped her see the blessing.

E'en down to old age all My people shall prove
My sove'reign, eternal, unchangeable love;
And when silver hair shall their temples adorn,
Like lambs they shall still in My bosom be borne.

Nora thought of Celest Delhomme and her crown of silver hair. She was a living example of God taking care of His lambs, even when they grew old. Nora wasn't sure she knew what sovereign meant, exactly. But she knew she longed for eternal, unchanging love. Even if Luc couldn't give her that, God could.

The soul that on Jesus still leans for repose,
I will not, I will not desert to His foes;
That soul, though all hell should endeavor to shake,
I'll never, no, never, no, never forsake.

When the new song leader rose to lead the closing hymn, something compelled him to say, "I can think of no better closing hymn today, than the one we have already sung. Please, allow my unorthodox request. Let us stand and sing together once more, 'How Firm a Foundation.'"

Nora sang this time, her face shining with joy. The words to the hymn rang in her heart, because at last, they were the testimony of her own, personal faith. No one could promise her eternal love but God, but if she and Luc both shared God's love, they had a chance for something wonderful. Something better than she had ever dreamed. Something just like the Ritters.'

As Nora left church that morning, she felt reborn. Some things hadn't changed. The thought of the unknown still terrified her. But the conviction that God was already there, in the unknown, gave her hope.

As Nora walked home from church, she hummed to herself . . . "He'll strengthen and help me, and cause me to stand, upheld by His righteous, omnipotent hand."

Thunderous applause and flower-strewn stages had never been so meaningless. Luc Delhomme's pasted-on smile disappeared the instant he stepped back from the floodlights. The curtain came down. The players congratulated one another. Mr. and Mrs. Kendal patted Luc on the back.

"Are you feeling all right, Luc?" Mrs. Kendal asked.

Luc mumbled an excuse and headed down the crowded hallway for his dressing room.

She had not come. He had promised her everything—commitment, faithfulness, and love. It was a crushing blow to realize that all he had to offer wasn't enough. Where had he gone wrong? What else could he have done? Maybe he would give up the theater. Maybe he would go home.

He stopped and leaned against the wall, reaching up to fumble with the buttons on his shirt. Why did it always have to be so blasted hot and stuffy backstage? He wiped his forehead across the back of his sleeve. Mr. and Mrs. Kendal walked by.

Mr. Kendal held out an envelope. "Someone asked us to give this to you."

Luc opened the envelope. Inside was a large mother-of-pearl button. He laid it in the palm of his open hand, running his finger over the letters engraved on its face. L, A, C, D. He remembered. Saying the letters in French sounded just like the sentence "Elle a cédé." His mother had given the button to Nora, explaining that it was a romantic play on words . . . L, A, C, D . . . *She gives up*.

Ned Gallagher tapped him on the shoulder. "Hey, Luc, there's someone here to see you."

Suddenly, there was no crowd backstage. There was only one person, standing at the end of the hall, just outside his dressing room. She was wearing a green bombazine dress, and just as he looked at her, she opened an elegant lace parasol.

Luc closed his eyes for a moment. But when he opened them, she was still there, her eyes shining, her lips parted in a little nervous smile. He walked toward her, and the closer he got, the more she smiled. When he put his arms around her waist, she said, "Where's my button? I want it back."

"Be quiet and come here," he said, pulling her into his arms.

From where he stood at the opposite end of the back-stage hall, Ned Gallagher saw the parasol dip. He opened the door behind him. "Uh, Mr. Froman, I think you can stop the search for a new costume mistress. Luc Delhomme has one all tied up."

Epilogue

1998

"And that's it," Noah said, "I certainly would have preferred the coward's way out, but I knew it wasn't right. I had to go back and talk to Angela face-to-face. I hadn't really cared for her in a long, long time, but after she put up with my nonsense for nearly two years, she deserved a good-bye in person. That's where I was when Aunt Rini had her stroke." He sat back and studied Reagan for a moment before concluding, "And I guess I wouldn't blame you if you ordered me to take you home right now."

Earlier in the evening, Noah had accompanied Reagan to a children's Christmas program. Then, the two had driven downtown, where thousands of white lights outlined the historic buildings of the Haymarket district of Lincoln. Parking Noah's pickup, they had walked the district talking quietly about nothing. It was not until they were seated at a small table in a coffeehouse that Reagan asked Noah about Angela. As far as Reagan could tell, he answered her honestly, without trying to paint himself in a sympathetic light.

"What did she say when you shared the faith with her?" Reagan asked quietly.

Noah grimaced. "It made her mad. She said that if I was ever going anywhere but church to give her a call—and she'd set me up with someone she hated." He took a gulp of coffee.

"I'm sorry." Reagan said.

Noah shook his head. "Don't be. I deserved that and worse. I can imagine how she felt. She gives me two years of her life, and then I 'get religion,' dump her and move back to Nebraska." He leaned on one elbow and rubbed the back of his neck. "Anything else you want to know?"

Reagan shook her head.

"Where do we go from here?"

"Home." Reagan said as she stood up. "It's getting late."

"Would you come to dinner with Aunt Rini and me after church tomorrow?" He tossed a five-dollar bill on the table and they left the coffeehouse. Reagan still hadn't answered Noah's question when he gently took her hand. She didn't pull away, and when they arrived at the truck, Noah kissed her softly before unlocking the door. When he drove into Reagan's driveway, she quickly opened the door and jumped to the ground.

"You didn't answer me about dinner tomorrow," Noah said as they walked to the door together.

She fumbled nervously with her keys before answering "yes." She had already opened the door when Noah cupped her chin in his hand and turned her face toward him. He searched her eyes, saying softly, "What are you thinking?"

Reagan pulled away, pushing her front door open and starting to go inside. At the last minute, she turned around, still keeping one hand on the door as she said, "I'm thinking things are happening too fast."

"And I'm thinking I can't wait to see you again," Noah said, smiling down at her.

Over Sunday dinner at a local cafeteria, Noah launched into a lengthy explanation of his plans for the homestead.

"Did you know that Nebraska has one of the premier wildlife-viewing events in the world? The cranes draw thousands of people to the area each year. Surely there are some bird-watchers among them who would enjoy an authentic homesteading experience. Once I get the soddy rebuilt and furnished, I could give people a choice of 1880s soddy or 1930s farmhouse."

"But Noah," Irene protested, "you can't just walk out on the prairie and build a soddy. How would you begin? I mean," she laughed softly, "it's not like one of the neighbors can just drive over and show you how."

"There are books that show how it was done. Just because it hasn't been done in a few decades doesn't mean it's impossible. It will only take about an acre of Opa's prairie. I think he would approve." Noah smiled. "No one has complained so far about my fixing things up, but what I really want to do is buy the homestead so I don't have to worry about convincing the entire family about everything."

"You mean you are worried about your father," Irene said.

Noah nodded. "He is not going to be very excited about this idea." He took a sip of coffee. "And I can't say that I blame him. I haven't exactly modeled consistency and dependability over the years. But Aunt Rini," he leaned forward. "This is what I want to do." He laughed and shook his head, "I think I finally know what I want to be when I grow up."

Irene smiled, "I'll help you all I can, dear. But the kind of things you are talking about take a great deal of money. Where are you going to get the funds? Even if the bed and breakfast idea is a success, the cranes come and go in just a few weeks. What would you do for the rest of your income?"

Noah grinned, "It's the age of computers, Aunt Rini. I've checked around, and I think I could get a respectable consulting business going. I have to learn some of the ag software, but that shouldn't take long. My employer is willing to try a long distance arrangement for a while."

He continued, "The town board is considering my proposal about restoring the old opera house. If it really works out, there is talk of some kind of festival built around the history of theater in rural America. It has the potential of bringing much-needed cash into the area. There aren't many of the original opera houses still standing, you know. We can't just let all our history fall into ruins."

Irene finally said, "I'll help you all I can, Noah, but it makes me tired just thinking of all you have to do!"

Noah winked at Reagan, "And that doesn't even take into account researching Nora O'Dell."

"You don't have to bother with that," Reagan protested.

"Of course I do," Noah said, "It is the perfect subterfuge for courting you."

"Courting?" Irene said, "Did I hear the word 'courting?'"

Reagan felt herself blushing. "Stop it you two. You are ganging up on me, and I won't have it." She slid out of her chair and went to the dessert bar in the cafeteria.

Noah followed her. "All right, I'll back off. But only if you promise that you'll answer my letters and come for a visit in the spring—with Aunt Irene as a chaperone, of course. In the meantime, I'll learn what I can about Miss O'Dell from the museum in the town."

He slid a piece of chocolate cake onto Reagan's tray before selecting gooseberry and rhubarb pie for himself and Irene. The three filled the rest of their dinner together with talk of Noah's bed-and-breakfast soddy.

Reagan's computer said the words, "you've got mail" at least twice a day throughout the winter of 1998–1999.

Have you considered the irony of getting e-mail from a computer geek dressed in a flannel shirt who's involved with restoring a turn-of-the century farmhouse and plans to build a soddy in the spring?

Have you considered moving to Custer County?

1892—There's a Nora Delhomme in the census. Could it be her?

Ask Aunt Irene if she remembers anything about a marriage between Oma's friend and a Delhomme.

I know you dreaded the thought of reading all the old newspapers, but I think the only way you are going to learn much is if you take the time to peruse the Millersburg Republican.

You won't believe this. I found a sign from Miller's Emporium in the back room at the county museum. You'll have to see it when you come out. You are coming out?

The opera house is a mess inside. Some of the guys from the lodge are getting interested in the project. One is a carpenter. He's going to inspect the sills and check for termites.

Tell Aunt Irene I'm having the Ritter babies' tombstone cleaned and reset.

Even my truck couldn't get through the snowdrifts today. I had to turn back before I got to the end of the drive, then ended up getting stuck and had to shovel for nearly an hour before I could get back up to the house. The snow is beautiful, though. Imagining Karyn and Mikal Ritter driving a sleigh down the drive to church. Glad I don't have to break ice and water livestock.

The census shows Sophie and Cay Miller as having three children by 1892.

I drove out to the cemetery and found the Delhommes' graves today. I'll take you there when you come.

Reagan answered every message. She began to spend every Saturday afternoon at the State Historical Society, reading the *Millersburg Republican*. For several weeks, she found nothing. Then, amazingly, there was an announcement that Miss Nora O'Dell had opened a millinery business inside Miller's Emporium. Two Saturdays later, Reagan came across the description of a wedding between "the newly arrived Miss O'Dell and favorite son, Luc Delhomme, who has long graced the stage as the well-known dramatic actor, Greyson Chandler. The couple will tour with the Daniel Froman Company and hope to receive guests in the home of Mrs. Celest Delhomme over the Christmas holiday."

Reagan wound the microfilm furiously, looking ahead to the December issues of the *Republican*. Finally, she located the mention of the reception given in honor of Mr. and Mrs. Luc Delhomme. The list of guests included Mr. and Mrs. Cay Miller and Mr. and Mrs. Mikal Ritter.

She made copies of the articles and raced home to e-mail Noah. A message was waiting that said, *The dry-wall is finished. I'm ready to paint. Could you take Aunt Rini to the paint store and ask her to try to remember what color the rooms were? Send me samples.*

After calling Irene, Reagan replied, *Bringing paint with us last weekend in March. Will stay and help if you want us. Have amazing news of the button keeper.*

"And so," Reagan concluded, "Miss O'Dell and Mr. Delhomme lived happily ever after. They were back in Millersburg by 1892, and I found records that indicated they had five children." She was sitting on the sofa in the Ritter's farmhouse living room, enjoying coffee and cookies with Noah and Irene. She and Irene had driven up late that afternoon. Cans of paint, rollers, brushes, and drop cloths were piled in one corner of the room, awaiting the next day, when the three would begin painting the house.

"The frustrating thing is," Reagan said. "There doesn't seem to be any end to all of this. Now I want to follow the bunny trails to the children. And I wonder about Greyson Chandler's acting career."

Irene spoke up. "It would be fun to see if the Daniel Froman troupe ever played in Lincoln. The Historical Society might have playbills."

"Or," Noah offered, "there are always old newspapers."

Reagan groaned. "Please. No more newspapers on microfilm. At least for a while. I'm going to need glasses if I spend many more hours squinting at scratched microfilm."

"Did you find their marriage license?" Noah wanted to know.

Reagan shook her head. "Not yet."

"Well," he said, standing up and stretching, "let's go into the museum tomorrow and see what we find. We don't have to take the entire day . . . but we can at least check." He looked down at Reagan. "In the meantime would you care to join me on a walk?"

Reagan looked at Irene who shooed her toward Noah. "Go along, you two. I'll wash the coffee cups, and then I'm heading to bed."

Reagan followed Noah out the front door. They made their way around the back of the house and up the ridge, past the little burial ground to where they could see the prairie rolling away from them in every direction.

"I try to imagine what it was like when Opa came," said Noah. "No trees, no tilled fields, just miles and miles of nothing for as far as he could see. And where the nothing ended the sky began." He shook his head. "I don't know if I could have done it."

Reagan smiled. "I have a friend who says that if it had been up to her to settle the west, we'd all still be in Boston drinking tea." She paused and nodded toward the horizon. "Looking at that I'm inclined to agree. I don't think I could have done it either."

She looked behind her at the two little graves. "What women they were," she said. "Nora and Karyn, and all the others like them." She shook her head. "Everyone has such romantic notions about the good old days. A lot of the old days were pretty terrible."

They walked the homestead together. When the moon finally rose over the landscape, they were sitting on the front stoop of the house.

"Thank you for all the help with my research," Reagan said quietly. "I'm going to write it up and give it to the Society when Irene donates the charm string." She added, "I still wish I knew what each button meant to Nora. I wish she could come back just long enough to tell me the stories."

Noah nodded. "I know what you mean. I've wished Opa could be here to tell me if I'm doing things right around this place."

"You're doing just fine," Reagan said. "You're doing it with your heart. It's going to be beautiful when you finish."

Noah said softly, "Beautiful maybe, but still empty." He hesitated, "Do you think you could ever see yourself living up here in the wilds of Custer County?" He reached down to turn her face toward his. "I'm thirty years old, Reagan. I don't want to be alone for the rest of my life. If this is going nowhere . . ."

Reagan reached up to take his hand. She turned it over and kissed the palm. "It's going—somewhere—I think."

Noah pulled her into his arms and kissed her. "I'm falling in love with you, Reagan."

She laughed softly.

"Is that funny?"

She nestled her head on his shoulder. "No, I was just thinking though, here we are sitting on the front porch of your great-grandparents' house, two people who courted after they got married. I guess courting via e-mail isn't so strange after all."

They sat together in the moonlight, looking down the gravel road toward town.

COMING SOON FROM STEPHANIE GRACE WHITSON THE DAKOTA MOONS SERIES

Too late . . . God . . . dear God . . . I'm too late.
Flinging herself down from her horse, Mary shoved and pushed her way through the unheeding crowd. From somewhere up ahead she could hear the death song. The men's voices floated across the crowd as Mary clawed at the back of a man who blocked her way. "Please . . let me pass . . . let me pass."

The man turned around half angrily, but at the sight of the diminutive girl, he smiled. "Want to get a better view miss? Here . . ." He grabbed her by the shoulders and propelled her forward into the teaming crowd of onlookers. She was lost in a sea of sweating bodies and dust, and for a moment, she thought she might faint. Still, she pressed forward, feeling as though she were caught in a dream where every moment took unbelievable effort, every whispered word had to be shouted.

Before she managed to claw her way to the front of the crowd, the order was given, and Mary's screamed protest was drowned out by the strange sound that went up from the crowd. Not a cheer, really . . . but a collective sigh of satisfaction followed by mutterings from the men around her.

No one really noticed Mary. No one saw her face go white as she collapsed in a heap. Someone helped her up. She pulled away and stumbled to the edge of a boardwalk and sat down. It was a long time before she could bear to look up. When she finally did, they were cutting the bodies down. The faces were hidden by sacks that had covered the heads of each one of thirty-five condemned men. Some of the bodies had already been put into a wagon. There was no way to know which one hid his face.

Suddenly, despair melded into an iron determination to find his body. She had failed to save him, but she would at least see that he was buried properly. The need for immediate action smothered the savage wound of grief that gnawed at her midsection. Someone had said that there would probably be a mass grave. Some local physicians had already offered to pay for the right to claim a body for research.

I can't let that happen. I can't. I won't plead. I'll demand. They can think what they want. At least I can see that he is buried . . . that he can safely be put to rest.

But would they listen to her? Already there were rumors that she had been far too friendly with the Dakota during her captivity. For the first time since she and the children had been handed over at Camp Release, Mary realized that she didn't really care what anyone thought. They could think or say whatever they wanted. She would find his body and see that he had a proper burial in some secret location where no one would ever disturb him. It was the least she could do.

About the Author

STEPHANIE GRACE WHITSON lives in southeast Nebraska with her husband of more than twenty-five years, four children, and a very spoiled German shepherd. The Whitsons are active in their local Bible-teaching church. Stephanie is the author of the best-selling Prairie Winds Series, *Walks the Fire, Soaring Eagle,* and *Red Bird,* as well as the Keepsake Legacies series, *Sarah's Patchwork,* and *Karyn's Memory Box.*

Stephanie can be reached at the following address:

Stephanie Grace Whitson
3800 Old Cheney Road #101–178
Lincoln, NE 68516